throb

vi keeland

Throb

ISBN: 9781682304266

Edited by: Caitlin Alexander

Cover model: Josh Kloss

Cover designer: Sommer Stein, Perfect Pear Creative

Photographer: Scott Hoover Photography

Print layout by Deena Rae Schoenfeldt, eBookBuilders

dedication

To my husband,
whose voice somehow always finds a way into my books.

contents

definitions

game \\'gām\

Verb

1. to play a contest of chance for money

synonyms: *gamble, bet*

2. manipulate, typically in a way that is unfair or unscrupulous.

Noun

1. a physical or mental activity or contest that has rules and that people do for pleasure

throb \THräb\

Verb

1. to beat with increased force or rapidity, as the heart under the influence of emotion or excitement; palpitate.

Synonyms: *pounding, pulsating*

2. to vibrate; ache

Noun

1. a strong, regular beat

prologue

Months later

I turn. He's down on one knee, a black velvet box perched in the center of his hand. My heart starts to pound wildly in my chest ... or is it more of a *throb?*

"Marry me, Beautiful."

... And just like that, the game is finally over.

chapter

one

Cooper

My phone buzzes on my desk for the third time in an hour. Looking down, my eyes narrow finding the same name flashing from the display again. I frown, but slide my finger across the screen to answer this time. She skips the formalities, jumping right in to what she wants. "Come downstairs to the studio at lunch."

"I have a lunch meeting," I lie.

"I'll give you a delicious dessert when you're done," Tatiana purrs through the phone.

"Thanks, maybe next time," I lie again. There will be no next time. I regret not learning from my father's mistakes sooner—his no mingling business with pleasure policy was a lesson he learned the hard way.

"This is the third time you're blowing me off. Do you know how many men would kill to spend time with me?"

"Many, I'm sure. Listen, Miles just walked in … I have to run." My little brother hesitantly smiles and waves. I hold up one finger, ignoring whatever Tatiana is still rambling on about. His visit is unexpected, but I'm grateful for the excuse to get off the phone.

Miles nods and walks to the mahogany table displaying liquor bottles and ornate crystal glasses, the same one we'd watched our father walk to so many times before. He pours himself a tall glass of golden liquid and tosses half of it back in one gulp as he looks out at the view of Los Angeles.

There's strain in his face. I'm not surprised; the only time he comes by is when he needs to ask for something.

I rush Tatiana off the phone and, just as I push end, Helen beeps in from the intercom. "You have Stephen Blake on line one."

"Just give me one more minute, Miles."

My brother's glass is drained by the time I'm wrapping up my short conversation with Stephen. His brown eyes are worn and tired, there's a tenseness set in his jaw. Whatever he needs is big this time.

"Ben and I are putting a lot on the line with this project. We want him, but not for forty percent more. Ten is the highest we can go. You're the super agent—sell him on the backend percentage we're offering." I know what's coming next before the words sound through the receiver. "Sure, dinner next week sounds good. No, tell Miriam not to bring a friend." A pause and then, "Thanks, Stephen, I look forward to it."

Hanging up the call, I turn to Miles. "To what do I owe this pleasure, little brother?" I have a good hunch why he's visiting, but I'll play the game anyway.

My brother avoids the question, preferring to ease into the real subject he came to discuss. "Miriam still trying to fix you up?"

I pour myself a drink from a crystal decanter and raise the bottle, silently offering Miles a refill, which he happily accepts. "She swears Dad told her that she had to make sure I married well." I sip from the glass. "There'll be a woman there when I see them next week, even though I just told Stephen no." We exchange a rare true smile. Stephen was our father's best friend, and is one of Hollywood's most coveted agents.

"Maybe Miriam's got the right idea. You're getting old. Time to stop fucking half of Hollywood and settle down."

"I'm twenty nine. I'd hardly call that old."

"It is by Hollywood standards. Plus, you practically live in this place lately." He looks around my office. "You're starting to turn into *Dad*."

Miles says *turning into Dad* like it's a bad thing. We grew up in the same house, becoming anything like our father is a compliment to me, yet my brother utters it like it's an insult. A change of subject, to one that moves us to the point of his visit, is in order.

"How are things going at Mile High?" I ask cautiously, knowing it could be a very sore topic of discussion. A year after our father's death, my brother and I split our family's legendary film production business. I chose to continue on our father's path, the one that had made Montgomery Productions a name every A-list actor and director wanted to work with. Miles, on the other hand, decided it was time for a change. Diving into the risky world of reality TV, he filmed his first series, *Stripped.* To this day, he can't comprehend why *Stripped*—a show following a collection of artificially enhanced large-breasted strippers—flopped. Unable to accept the failure, he spent the last five years trying to prove he could make it as the King of Reality TV. In the process, he nearly depleted his trust fund, watched two of his "sure thing" reality shows fail, and got dumped publicly by the twenty-year-old starlet he'd just bought a Porsche.

Our strained relationship seemed to worsen as Montgomery Productions flourished over the last few years. My success fueled the grudge my brother has always harbored against me.

"Things are going great," he says. "Really great. We just started production on a show that's going to be huge. A ratings blockbuster, I know it."

I've heard those words from my brother's mouth on one too many occasions to believe him, although deep down I still hold hope that one-day he'll succeed. "That's great. What's the show about?"

"It's part *Survivor,* part *Bachelor.*" Miles's eyes light up. "*Throb.* Even the name of the show is marketing genius." He truly is passionate about his work. His lack of success has little to do with his own determination. It's the reason I always had difficulty saying no to him, even though I knew whatever I was asked to invest in was not a smart business move.

"Twenty bikini babes on a deserted island. One good-looking single guy, who also happens to be an up-and-coming rock star, and lots of physical competition for dream dates. Mud fights and all. Even have one of the contestants on my payroll, a ringer—she's playing the game for me—not for the bachelor. The advertisers are going to eat it up."

I have to work hard not to let my face show my true thoughts. It used to be if you were sixteen and got pregnant you would get in trouble. Now you get your very own reality show. "Interesting. When does it shoot?"

"We already have the first few weeks in the can. Twelve girls were eliminated and now we're down to eight. The last four are going to be shot live over two weeks in the Caribbean."

"I haven't seen any advertisements for it. When does it premiere?" I'm hoping, for Miles's sake, that it's at least six months away.

"Three weeks."

"Three weeks?" I try, really, I do, but the alarm is evident in my voice. A brand new show with zero advertising, and every other station touting a different reality show? It's almost certain to fail.

"Yeah." Miles's confidence falters for a fraction of a second, but I catch it. "Listen, Coop." He swallows hard and takes in a deep breath before continuing. "I'm not going to lie. I need some help. I just negotiated a great deal for ten solid days of prime-time advertising, but I'm running a little short on cash."

"How short?" I respond curtly, knowing my brother is padding the magnitude of the mess he's in.

"All of it. I need one-point-two."

"Miles," I sigh and drag my hands through my hair.

"It's a really good show, Coop. I just know the ratings will go through the roof with a little advertising."

I've heard all this before. It'll take more than Miles's biased and unreliable assurance to convince me. "Send me some dailies. I want a look before I can answer."

"You got it." He smiles, tossing back the rest of the liquor in his glass. "I'll have Linda send you over the first few episodes. You're going to be dying to get in on this one."

Dying, I think to myself, might be preferable to having to watch more reality TV.

Finally home after a fourteen-hour day that ended even worse than it started, I call Helen and ask her to have someone pick up my brand-new Mercedes from the repair shop in the morning. Three days old, and I was rear-ended while I waited for the light change, already ten minutes late for my first meeting because of yet another problem with the elevator in my building. I eventually walked down forty-two flights, thinking the morning couldn't get any worse. Damn was I wrong. Miles's visit came next.

I hop in the shower, allowing the steady stream of pulsating water from the shower massager to work its way into my tightly knotted shoulder muscles. I'm just letting out a deep breath, finally starting to relax, when the doorbell interrupts. "Goddamn it," I growl, grabbing a towel and heading to the door. Somebody better be dying.

Lou, the night doorman, stands holding a package. "A courier dropped these off for you today. I missed you come in. Must have been on my bathroom break. Sorry about that, Mr. Montgomery, the bladder isn't what it used to be."

"No problem, Lou. Thanks for bringing it up."

"Also, you had a visitor before you got home tonight. She wasn't on the list of approved visitors and you didn't answer the buzz, so I sent her away." Lou pauses. "She wasn't happy."

"Did you get her name?"

"Didn't need to. It was that actress, Tatiana Laroix."

Perfect. I've tried the nice route, but she just won't take a hint. "Thanks, Lou. You did the right thing."

"That's one beautiful woman, even at my age, ya can't help but notice that one. Hope you don't mind me saying so."

"You're right there. She is beautiful." *And damn crazy too.*

I change into some sweats and take a look at the package. *Mile High Productions.* Great. I can't think of a more appropriate way to end this crappy day, reality TV.

I grab a beer, take a long draw and slip the DVD in. The first ten minutes introduces half of the women. The method is interesting enough, although the responses fall flat. The host, who I'm actually pretty impressed Miles was able to score, is a well-known name. Each girl is on screen for a minute as he plays word association with them. Great concept, predictable answers. By the sixth woman who associates the word *profound* with the lyrics of Macklemore, I'm done. Maybe tomorrow, things won't seem so bleak.

Friday is appointment-free day. My father passed the tradition down to me, and it makes the day before the weekend something I look forward to. It's the one-day that Helen keeps clear. No appointments, no conference calls, no lunches, no meetings. It's my choice, all day. This week I need it more than ever. I do my morning run at the studio lot, knowing Miles is going to be shooting some promo work for *Throb.* I decide I'll drop in unannounced and check out what's going on.

I'm surprised to find the lot empty, so I head over to security to see what Mile High has planned for the day.

"Hey, Frank."

Frank Mars is sitting in front of a dozen security monitors, alternating between flipping cards on his desk and studying the video feed. Same uniform, same mustache, same cigarette behind his ear—even though he quit twenty years ago. He looks a bit more seasoned, more salt than pepper in his thick mane, but he hasn't changed all that much since I was a kid.

Frank's been our head of security as far back as I can remember. He was also a standard in my father's poker foursome, along with the CEO of a rival movie production company and one of the lighting grips. Every other Friday night, I could always find them in the empty studio hangar with a card table and a few cases of beer. Walking into that room, no one would ever know that two of the players were rich, powerful, Hollywood execs and the other two were average guys on their payroll.

"Cooper! Where you been hiding, kid?" Frank stands, shakes my hand, and slaps me on the back.

"Busy. It's been a while, hasn't it?"

"A while? Last time you were down here Grip hadn't even retired yet."

"Grip retired?"

"Going on two years now."

Two years? The thought scares me. I would've guessed the last time I was here was more like three months ago. "Damn. I can't believe it's really been that long. You still have your Friday night games going?"

Frank pats his chest, hand over his heart. "As long as my ticker keeps going, that game will be around."

"Grip still playing even though he's retired?"

"Winter months. Summers, his wife drags his ass to Arizona. Their daughter lives out there now, got two grandkids too."

"Still rotating Dad's chair?"

"Yes, sir. No one man can fill that chair. Hey, why don't you join us tonight? We were going to ask Ted over in finance to play, but that guy always takes my money."

"Are you saying I won't take your money?"

Frank laughs. "You got your father's good looks, you didn't get his poker playing abilities, kid."

"Might have to take you up on it, just to kick your old ass, Frank."

"You do that." He smiles, the creases on the sides of his eyes deepening. "Eight o'clock?"

"Why not. Hey, do you know where Miles is? I thought he was shooting a promo here today."

"He's shooting on location, down at a beach in Malibu."

Figures—any chance Miles gets to throw a girl in a skimpy bikini. "All right. Well, I'll be back later to take your money, old man."

"You keep telling yourself that, kid."

It's eight on the nose when I return to the studio lot, looking forward to sitting in on one of my father's favorite pastimes. Frank's setting up the card table and Ben is packing a cooler with Heineken.

"What? You think you're rich or something? Heineken? What happened to Budweiser?" I call out, walking toward Ben with a case of Bud in tow.

"Only your old man drank that shit." Ben Seidman, the founder and CEO of Diamond Entertainment, clasps my hand as he takes the case. Diamond Entertainment is the second largest movie studio in Hollywood—second to Montgomery Productions, of course. Ben also happens to be one of my father's oldest friends and my godfather.

"He drank it because it's good. Not like that imported shit you're packing in there."

For a few minutes the three of us catch up and reminisce about some of the old card games. I'm glad I came tonight. A night with these guys is just what I need. Good memories, cold beer, no talk about the looming union strike aging me prematurely.

I crack a Bud and clink the bottle with Ben's before taking a sip. Budweiser tastes like crap. I'd much rather be drinking the Heineken that Ben's drinking—or a Stella from my fridge at home—but I'11never admit it to him. Some things are just part of tradition. "Where's Grip?"

"Couldn't make it tonight, wife's sister had cataract surgery, so he took her up to Seattle to see her or some shit."

"Ted filling in?"

"Nope." Frank grins.

"Who's playing the fourth?"

"Her." Frank motions to the other side of the room, where a woman is carrying a case of beer. A case of damn Stellas.

"Hey, Frank." The woman smiles and I almost drop my beer. And it's not just because she's drop-dead gorgeous. I can't believe Frank's letting a woman play.

"Really?" I say incredulously.

Frank smiles knowingly. "Really."

"Never thought I'd see the day." I shake my head.

"What?" The beautiful woman directs her question at me.

"You're a woman." I smile, shrugging my shoulders.

"I am?" Eyes wide, feigning surprise, she looks down and playfully pats her body. "Oh my god. I am."

"That's not what I meant."

"So a girl can play?" She's petite, maybe only 5'4, the top of her head barely reaching my chest, but she squares her shoulders and dares me to respond. Oddly, I feel a little twitch in my pants when she challenges me.

"I don't know, can you?" I decide to stop backpedaling and go on the offense, wanting to see her push back more.

"I can. Can you?" She arches one brow. Damn, it's sexy. Another twitch.

"Guess you'll find out," I tease.

"All right, you two," Frank breaks in. "Kate, this is Cooper and Ben." She shakes my hand; her skin is so smooth and soft. Long, blonde, wavy hair loosely frames her pretty face. Unlike most women around this place, it's almost makeup-free. A hint of pink color and gloss on her lips picks up the lights above. The way it reflects and shimmers has me staring at her full lips a bit too long. It's an effort to drag my eyes away.

"Do you work at the studio? I haven't seen you around," I say curiously.

Frank speaks up before Kate. "Ben, smack this kid in the head, he's forgetting the rules already."

I actually did completely forget. No mention of work at all. It was my father's favorite rule. After the studio started to take off, this hangar was the only place he could really relax and forget who he was for a while. Normally I'd love the rule too, but I find myself eager for a little background on the sexy woman tugging my errant cock from its self-imposed hibernation.

Kate smiles and shrugs.

Half an hour into the card game, she tosses a straight flush down on the table, just as I'm about to reach over my three aces and sweep the pot.

"You've got to be kidding me. Again?" I lean back and slump in my chair, defeated.

She smiles and pulls the heaping pile to her side of the table.

"Where'd you learn to play like that?" Ben asks her.

"My dad."

"Dad's a poker player, huh?"

"Ever hear of Freddy Monroe?" she asks casually while stacking her chips.

"Five-card Freddy? Sure. He always wore those diamond four-leaf clover cufflinks. He took the Texas Hold 'Em World Championship three times."

"Four," Kate corrects. Then adds sheepishly, "He's my father. I'm a St. Patrick's Day baby. He had the cufflinks made when I was born."

Ben laughs and throws his hand in the air, looking at Frank. "You invited a shark to play with us?"

"I was playing solitaire one night when she was in the studio late. We played a few hands of rummy. She beat me twenty-two hands in a row. Figured I'd see if it was beginner's luck."

"It ain't beginner's luck," Ben guffaws.

Two more hands and Ben and Frank fold again, leaving just Kate and me. My cards are shit, but I like the way she pushes back every time I raise the ante, so I just keep throwing good money after bad.

After my last raise, Kate brushes her thumb over the worn chip she's kept at her side all night, looks down at her pot, then back to me, studying my face. I return the challenging stare. Her blue-green eyes squint ever so slightly as she tries to read what I've got sitting face-down on the table. For a second, she drops her gaze and lingers on my mouth before returning to my eyes. I have no idea what she sees, but something makes her smile. It's slow and confident and she arches one eyebrow before she pushes her chips in. "Call."

I don't take my eyes off her as I turn over my pair of twos. She smirks, then turns over a pair of threes. Ben and Frank laugh their asses off and decide we need a short break, one long enough for me to "pull my head out of my ass."

The two men disappear to the men's room, leaving just Kate and me sitting at the table. Leaning back in my chair, I ask. "How did you know?"

She shrugs and smiles. "It's all about reading people."

"So you can see what I'm thinking?" I lift my beer to my lips and take a slow draw without breaking eye contact.

"Sometimes."

"What am I thinking about now?" I try in vain to keep a stoic face, but the corner of my mouth tilts up to a dirty grin.

She shakes her head and walks to the restroom smiling, leaving me watching the sway of her ass.

A few hours later, Frank calls for the last hand. I pull a money clip out of my pocket and lay it on the table. Ben takes out a business-card holder engraved with his initials and Frank tosses a pair of my father's cufflinks to the middle.

"What's going on?" Kate questions, a look of confusion on her face.

Apparently Frank failed to tell her about the tradition of last hand of the night, so he begins explaining. "Last hand isn't for cash. It's something that means something to you, that all of us might want."

Kate lifts her purse and spends a minute looking through it. Finally, she takes out a pen and paper, writes something down, and folds it up.

"We don't take IOUs," I tease.

She looks me in the eye. "It's my phone number. Didn't think any of you would want my lipstick or a tampon." She arches one eyebrow, daring me to question her choice. Another damn twitch. I might have to sit at the table for a while if this is another quick hand.

I laugh, but damn she anted up something I want. Badly. Unfortunately, true to the rest of the night, Kate is the one pulling in the pot at the end of the game.

"You better give me a chance to get my friend's cufflinks back tomorrow, little lady." Frank wags his finger at Kate. *So she works here. Good to know.*

Frank tells us to go, he has a few things to do before he can lock up. Ben takes off quickly, answering yet another call from his third wife. I walk Kate to her car.

"Lucky chip?" I ask, referring to the solid black worn chip she took from her purse and slid her thumb over on more than one occasion while playing.

"It brought my dad a lot of luck over the years."

I nod. "I'm glad I came tonight. I had a great time. It's been a while since I played with those guys."

"Seems like you guys go pretty far back."

"Pretty sure they were all playing cards in the hospital lobby when I was born," I joke, but I wouldn't be surprised if they were. I'll have to ask one day.

"This is me," Kate says as we arrive at an old Jeep in the parking lot. It's a beautiful night and the top is already off. She clicks her keys to unlock the door. I open it for her to get in, but hang on to the top, not letting it close.

"Listen, I'd love to take you to dinner."

"Dinner?"

"You left me a couple of bucks, figured I'd like spending them on you as much as I liked losing them to you."

"You *liked* losing to me?"

I contemplate the question for a moment. "Oddly, yes. Which is strange because I hate to lose."

"I'm guessing it doesn't happen often."

"What? Losing?"

She nods.

"No, actually. It doesn't. I tend to go after what I want until I win." Our eyes lock on each other, something passing between the two of us, a thick tension swirls in the air. "So...dinner?"

Kate smiles, but the uptick at the corners of her mouth quickly turns down. "I can't." She looks hesitant, but offers no further explanation. "I had fun tonight." She reaches into her purse, pulls something out, and extends her hand to me. "I don't really want to keep your money clip. I noticed it wasn't your first initial engraved on it. Maybe it means something to you?" She tilts her head, observing me.

"It does. But that's okay. You keep it. It'll give me a reason to see you again." I reach down, close her fingers back around the money clip, and lift her hand to my mouth. My lips brush the top lightly, my tongue sneaking out to fleetingly touch her skin. The brief contact stirs an ache inside me. This woman tugs at something—more than arousal—something that makes me want to slow down time just to spend a few more minutes standing here.

"Did you just …" she stammers a bit.

"Did I just what?"

She squints at me. "You know."

"Do I?"

"I felt your tongue on my hand. You … you licked me."

I'd been dying to run my tongue along her neck all evening, although I hadn't really meant to be so crude about it. It just sort of … happened. "I wouldn't say licked, maybe just a little taste."

"So you tasted me?"

My entire body suddenly has interest in this conversation. "I suppose I did. But it wasn't nearly enough. That brings us back to my invitation for dinner. Tomorrow night?"

"I can't."

"The day after then?"

She laughs and shakes her head. The sound makes me smile.

"Good night, Cooper." She pulls the driver's side door shut and leaves me standing there … for a full five minutes after she's gone.

chapter

two

Kate

Distracted as I drive home, my mind replaying the evening over and over, I miss my damn exit as a picture of Cooper standing beside my jeep pops into my head for the twentieth time. Dress shirt unbuttoned at the collar, shirt sleeves rolled up to reveal sexy strong forearms, he exuded power, yet something about him was playful ... down to earth. Not like the typical guys I've been meeting the last few years.

His square, deeply defined jaw had just a hint of a five o'clock shadow on his perfectly tanned skin. Bright, startlingly green eyes stood out, the shade somewhere between jade and moss. Beautiful, but the color wasn't the part that mesmerized me. It was the gold ring around his pupil that captured my attention, surrounding the rich dark brown. It reminded me of a sunflower, painted in a field of green grass. And every time he tried to bluff, the sunflower grew bigger, making it that much more difficult to focus on my hand. It didn't help that the soft green and glittering gold were set off by the thickest eyelashes I've ever seen on a man. Why do men get the good eyelashes?

I hold my breath and make a wish as I enter the tunnel. I've been making the same wish as I drive through the burrowed rocky canyon for years. It's always about my brother. Selfishly, today my wish is for me.

After a twenty-minute detour, I'm surprised to find my roommate, Sadie, still awake when I walk into my apartment.

Collapsing onto the couch dramatically, I slouch down, stretching my long legs across the coffee table.

"Bad day, Angelina?" she says. Every day since I started filming the reality show, she has a new actress name for me. Yesterday I was Reese.

"Long day of sitting around doing nothing. But, actually, it was a good night."

"Did you get to see Flynn?" She sits up on the couch, hoping to hear some good gossip. Gossip I'm not supposed to share by the terms of my contract, one that I violate pretty much daily. Even if I weren't anxious to tell my best friend about a guy I was seeing, she'd get it out of me. Sadie Warner could pull gossip out of a priest.

"No, he wasn't on set today."

Deflated she won't be getting the juicy inside scoop about Bachelor Flynn today, she continues anyway. "What did you do tonight that was fun then?"

"I played cards."

"Cards? Booooring." She drags out the word in that singsongy way.

"Not when one of the players is hot."

"Why didn't you say that sooner?" She tucks her feet underneath her, giving me her full attention.

"You lost interest the minute I told you Flynn wasn't there, and only regained interest once I mentioned a hot guy."

"So?" Clearly she can't fathom what is wrong with my statement. I roll my eyes.

"What if I had a nice night catching up with an old family friend? A *female* old family friend who is important to me. Would you have wanted to hear about my night then?"

"Absolutely not."

I laugh. "I shouldn't tell you about the hot guy then, if you don't want to hear about our old friend Edna."

"Who's Edna?" She looks confused.

"The old family friend I just made up that you had no interest in?"

"And you felt the need to give her a name?"

"Maybe I love dear old Edna a whole lot and she's special to me."

"Then call your mother and tell her about Edna."

"Maybe I'll call my mother and tell her about Cooper too then."

"Cooper, huh?" Her eyes widen in an *ooh*. "How tall was he?"

I can't help but smile. "I didn't measure him … but tall … maybe six foot one or two."

"Nice." Sadie wiggles her eyebrows. "Tall is good. What else you got?"

"Square jaw, chiseled nose, inky dark hair and matching thick lashes that set off incredible light eyes. Green with sunflowers in them."

"Mouth?"

"Ridiculously sexy kissable lips. Oh … and he licked me."

"He licked you?"

"He did it discretely, kissed the top of my hand, but I felt his tongue. Made my skin heat. Like throwing water into a heated frying pan."

"Mmmmm … the kind of sexy that makes your temperature rise. I need more. How's his ass?" Sadie closes her eyes as if she's imagining the man I'm describing.

"Like you could bounce a quarter off of it."

"Arms?"

"He was wearing a dress shirt, so I only got to see his forearms."

Her eyes are still closed. "Okay … tell me about those."

"Strong, incredibly sexy."

"Chest?" Her voice is lower.

"Broad. Thick wide shoulders. Narrow waist."

Sadie's eyes fly open.

"What?" I say, wondering what part of my description could possibly have derailed her fantasy.

"Why are you home, if he's out there?"

I laugh, but then I remember the reason. Leaning back with a sigh, I admit, "He asked me out too."

"And … ?"

"I said no."

"Why?"

"You know why! The contract."

"Screw the contract."

"Screw the contract? You're the one that made me sign it!"

"I made you sign it. I didn't tell you that you have to follow it to a tee!"

"But that's the way it works. I promise them something and they promise me something. Isn't that how you explained it to me?"

"Pfffft ... No one ever pays attention to those things," my best friend, who also happens to be my attorney, says.

"I need to focus on the show. I don't need a distraction right now."

"You haven't gotten *distracted* in a long time. How long has it been?"

Too long. "I've been busy."

"I know. You've been running yourself ragged since the accident."

"Someone has to take care of things."

"Yes. And you will. But there's no reason you can't take care of *other things* too. Have you checked for cobwebs down there?" She teases, then her face turns serious. "Look, I know you have a lot on your plate. But sometimes I worry it's less about you being busy, and more about you denying yourself happiness from misplaced guilt."

"I'm fine. Stop worrying about me. Plus, who knows, I could win a lot of money on this show *and* get my cobwebs dusted."

I'm up early, nervous as hell about going back to the *Throb* set. Today is the first day of *bachelor's choice,* meaning Flynn gets to pick which girl he wants to spend twenty-four hours alone with on a deserted island. Sure, the island is only a few miles off the coast of California, and the deserted couples get delivered a gourmet food basket—*Survivor,* it's not. But still, who knows what can happen when two people who are attracted to each other are alone for twenty-four hours in that setting?

I hastily park my car and jog to the door of the studio a few minutes late. The other contestants are sitting around waiting still, so I stop by Frank's office and say good morning.

"You know, missy, normally I'd have to be married to let a woman take that much money from me." Frank smiles warmly as he jokes.

"And normally I wouldn't let a man off so easily the first time I play with him," I say joking—but there's truth in my words. One of the cardinal rules my dad taught me: you only get the element of surprise once, so win big the first time.

Frank chuckles. "What's Mr. Montgomery got planned for today?"

"We're all going over to the beach house in Malibu. We spend a few hours with Flynn and then he gets to pick his choice for his next date."

Frank sighs. "Whatever happened to meeting women the old-fashioned way ... picking them up in a bar? I don't get the whole reality TV thing. Why would a beautiful girl like you have to go on national TV to *maybe* get a date?"

"Seemed like a good idea at the time I signed up." I shrug, trying to come off casual. The terms of our contract are confidential, so I can't share with him the real reason I decided to go on the show ... the $250,000 grand prize.

Behind me, I hear the director calling everyone together. "I better go. Have a good day, Frank."

"You too, Kate. The seat is yours if you want to sit in on the next game, kiddo. I know some of the guys would love a chance to win back some of their money." Frank pauses. "And maybe their pride."

"I'd love that. See you soon."

The age range of the contestants runs from twenty-three to twenty-eight, yet it feels like high school all over again. I look over to the padded lounge chairs along the side of the pool, where six of the remaining ladies sit gathered in a tight group, gossiping.

"Bet they were cheerleaders," Ava says as she joins me in the pool, the two of us outsiders looking in on the cool-girl posse from a distance.

"Without a doubt." I nod my chin in the direction of the ringleader who sits in the middle of the clan. "Jessica was definitely prom queen too."

"You know they aren't coming in because they don't want to mess up their hair and makeup."

"Of course … God forbid." I should probably be doing the same thing, keeping my eye on winning the prize, but it's over ninety degrees today, and sweltering in the sun while staring longingly at the glistening pool just seems stupid to me.

"Who do you think he picks for the first stranded date?" Ava's fisted hands clench and unclench in the water, each squeeze sending a stream of water soaring into the air.

"Jessica. That little white string she calls a bathing suit will definitely catch Flynn's attention. You think they're real?"

"Her boobs?"

"Yeah."

"No, they are definitely not real." We both stare over at prom queen; her nipples are barely covered by the small triangle top that tries to contain her overflowing breasts.

I look down at my barely C cups: they're perky, but definitely not the attention-getters that Jessica's are. "Remind me not to stand next to her in a bathing suit." I laugh.

"You?" Ava looks down and then back to me. "Hello? I look like a boy!"

I hadn't really noticed her flat chest until now, but she actually makes me look endowed. "Maybe I should stand next to you, might help put my girls into perspective." Ava splashes me, smiling.

"Hi ladies." Flynn Beckham interrupts our girl talk, walking into the spacious yard wearing nothing but swim trunks. Every head turns. I may have entered this contest for the grand-prize money, but I'd be lying if I said that the bachelor hasn't sparked my interest. He's nothing like I expected. The outside may scream rockstar, but in the small amount of time I've spent getting to know him, he's seemed like a pretty normal and great guy.

"Hi Flynn." The lounge-chair ladies swoon in unison.

He smiles and waves, but keeps going as he passes, heading straight for the pool—to the blatant dismay of the poolside posing beauties.

As he gets closer to the pool, he winks at Ava and me ... right before cannonballing into the middle, splashing water all over the ladies who weren't planning on getting wet.

When he surfaces with a huge boyish smile on his face, I'm laughing. If I was in his position, it's exactly what I would have done. "Wish I could have seen their faces," Flynn grins as he speaks to us low.

"I don't think they were happy getting their hair ruined," I say through a genuine smile. He's facing us, his back to the other women. I glance over, then return my attention to him. "Bet they all come in the pool now though."

"I say four come in."

"All six."

Flynn arches his eyebrows. "Bet you a foot massage."

Crinkling up my nose, I respond, "I'm not really a foot person."

A lopsided smile reveals one of his two deep-set dimples. God, he really is adorable. "Chicken?" he challenges.

Looking over at the girls, I see three already coming toward the water. "You're on." I extend my hand and we shake on it.

"That feels so good." I close my eyes and lean back, relaxing into the pleasure with a deep sigh. I wasn't kidding when I said feet weren't really my thing. But Flynn definitely knows what he's doing as his two thumbs rub firmly into the ball of my foot, each stroke releasing a little more tension from my body.

"I'm glad I lost." His murmur is a low rumble. I can tell he's smiling, even though I don't open my eyes to check. I smile back too.

"Mmmmmm. I'm glad you lost too" is all I can muster as he alternates between kneading and long gliding strokes on the instep of my left foot.

"Not to be a pig here, but Jesus, Kate, you look like you might have an orgasm."

My smile widens. "I might." It would be the first one in *way* too long.

He laughs. "That good, huh?"

"Shut up and rub." I don't even care that cameras are probably filming my succumbing to a pre-orgasmic induced haze.

"Yes, ma'am. Watching your face is better than getting a foot massage myself anyway."

chapter three

Cooper

Early afternoon sunlight streaks in through the tall windows in my office, a ray landing directly on the shelf against the wall where my father kept his most coveted prizes. Nine Academy Award statues, a picture of my mother smiling on the beach in Barbados, and a framed photo of me, Dad and Miles on a fishing trip in Alaska.

My father beams proudly, standing between Miles and me, both of us holding up king salmon. I was probably eleven or twelve, Miles six or seven. It was the summer after our father divorced Miles's mother.

My mother, Rose, had been the love of Jack Montgomery's life. But a tragic car accident tore her from us not long after I was born. Her untimely death left my father reeling … and raising a six-month-old son on his own.

Although my father never truly got over Rose, a few years later, desperate to fill the void and find a mother figure for me, he met, and quickly wed, a beautiful, budding young actress. The first few years were marital bliss—my father was thrilled when Courtney gave birth to Miles less than a year into their marriage. Unfortunately, it didn't take much longer than that to realize Courtney was more interested in partying and an acting career than mothering their two children. She began making the rounds at all the usual Hollywood parties, the Montgomery name opening doors for her like a magical key. For the sake of his children, Dad tolerated her late nights and overindulgence in a lifestyle she wasn't accustomed to—

until he discovered she was carrying on an affair with a twenty-three-year-old unemployed wanna-be rockstar.

When they divorced, Dad took full custody in exchange for a substantial financial payout to Courtney. She disappeared on a worldwide tour with her rockstar and never looked back. Although Dad loved both of us fiercely, Miles somehow resented my mother. And over the years, that resentment spread to me—the child of our father's *precious Rose*.

"This is from today," Helen says as she hands me a DVD. "Miles brought it over himself an hour ago. Said to tell you tonight is the first stranded date." She stops on her way out, turning back to me. "He seemed a little anxious."

I bet he is. After a tense two-hour meeting with the president of the stagehands' labor union, I'm really not in the mood for more of Miles's reality crap. But I pour myself a late afternoon drink and pop the DVD into my Mac anyway. I watch the first few minutes, dreading the conversation I'm going to have with my brother when I tell him I'm not giving him the loan he needs.

It's no secret that Mile High Films is struggling financially since the split five years ago, but I had no idea how bad things were until I made a few calls this morning. My brother owes half of the film industry's biggest suppliers a ton of cash. If it were any other film house, the credit would have dried up months ago, but the Montgomery name carried him far. Now the name is almost all he has left ... aside from this show he's banking on.

The contents of the crystal tumbler burn as the liquor slides down my throat in one hefty medicinal gulp. I lean back in my chair, closing my eyes for a few minutes as Miles's daily feed drones on from my computer. The alcohol seeping into my blood, I actually begin to relax for a minute.

Then I hear *her* voice.

My eyes jar open. I'm positive it's her before I even look up at the screen to confirm it. All morning, my mind has drifted back to her over and over again.

Her hair's wet, slicked back from her face, and she has no makeup on, but I'm sure just from the sound of her laugh. A tall, thin-but-solid, tattooed, longhaired guy stands next to her in the pool. The filming doesn't pick up what they're whispering, but I can tell that he's flirting with her. The way he looks at her, watches her mouth move, stealing glances at her perfect tits on display in her bikini top. I have no idea why, but it pisses me off. A fuck of a lot.

Sitting up in my chair, I move closer to the monitor and turn up the volume, hoping to eavesdrop on their conversation. But all I can hear is a bunch of complaining, whiney women in the background, standing around lounge chairs. The tatted rock-and-roll-looking guy in the pool says something and lifts one eyebrow. *What the fuck did he say?* I rewind, but still can't make it out. So I do it again. And then again. Each time getting more annoyed watching that stupid eyebrow raise as he grins at Kate.

I speed up the parts where Kate isn't on the screen, stopping each time she reappears. And when I come to a shot of her getting a foot massage, I feel like breaking something.

"Helen?" I bark. "Clear my afternoon schedule. Where is my brother filming right now?"

Rounding the turn to my brother's office in the building we still share, I walk straight into a brick wall of a man. Damian Fry. I haven't seen the guy in years. Dressed in head to toe black, his bald head gleaming, he looks exactly like what he is—a menace. Untraditional, unethical, a heart made of stone … the perfect private investigator for dirty jobs. It's no wonder the police force kicked him off ten years ago. They called it excessive force, but Damian called it a waste of talent.

"Damian." I nod.

"Make sure your brother pays my bill on time," he sneers and walks away. He's as friendly as usual.

When I stroll into Miles's office unannounced and without bothering to knock, he, at first, looks annoyed. Then he remembers he needs something from me, and forces a smile onto his face.

"To what do I owe the pleasure, bro?"

Bro? A month ago he couldn't stand the sight of me. The last time I was in this office, I'd confronted him about paying Mile High bills through Fallen Rose Petals, our father's charity for children who lost parents. I'd let it go the first time I noticed it happen, knowing he was struggling financially. But when he didn't get caught the first time, he got greedy, going back for seconds … and thirds and fourths and fifths. When I called him on it, he didn't even bother to pretend it was inadvertent. Instead he screamed that he was taking *his mother's* half of the charity, since our father hadn't sought fit to set up one in his mother's name, and I should *get the fuck out* of his office.

Miles sweeps together a pile of documents strewn around his desk and opens a thick folder. My eyes narrow on the Fry logo emblazoned on the outside; anything to do with Damian raises my suspicion. A few black-and-white glossy photos spill out, but he quickly gathers the file and puts it into drawer.

"Tell me more about the show."

Miles's eyes light up, excited that I'm interested.

"The bachelor is Flynn Beckham. An up-and-coming singer with a pretty decent-size following. The ladies love him. He's got that rockstar aloof, I-don't-give-a-shit attitude down pat. There were twenty ladies originally. We're down to eight. When we get down to four, we go live. So there's a planned hiatus coming up to let the taped shows catch up with the live shows."

"Who are the eight?" I'm starting to lose my patience, anxious to find out more about Kate.

"Did you see them? We got a smorgasbord of beauties. One for every demographic. The advertisers are going to love it."

Right now, I don't give a crap about the advertisers. I just want to know more about the woman who took all my money, turned me down for dinner, and made my dick come alive, all in the same night.

"I saw them. What's their background?"

Miles takes out another folder from his top desk drawer. Opening it, he reveals a black-and-white glossy of a woman who looks like she could be Miss California. She's pretty, but not Kate.

"Jessica Knowles." He holds up the candid photograph. "Twenty-three, former Miss Teen USA runner-up. Aspiring model and actress. She's built like fucking Jessica Rabbit. Tits are fake, but huge. Every eighteen-year-old will be having a wet dream when she comes on screen in that white bikini of hers."

He turns the photograph. There's another beautiful girl, but still not Kate. "Mercedes Mila." He smiles like a Cheshire cat. "I'd like to take a ride in this Mercedes. Twenty-four, nurse."

Ten minutes of résumés later, we've covered everything from student to lawyer to stripper. I'm growing impatient. Finally, Miles flips the photo and my eyes land on Kate. "Kate Monroe. Twenty-five. Blackjack dealer. Working on her doctorate in physical therapy. She's my girl next door. Looks sweet and innocent, but she has a streak of something wild. Father was a hotshot card player." Miles pauses. "I'm curious if this one's wild in the sack."

My brother's insolent commentary was already wearing thin on my nerves, but his disrespect for Kate gives me the urge to kick him under the table. Jaw clenched, I stare at the remaining headshots, but my mind is a million miles away. I ponder the strange combination ... medical student and blackjack dealer. Strangely enough, from the little that I know, it fits her.

"I saw this morning's dailies," I say. "What happens next?"

"Tonight he picks his first stranded date."

"Stranded date?" With my brother's penchant for risqué, I'm almost afraid to ask.

"He picks one woman and he gets a twenty-four hour date with them on a deserted island. We set up cameras all over the place, so there isn't even a cameraman following them around." Proudly, he continues, "We're hoping to take away all their inhibitions. Other reality TV shows, the contestants are constantly reminded they're being watched. Filmed. Having cameramen around makes the women think twice before they go too far."

"What happens if Beckham and his date aren't into each other?"

"Oh, they'll be into each other. We make it impossible for them not to be. They might be stranded, but we set them up for romance. Think of the perfect romantic date—the kind that gets you both in the mood. Then multiply it times a hundred. We know how these contestants tick. We've done our homework. There *will* be action on that island."

Perfect. The first woman I can't stop thinking about in years, and she's about to have the most romantic date of her life … with someone else.

"Does Beckham have favorites? Any idea who he's going to pick for his date tonight?" I ask Miles as I downshift, slowing into traffic on the Pacific Coast Highway. My request to visit the set was eagerly accommodated by my brother. He's anxious to show me his show. I'm only anxious to see one contestant.

"He has a thing for Jessica."

I let out a breath too soon.

"And Kate."

Fuck. "And if he picks someone you don't think will make for good TV, you can override his decision."

"Scripted reality TV, bro. It's what makes ratings. Can't always let the bachelor think with his dick. We need to think with our wallet. But I won't have to interfere with his pick this time. He's salivating to get his hands on one of those two. Either will do. Hell, I'd like to get my hands on one of them."

I weave in and out of traffic, enjoying my brother grabbing onto the door handle once or twice as I cut a swerve that makes him a bit nervous.

"This thing is thirty years old. Time for a new one that handles better, Coop," Miles says, referring to our father's Porsche. The car he loved. It wasn't worth nearly as much as the other cars he had, but he went through two clutches in this thing teaching me to drive. Great memories. Miles was only too happy I took the less valuable car. Unfortunately, our ideas of value have always been measured on different scales.

"I bought a new car. A bump in the rear at a light cost eight thousand for damage repairs. I like driving this one better anyway."

We arrive at the Malibu house that Miles rented to shoot most of the show. I choose to hang back, watching the action through the camera feed in the three-car garage they've turned into a makeshift studio. Miles jumps right into the thick of things.

Some of the crew I know from Montgomery projects, others are new. Joel Blick comes over to greet me. "They let anyone in around here." He slaps me on the back, grabbing my hand for a shake.

"Joel. How the hell are you? Didn't you retire yet?" I prod, knowing he's only in his fifties.

"I'm never retiring, I'd have to hang out with Bernice all day." He rolls his eyes and says it like he's joking, but he isn't. And I don't blame him, I've met his wife. I'd work as much as I could if the alternative was spending my days with Bernice complaining all day.

"You the director?"

"Yep. I didn't know you had an interest in reality TV," Joel says.

"I don't."

He smiles knowingly. "Miles drag you into investing?" He lowers his voice so no one else in the crowded room can hear him.

I turn to face him, growing serious. "Is it a bad investment?"

Joel looks away, coming back with the only answer he could give that wouldn't throw Miles under the bus, yet still not require lying to me. "Reality TV is risky. When you hit, you hit it big. Look at *Survivor* or *The Bachelor*. But it's anyone's guess what will hit these days. Young people are a fickle audience. Their appetite changes faster than we can keep up. I'd say faster than they change their underwear, but sitting behind the camera all day, I know most of 'em don't wear any." He shakes his head ruefully.

I nod. The monitor I've been halfheartedly watching pans to focus on Kate. Joel keeps talking, not realizing he's lost my attention. Kate looks beautiful, all dressed up in a pale blue gown that shows off the tan she deepened while playing in the pool today. My moment of joy is quickly replaced by an ache in my chest as Flynn Beckham walks to where she's standing alone outside on the deck. The lighting from the sun beginning to set creates a romantic backdrop.

"Pull in on three," Joel yells into a headset. I watch as the camera pans in on the couple.

"Wow. I didn't think you could look more beautiful than you did today in the pool." Flynn takes Kate's hand. She looks down at their joined hand as he twines his fingers with hers.

Kate smiles, her response timid, like she's not used to receiving compliments regularly. Only, I can't imagine that to be true. "Thank you. You clean up pretty good yourself."

"What were you just thinking about? You looked a million miles away." Flynn takes a strand of her hair and tucks it gently behind her ear. His eyes never leave her face. It's difficult for me to watch, disappointment mixed with a hint of jealousy builds inside of me at seeing another man touch her. Yet I know I have no right to feel this way.

She hesitates, looking away for a second, and then back. "Sorry. I was just thinking about last night."

I knew it. You're thinking about me too, aren't you?

"You should be thinking about tomorrow, not yesterday." Flynn leans his head down, dragging her eyes back up to his.

Tilting her head to the side, she asks, "What's tomorrow?"

"Our date." The asshole smiles so big, I want to smack the smugness from his face.

"You want me as your first stranded date?"

"Cut! Camera three, fade to black," Joel yells, and the picture I'm staring at fades away, along with my hope.

An hour later when Miles finally comes back from the set, I feel deflated. "Have you been watching?" he asks excitedly.

"I watched for a little while." My tone is curt. I've never been one to easily hide my emotions too well. But Miles is riding high and doesn't even notice.

"There's so much chemistry going on in there, the set might explode."

"That's great, Miles."

"We're on a fifteen-minute break and then Flynn is going to announce his pick for the first stranded date. I'll be able to wrap up in an hour, then we can head back to the studio."

"Great." My brother completely misses the sarcasm in my tone.

Joel comes back out of the house, just as Miles goes back in. Taking the seat next to him, I decide to watch the final scene, against my better judgment. Roaming cameras tape random exchanges between the contestants, finally settling in on a couple as they pan in outside near the pool area. Flynn appears on camera again, only this time he's with Jessica.

My interest piques back up as she lays both her hands flat on his chest. She looks up at him from beneath big, round, hooded eyes laced with long, thick black lashes that offset her sparkling blues. She really is attractive. A bombshell, one whose curves radiate sex appeal. Apparently Flynn thinks so too. "I'd love to get to know you better in private," she coos at him, her voice sultry and seductive, full of hidden meaning. Normally, she'd be exactly what I would be into.

Flynn seems to get caught in the web she weaves, as easily as she spins it. "I'd love to get to know you, too." He rubs her bare shoulders before he continues, but the exchange is different than it was with Kate, less intimate. "There are a lot of stranded dates coming up." *Fuck!* He's hedging.

Not thinking it through before I open my mouth, I turn to Joel and do something uncharacteristic of me. In fact, it seems more like a Miles thing to do. "Tell Flynn to ask Jessica on the stranded date," I demand.

Joel's brows furrow. "Pardon?"

"This is scripted reality, right?"

"Yes ... but—"

I'm in no mood to argue. "Script him to invite Jessica for the first date," I demand.

"Can I ask why?"

"No." My response is clipped.

Joel's eyebrows shoot up.

"You have my word: This show doesn't make it, you direct the next project over at Montgomery Productions."

Seeing I'm dead serious, knowing I'm a man of my word, it doesn't take long for Joel to see things my way.

"Cut camera five!" he yells into the microphone. "I need a moment with Flynn."

Joel looks to me for approval. I stop him as he heads toward the set. "Don't mention any of this to Miles."

He nods and walks off.

chapter four

Kate

Not sure if I feel disappointment or relief that Flynn picked Jessica for the first stranded date, I plop my unused overnight bag inside my front door.

"Guess Flynn picked someone else, Miley?" Sadie says, pulling a bottle of wine from the fridge and pouring two glasses. "What a loser."

Tossing my keys on the counter, I join her in the kitchen. "Actually, he asked me to go, but I said no. Told him I'd rather come home and share a cheap bottle of White Zinfandel with my best friend." I take the glass she just poured from her hand before she can sip.

"I wouldn't put it past you." She squints, assessing me.

"He picked Jessica." I sigh and sit on the stool on the other side of the counter.

Sadie leans in. "Aren't you violating your contract, disclosing who he picked to me?"

I sip my wine. "My attorney advised me to violate that pesky thing every chance I get."

"Good advice. I bet your lawyer's got a great rack too."

"The weird thing is … I really thought he was going to ask me. He pretty much told me he was going to."

"So what happened?"

"I don't know. Guess he changed his mind when he got a load of Jessica's boobs in that dress."

"Well, he doesn't know what he's missing." Sadie holds the second glass up, an unspoken toast to me before drinking.

"It's okay, I needed to bring the Jeep into the shop tomorrow anyway. And I'm going to see if I can grab a shift at the casino tomorrow night, since I'm off till Monday now. Think you can give me a ride to the studio in the morning? I can find someone to give me a ride back to the shop after it's done."

"Sure. But if Mr. McNiceAss is there, you have to introduce me."

"Miles?" But I know who she's talking about. She's been obsessed with his ass since she came with me to the interview portion of the application process for the show. Some women have a weakness for dimples, others have a thing for broad shoulders or height. Sadie is most definitely an ass girl.

"Who else?"

"There's something weird about that guy. He's nice and all, but I don't trust him. I keep my distance."

Sadie shrugs. "I don't want to marry him. I just want to get him naked." She sips her wine. "And dig my nails into that fine ass as he plows into me."

"How do you practice in entertainment law? Aren't most of your clients handsome actors? It must be difficult for you to get any work done, with your brain constantly in the gutter all day."

"Tell me about it." She exhales loudly and together we finish the bottle before going to bed. We've both had a long stretch of self imposed abstinence. Sadie's to recover from a broken heart her fiancé left her with when he broke things off. But my broken heart doesn't come from the hands of a man. Well, not one in the same respect as Sadie anyway.

I'm early for the production meeting when we pull into the studio parking lot. The silent click of the minutes on the dashboard catches my attention as the number changes. 11:11. Four of a kind. I close my eyes and make a wish. Today may turn out better than I expected after all.

"Thanks for the ride." I reach for the door handle and Sadie cuts the engine.

"I'm coming in with you."

"You really want to meet him? He's a womanizer."

"I'm hoping he'll womanize me."

We walk through the studio toward the conference room where the remaining contestants are meeting this morning to discuss the shooting schedule. Of course, Flynn and Jessica won't be there—they have the day off to recover from their stranded date. I'm guessing any man needs a day of recovery after a date with that woman.

Walking down the long hall to the conference room, I stop in my tracks as I catch sight of someone barreling down the hall, typing away on his iPhone, about five seconds from crashing into me. Sadie walks right into me as I halt. "What the ..." She's just about to yell at me when she spots the man that has halted my path. She gasps, instead of finishing her sentence. The sound catches the attention of the otherwise occupied man.

The casual appearance and demeanor of the other night gone, Cooper looks every bit the picture of power and authority in a custom-tailored three-piece suit. His longish hair grazes his collar, giving him the appearance of a model dressed for an Armani ad. My stomach flutters before he even utters a word.

"Kate." He closes the distance between us, holding out his hand to me, palm up. Shaky from seeing him again without warning, I place my hand in his. My pulse reacts on its own accord, my stomach churning nervously, like a damn schoolgirl's. I stare at him wordlessly, my mind filled with racing thoughts I can't seem to make sense of and pull into words.

"Kate?" he repeats, concern in his voice.

"Cooper. I … I … you caught me off guard, I didn't expect to see you here."

"I didn't expect to see you either." He smiles. "But I'm glad I did." Amusement dances in his eyes, obvious male satisfaction at my being flustered.

Breaking eye contact to collect my wits, I take in the full sight of him. Broad, thick shoulders, the way his shirt tucks into his pants, hanging so perfectly from his narrow waist. Scanning the length of him down, I flush more than when I was caught in his gaze.

He raises one eyebrow playfully, having watched my slow assaulting inspection of him. A lopsided grin graces his face as he speaks, "Let's grab a cup of coffee."

"Coffee?" I mimic, still unable to comprehend even the simplest of conversations. What the hell is wrong with me?

"Yes. Do you drink coffee? If not, I'll buy you tea. Or water. You do drink water, right?" he teases.

"She drinks coffee," Sadie interjects from behind me. I'd completely forgotten there was anyone else in the hall. Anyone else in the universe, in fact, at this moment.

Cooper smiles, addressing Sadie, instead of me. "Good to know. How does she drink her coffee?"

"Cream, no sugar."

He nods, smiling. Something unspoken passes between the two of them.

Thankfully, Sadie snaps me out of my haze. "I have to run, Kate. Do you want me to pick you up?"

"No, I'm good. I'll get a ride."

"You sure?"

Cooper responds, "I'll drive her."

"You don't even know where I'm going," I say.

"It doesn't matter."

"Bye, Ms. Biel-Timberlake." Sadie saunters off, a shit-eating grin on her face.

"So … coffee?" he asks, already guiding me with his hand on the small of my back.

"Sure." I'm early and a cup of coffee isn't a date, I justify in my head.

We only make it a few steps down the hall together before Cooper's cell phone rings. He mutters something I can't make out before he excuses himself to answer. "What?"

I'd hate to be on the receiving end of that phone call.

"No. You can't offer that. Every union will be breathing down our neck if you do. That's not negotiating, that's throwing in the towel." He pauses, listens for a minute and then growls, "Christ, Evan. I'll be right there. No. Don't let them walk out the door. Tell them to wait."

"I'm sorry. I have to run. What time are you leaving?"

"Five?" I guesstimate, since I actually have no idea how long a reality TV planning session will take. Foolishly, I used to think reality TV was about reality.

"I'll pick you up here."

"Thanks. But you don't have to. I can get a ride."

Stepping in my path, he turns to face me, halting my stride. Eyes lock on my mouth for a long moment, then his lips curl as he meets my gaze. "I'm taking you," he says in a raspy voice. "It's probably the one thing that is going to keep me sane today. Thinking about seeing you again later."

How can I argue with that logic?

Sitting around a long conference table, two rows deep, the "talent" in the front, crew in the back, I listen as Miles Montgomery spends hours detailing his vision. He lays out who we are. Who we are. I guess I should be happy he's dubbed me "the girl next door," especially since the room apparently contains one "town slut" and another "drunk gossip." He actually gives us these titles, as if he's the king at the coronation and we're his subservient minions. I wasn't a big fan the first day I met Miles Montgomery, even less of one after today.

I find myself daydreaming for a good portion of the meeting, my mind continually wandering back to one person, Cooper. He was even more striking than I remembered; his captivating green eyes were difficult to tear mine away from. And the way he spoke today, the command he held, heightened how sexy he is to a whole new level.

As if reading my mind, Miles throws a file onto the table. "This, ladies and gentlemen, is a copy of your contract. Putting aside the legal ease, this is what it boils down to. He motions to his assistant and she flicks off the lights. A screen projects up on one side of the room. The first few bullet points fill a page. Miles reads them aloud.

"You are a character in a loosely scripted play. You are not free to choose to play a new one.

Forget the cameras are there. Don't whisper; we need to capture that secret you're telling.

Discussing anything that has not been aired with anyone outside of the show is a violation of your contract.

Cameras and cell phones are prohibited. You are to have no outside contact of any kind during the hours you're filming.

Dating or sexual relationships, of any kind, other than with the bachelor or a fellow contestant, are prohibited until the last episode has aired.

Violation of any of the terms of the contract will result in forfeiture of any prizes. And you can, and will, be sued for breach of contract."

He smiles as if he's enjoying himself. Something about the guy just makes me want to shower after spending time in a room with him.

I'm outside talking to Ava when Cooper pulls up in a classic convertible Porsche. Her eyes go wide when he hops out of his car and heads over to me as if he's on a mission.

"Ready?" he asks in a businesslike manner. His hand reaching out to the small of my back is the only indication he could be more than my ride.

"Yes." I smile somewhat wearily at Ava. "See you tomorrow." Her mouth is still hanging open as we walk away.

Remaining silent as he opens the door for me and waits for me to get in, Cooper jogs around to the driver's side and pulls out of the parking spot in a rush. "If you're in a hurry, I can get a ride," I offer, but he's already barreling out of the lot.

"Sorry. I just want to get out of here. It's been a long day." His hand flexes, shifting the gear stick into third and, as ridiculous as it seems, even the sight of him taking control of the car does something to me. *What the hell is wrong with me?*

"Everything okay?" I ask, turning to watch him drive. There's tension on his face ... in the clench of his handsome jaw.

"It's better now." He flashes me a sexy grin.

As we make our way through traffic and reach the highway, he turns east, rather than west. "Ummm ... I live the other way."

"Not taking you home," he says with a smile. One that reaches all the way up to his eyes. They're now covered with sunglasses, but I picture the sunflowers growing bigger as his smile broadens.

"Where are you taking me?"

"For something to eat."

"And you're not going to bother to ask if I want to go?" My eyebrows rise, intrigued more than offended by his assumption.

"This is the third time I'm asking you out. The first time you shot me down. The second time we were interrupted. So I'm not taking any chances by hesitating."

"What if I were to tell you to take me home right now?"

He glances at me and quickly back to the road. "I'd take you home." His unwavering response solidifies what I've felt since the moment I met him. Underneath the bossy exterior lies a gentleman at heart. The combination is sexy as hell.

"I guess I am sort of hungry …"

Cooper chuckles. "You're difficult, aren't you?"

"Is that a problem?"

"Not all. Good things don't usually come easy. And I love a challenge."

A flutter grows deep in my belly. I consider arguing with him for a second, telling him I'm not a challenge for him to conquer. But instead, I relax into the seat, deciding to enjoy the wind in my hair and the beautiful man sitting next to me.

"So you work at Mile High?" I ask, breaking a comfortable silence.

"No." His response is fast, almost as if the notion insults him.

"You just hang around there in a business suit and drop in to play cards sometimes?" I say, waiting for him to fill in the blanks.

"Something like that." The corner of his mouth twitches up, but he tries to hide his amusement.

Merging on to the scenic Pacific Coast Highway, Cooper hits the gas and the car's power pumps up my adrenaline. The roar of the engine coupled with the beautiful late afternoon sun warming me as the wind streaks through my hair is invigorating. Freeing. A feeling I realize I haven't felt in a very long time. I lean back into my seat, shut my eyes, and let myself sink into the sensation.

Cooper reaches across and gently lifts my hand from my lap, wrapping my fingers around the gearshift before his hand covers mine. Our eyes meet for a split second and we both smile.

"You like the car?"

"I like how I feel right now," I reply honestly. Cooper's hand tightens around mine.

A short time later we exit the highway, traveling off the beaten path for a while until we pull into a parking lot. I'm surprised to find we're at a roadside food truck. This seems more my style than I would have taken Mister Custom Three-piece Suit for. He comes around to open my door and offers me his hand.

"Not what I would have expected," I say.

"Sometimes the best things in life are the unexpected."

The parking lot has a half a dozen worn picnic tables and the food truck looks like it's seen its glory days ... about a decade ago. Cooper doesn't let go of my hand as he walks over to the older couple loudly arguing from inside the truck.

"Ah! Señor Cooper. Long time no see. We've been wondering where you've been," the man exclaims in broken English.

"Busy, Carlos. Busy."

"You work too much. Just like your father. God rest his soul." The man makes the sign of the cross.

The man's wife smiles at me and then speaks to Cooper in Spanish. *"Esta es su novia? Ella es Hermosa."* The only words I understand are *ella es hermosa*—"she is beautiful."

"Sí, ella es muy hermosa," Cooper says, squinting at me with a devilish look on his face. *"Y estoy trabajando en la parte novia."*

"Ahh." The woman smiles at me and then says to Cooper, *"Ella no tiene oportunidad."* She laughs.

"What did she say?" I ask Cooper.

"She said you don't have a chance."

"About what?"

He ignores my question. "They make the best tapas on the West Coast here."

"You find someplace better on the East?" Carlos interrupts, looking highly offended.

"Just a figure of speech, Carlos. Just a figure of speech," Cooper says, amused. "They have salads if you prefer," he adds as I study the menu board.

"I like real food."

He smiles like I've just given him the answer he hoped for. "Two Platos Combinados."

"Dos cervezas por favor," I add and Cooper arches an eyebrow.

I shrug. "Don't be too impressed. I can only order two beers and ask directions to the bathroom." We sit down at one of the picnic tables with our heaping plates. The smell is incredible. "So how many other languages do you speak?"

"Two—French and Italian. And what did you just do?"

"Nothing."

"I saw you tap your knuckles on the table. Did you just knock on wood?"

I do so many things on autopilot, I seriously didn't even give it any thought. I suppose most people I surround myself with are either used to it, or don't pay close enough attention to catch my little idiosyncrasies. I shrug, trying to make light of it. "It's good luck."

"I thought it was more of an expression than an actual thing."

"It's a thing," I say defensively.

"Guess it's more your thing, than mine."

"What's your thing then?"

He doesn't respond. Well, at least not verbally. But his eyes drop to my mouth and his lips curl to just a hint of a grin when his gaze returns to mine … damn it's sexy. My insides do funny things thinking of what his *thing* might be.

"So. Three languages." I lift a tapas to my mouth. "Prep school brat?"

Cooper chuckles at my quite obvious attempt to change the subject, but goes along with me anyway. "Actually, just the opposite. My father thought our school system was too segregated, so he put us in public school in a lower income area. Thought it would teach us about real life more than spending our days with a bunch of silver spoons."

"Wow. Totally wasn't expecting that response."

"Told you to watch out about those expectations."

I bite into the first of a packed plate of tapas. "Oh my god. This is incredible."

"I wouldn't steer you wrong."

I inhale two small tapas. "How did you find this place?"

"Carlos and Glorya have been in this spot for almost thirty years. It was my parents' favorite place to eat. My father always told everyone that he fell in love with my mother because she never ordered a salad."

"Smart woman."

"My mother said he took her here because he was cheap."

"Which one was the truth?"

He smiles. "Both."

When I've devoured almost everything on my plate and am reaching for the last sip of my beer, Cooper's fingers circle one of my wrists. "They're so small."

I have to blink myself out of the dirty thoughts seeing his hand locked around my wrist conjures up. I swallow hard. "Is that a problem?"

"Not at all. I was just thinking I could probably fit both in one hand."

Flustered, I ignore his comment and change the subject. "It sounded like you haven't been here in a while?"

He nods and looks around. "It's definitely been too long."

"Too busy being a tycoon?"

"A tycoon, huh?" Lifting an eyebrow, he grins. "How do you know I'm a tycoon?"

"I can just tell." I pause, but Cooper neither confirms nor denies my assumption. "Am I wrong?"

"No, you're not wrong, actually. And what do you do? Aside from hustling cards?"

"Playing cards is sort of my job these days," I say, trying to act like it's a choice I've made, instead of something that I dread doing daily. I'd much rather be finishing up school than spending my nights in the high-stakes room, flipping cards to men who deal out hundreds like candy. Especially since most of them seem to think their stack of chips will impress me.

"You're a dealer?" He doesn't seem surprised. After all, I told him who my father was the other night.

"For now. I was in school, but had to take some time off."

He nods, accepting my response without further prodding.

Another hour passes by in what seems like five minutes. Our conversation jumps from topic to topic, but there's a buzz in the air that makes everything seem like it has a sexual undertone to it. He's playful, some of his flirting innuendo is intentional, but my mind seems to want to read something filthy into everything he says. I finally eye the time on my watch. "Shoot. I didn't realize it was so late. I have to work tonight."

He nods and offers me his hand to stand up. The way he doesn't let go and we walk to the car with our hands twined makes me feel like a teenager again. He opens my car door and I stop before getting in. "I probably would have passed right by this place and never even noticed it. It's sweet that you come to your parents' favorite place."

"Pretty sure I've never been called sweet by a woman." Cooper adds with a wry grin, "But if you like sweet, I'll take it."

My heart is heavy when we pull up to my apartment building. Cooper gets out to open my car door.

"Thank you for kidnapping me."

"Anytime." He says. "Are you going to agree to go out with me now, or do I need to kidnap you again?" He takes a step closer to me. "That one little taste wasn't enough."

My eyes close with dread. Everything about this man seems perfect, and yet I have to turn him down. Again. When I signed the contract for the show, I didn't give any thought to what would happen if I met someone. Most likely because I hadn't met anyone worth worrying about the last year. But of course, now I meet a man who gives me butterflies. And I can't tell him about the show. Just like dating, disclosure of my involvement with the show itself is a violation of the terms.

Opening my eyes, feeling disappointment and regret at what I must do, I'm met by a sparkling sea of green intensity that threatens to drown me in lust, making what I have to say that much harder. "I can't."

Picking up on my lack of conviction or word choice, Cooper says, "Can't? Or don't want to?"

"Can't." I know it would be easier to lie and say I don't want to, but something tells me he'd see right through me.

"Why?" He leans in just an inch or two. Our bodies aren't touching, but the heat emanating from his skin ignites mine. Or maybe it's the heat from my own body that sparks his. Either way, I can't think straight with this beautiful man so close.

"I ... I ... I just can't."

"You can't date me?"

I shake my head.

He leans forward to whisper in my ear. Voice gritty and strained, his warm breath sends a shiver through my body that I can't even try to hide. "Can you kiss me?"

Too distracted to form a cohesive thought, I don't respond right away.

Cooper pulls his head back slowly, the stubble on his cheek lightly grazing my sensitive skin, until we're face to face. Smoldering eyes staring intently into mine, mixed with a hard, muscular body just inches away, make it easy to forget that he's off limits. Banned. Forbidden. A complete violation of the rules of my contract. It only makes me want him more.

Swallowing hard, my mouth suddenly parched, I unconsciously run my tongue along my lips to moisten them, readying myself to finally speak.

Cooper's eyes drop, following the path of my tongue. As his eyes finally find their way back up to mine, I open my mouth to speak just as his lips crash down on mine.

I don't even attempt to protest, immediately surrendering to the ferocity of a kiss that sets my entire body on fire. Our tongues find each other quickly, his leading mine in a just slightly aggressive way that excites me. Gently at first, the hard contours of his body press flush against the soft of my curves. Then I reach up, my hands threading the hair curling up at the edge of his collar. Cooper growls when I tug, pushing harder against me, deepening the kiss as we move from exploring to feverishly groping each other.

Both of us are panting wildly as we break the kiss. He tugs at my lower lip, claiming it roughly between his teeth before fully releasing my mouth.

"Wow," I croak out, my mind still in a daze as my eyes flutter back open. Cooper's thumb rubs tenderly across my now swollen bottom lip as his eyes come up to reach mine again. Flicking down to my mouth and then quickly back to my eyes, he looks torn between kissing me again and saying something.

"See, that wasn't so hard," he rasps, one side of his mouth tilting upward into a sexy half grin. "And that, Kate, won't be the last time that happens. I promise you that."

My wobbly legs carry me up the stairs, but I feel Cooper's eyes on me every step as they lead me away. When I reach the top, I make the mistake of looking back. He's leaning against his car, arms folded over his chest, watching me intensely with those piercing green eyes. Eyes that tell me he's a man that keeps his promises.

Inside my apartment, I lean my head against the door for a few minutes as the haze of lust clears and my knees find their strength. Replaying Cooper's vow in my mind, I reach up to feel my still swollen lips. And all I can think of is *Oh shit.*

chapter five

Cooper

"**M**r. Montgomery?" Helen peeks her head in the door hesitantly. "The division heads are all in the boardroom for your weekly pitch meeting."

I look at my watch and back to Helen. "Tell them I'll be a few minutes."

Helen looks confused. I'm never late and she's no doubt wondering why I am today, since I've been sitting at my desk for the last hour doing absolutely nothing. I just can't seem to concentrate this morning. She nods without saying anything else.

"Helen?" I call after her before she heads back out to her desk. "What time is Miles's production meeting this morning?"

"I'm not sure. Let me make a quick call."

A few minutes later she returns and hands me a few papers. "This is the schedule for the next week. Looks like the production meeting started a few minutes ago."

I stand.

"You forgot your jacket," Helen points out as I make my way to the door.

"Reschedule the pitch meeting to this afternoon."

"Really?" She sounds shocked. I rarely go off schedule, especially with weekly meetings. Another trait inherited from my dad. Don't cancel meetings, it tells people there is something more important than them. Today, that's exactly the case.

"Make it late afternoon. I might be a while."

Miles's production meeting is already in full swing when I slip in unnoticed. I pick up a pad and pencil from the pile on the table in the back of the room, as if I might really take notes on anything he's saying. He's rambling on about the art of sexuality, but I don't really hear a word. My brother notices me and waves, his already robust delivery of his lecture becoming even more animated for my benefit. He's always been the showman of the family. I'm surprised he never wanted to be in front of the camera.

I nod and quickly scan the room, my eyes landing immediately on her. Unlike the other attentive women clinging to Miles's every word, Kate is doodling something on the pad in front of her, not paying a lick of attention. It makes me smile.

"Let's start out with an example of what is *not* sexy. We have some clips from the show that landed on the editing room floor. This isn't the first day of shooting, ladies. We need to forget the cameras already." Miles motions toward his dutiful secretary, and the concealed screen at the front of the room begins to inch down.

The video starts off with a kiss so awkward, it makes me uncomfortable just to watch it. Jenny Clark and I did better than that behind the dumpster in the back of the school in sixth grade. At least the way *I* remember my first kiss.

A second kiss comes on, this one a little better, but the woman looks right into the camera the second it's over. Not exactly the voyeuristic feel my brother is going for. A few more roll across the screen, none of which hold my interest for long.

I watch as Kate glances up at the screen on occasion, but her doodling seems to have her rapt. The corner of her mouth quirks up slightly as her pencil swirls around the corner of the page. It makes me curious what she's drawing. Then suddenly her pencil stops, she raises her head, and our gazes meet. And hold. She blinks a few times, almost as if she's deciding if I'm really standing here or not, then her eyes widen when she decides I'm really on the other side of the room.

Amused at her reaction, I flaunt a smile and watch as she becomes flustered. Nervously, she looks to see if Miles is watching our exchange, then looks back to me. My brother is oblivious. He's busy pausing the video so he can berate the poor women who he's caught uncomfortably sharing a kiss with the moron bachelor.

Not quite sure what to do, Kate tries to ignore me. Her eyes dart all over the room—to Miles then back to me, down at her pad for a second, then quickly back up to me. My stare never waivers. She fidgets in her seat when she realizes I'm not looking away anytime soon.

I casually move from my position near the back door. Kate's eyes flare wide when she realizes I'm walking toward her. I stop a few feet behind her. She shifts her hand to cover her doodle, but I catch it before she does. A script C is scribbled over and over. Again I'm brought back to sixth grade. Jenny used to scrawl my name all over her notebooks. I smile triumphantly. Kate's fidgeting in her seat becomes more pronounced as I take a step closer to her from behind.

I've lost track of what Miles is talking about as he drones on ... until a close up of Kate freezes on the screen.

"Well, ladies. We've learned what a bad kiss looks like, now let's learn what a good kiss looks like."

Miles nods and his assistant begins the video again.

"Did you know," says Flynn, the bachelor I've come to despise, yet never met, "that on the majority of dating shows, the first kiss on the show winds up being the last?" He reaches for Kate's hand.

Kate looks down, watching him lace their fingers together. "I didn't know that. But sounds like you may want to be selective with who you bestow the coveted honor on." There's a hint of sarcasm in her voice.

"Oh, I'm selective all right. I've been saving the kiss for the right one."

Kate squints. "So you haven't kissed anyone yet? That's not what the ladies are saying."

Flynn's face shows surprise.

"According to rumors, you've kissed plenty more than one."

"I haven't," he protests.

Kate looks up at the longhaired dickhead. "Why would they lie?"

"Strategy, I guess."

"Hm. The thought of kissing someone right after they've kissed someone else does kind of gross me out."

Dickhead takes their joined hands and wraps them around Kate's back, pulling her close to him. "Well, I haven't kissed anyone else, Kate." He pauses and waits for her to look up. "I was saving it for the someone I thought might be my last kiss of the show."

Kate opens her mouth to say something, but Dickhead doesn't give her a chance. He seals his mouth over hers and kisses her. At first, it's stiff—he's kissing her, but she isn't sure what to do. *Come on, Kate, don't kiss him back.* Then the reality hits me like a blow. Her body melts into him and she kisses him back. *Kisses the fucking asshole.* I see Kate turn to sneak a look at me a few times, but I don't ease my glare at the screen. The loud snap of the pencil I'm holding in my hand echoes through the room two seconds before I storm out.

Back in my office, I pace as I rake my fingers through my hair, tugging as I bellow harshly at Helen. "Go find Kate Monroe. She's in my brother's production meeting. Wait till it breaks and bring her to my office."

chapter six

Kate

"Ms. Monroe?" a kind-looking older woman asks as I exit the production meeting.

"Yes?"

"My name is Helen. Could you come with me?"

"Umm ... sure. Where are we going?"

"Mr. Montgomery would like to see you."

I turn and look back at the room.

"He asked me to bring you to his office after the meeting was over."

"Oh." *Shit*. Miles knows. He must have caught on with how the two of us were looking at each other. The guy would probably be thrilled if I'd been making out during the meeting with one of my fellow bachelorettes, but I'm likely to get fired for even flirting with one of his colleagues.

Together, Helen and I make our way across the complex and up to the top floor of the building. She brings me to an open door at the corner of a luxurious-looking suite of offices. Much nicer than I would have expected of Miles. Classier. I would have thought he would be more a metal-desk-and-worn-shag-carpet kind of guy. The sleek, intimidating swank of this place doesn't fit.

"Ms. Monroe is here," Helen announces and steps aside for me to enter.

I walk in with trepidation. I really need to make it to the top four.

"Did you like kissing him?" The voice catches me off guard.

"Cooper?" I look up, confused.

He stalks to me. "Did you?" He infiltrates my personal space but I don't move.

"Where's Miles?"

"I don't care where Miles is. Answer my question."

"But ..."

"Please, Kate. Just answer the question."

"I don't understand."

He takes a step closer. I take one back.

"Did you like kissing him? It's a simple question, Kate. Yes or no." His voice is flat, monotone, but it's not the kind of flat sound that makes you think the words aren't important. Just the opposite. The way they're said in such a controlled tone makes me think the answer really matters and he's controlling himself to even ask the question.

"It isn't a simple question. Nothing about what I'm doing is simple."

Another step closer. One more back for me.

"Did you feel the same thing kissing him as you did when I kissed you yesterday?"

I don't say anything.

He takes one more step toward me.

I retreat another step. My back hits the wall behind me.

Cooper leans in, one arm pressed into the wall on either side of my head. I look to the right, then the left. His stare is unrelenting, even while I avoid his eyes.

"You're not answering me."

I'm not sure how to respond, so I don't. At least not with words anyway. Instead, I give in to what I'm feeling and let my body tell him the answer. My mouth closes the small distance between us and I literally devour his lips.

I may have started the kiss, but it takes less than a heartbeat for Cooper to take over. With a growl, he pins me against the wall and devours me. Wrapping my hair tightly in his fingers, his grip is so firm, I couldn't escape if I wanted to. But it's irrelevant, because there's nowhere else I'd rather be in this moment.

"Wow," I breathe when we come up for air.

"Jesus, Kate." His voice is low and thick, chest heaving.

"No," I whisper.

Cooper's eyes question me.

"No, it didn't feel like this when I kissed Flynn."

"Who?"

"Flynn … the bachelor?"

"Oh. I've taken to calling him Dickhead."

Cooper's serious, although it doesn't stop me from laughing. In fact, his stern demeanor makes me completely crack up. He doesn't seem happy that I'm finding amusement at his expense. "Dickhead? Really?" I laugh.

He tries to remain serious, but I catch the corner of his mouth twitch. "I have a few other names, if you'd like to try one of those on to see if it fits better."

I shake my head. "What did he do that made you conjure a vast dictionary of nicknames?"

"He's in my way."

Cooper hasn't moved, and I suddenly realize where I am. "Ummm … where is Miles?"

"Probably on the casting couch with one of the contestants from your show."

Miles is undoubtedly the casting-couch kind. I smile and look around. "Wouldn't he be casting in this office though?"

"My office? Miles tries to avoid me at all costs most days."

I pull my head back, confused. "This isn't Miles's office?"

Cooper furrows his brow.

"But Helen said Mr. Montgomery wanted to see me, and she brought me here."

Cooper inhales, then blows out a deep, audible breath. "Sit."

"Okay, now I'm ready," Sadie says as she hands me a very full glass of wine. She kicks off her four-inch heels and settles in on the loveseat for the story of my bizarre day.

"You do realize you aren't supposed to fill the glass to the brim, right?"

She shrugs. "I'm efficient. If I pour a half glass now, I'm only going to have to get up again in five minutes."

She has a point. I gulp a mouthful of wine and dig in. "Cooper is Miles's brother."

Sadie is a lawyer—not showing surprise is her forte—but her eyes bulge when I give her the news. "We're going to need a second bottle."

"Picked it up on my way home."

"So he knows you're on the show?"

"Yep. He didn't know when we played cards last week. But he saw the dailies from the show and recognized me."

"And?"

"And I kissed him when we were in his office."

"How was his office?"

"Really? That's what you want to know. Not how was the kiss or aren't you in breach of your contract? How was his office?"

"You can tell a lot about a man by his office."

I gulp another unladylike sip from my wine glass. "His office was beautiful. Sleek, overlooking the city. It oozed power."

"Nice. Bet he fucks like he owns you."

The thought of what he's like in bed is enough to make me lose my train of thought.

"Go on," Sadie prods.

I don't continue immediately.

"You forgot what you were up to because you were thinking of him fucking you like he owns you, didn't you?" My best friend smirks knowingly.

"Shut up." I pause. "Anyway, I don't know what I'm going to do."

"Well, him. Obviously."

"I wish it were that easy."

"What was his take on the whole thing?"

"He said he didn't care if I was breaking the rules. He wants to get to know me."

"And by 'get to know you,' he means starting with the inside and working his way out. I saw the way that man looked at you. I almost had to come home and change *my* wet panties." She pauses. "But I took them off instead. There's something really empowering about walking around in a skirt and no panties at work, don't you think?"

"Can we get back to my issue? Dealing with yours will take years."

Sadie shrugs. "So, you both keep quiet, what's the big deal?"

"Forgetting about the contract, and the fact that Miles can sue me for more than I will probably earn for the rest of my life, I just don't think I can be involved with two guys at once. Even if I don't win, I really need to get to the top four to win enough money to buy some time to come up with the rest my mom needs."

"How long do you have left?"

"Seven weeks."

"So tell Cooper you need a couple of months."

I drain the rest of my wine glass. "Something tells me that won't go over too well ... asking Cooper to wait around while I date someone else."

"What choice does he have?"

"I don't know. But Cooper Montgomery is not the type of man you give an ultimatum."

chapter

seven

Cooper

"I thought that stupid meeting would never end," I grumble, falling in step with Kate as she walks down the hall after her morning production meeting.

She smiles and keeps walking. "Were you standing out there long?"

"Long enough to have lost my patience. Meet me in my office in ten minutes."

She stops mid stride. It takes me a few paces to realize I'm no longer next to her. "Bossy, much?"

"I'll show you how bossy I am right here in the hall, if you'd prefer." I arch an eyebrow.

"Coop," Miles's voice carries from down the hall. I wave and then return my attention to Kate.

"My office ten minutes or do you prefer the hall?" She looks back at Miles and then me, quickly making the right decision.

"Your office."

I gloat my victory with a smile and turn just as my brother approaches. Kate walks a bit ahead, but Miles stops her. "Kate, have you met my brother?"

"Ummm ... I don't think so." She turns cautiously.

"Nice to meet you." I extend my hand and my fingers stroke the inside of her palm inconspicuously.

Her eyes widen and I take my time to release her from the shake.

"Kate here is one of the contestants on *Throb*." Miles puts his hand on Kate's shoulder. I fight the urge to remove it for him and simply nod.

"She's one of Flynn's favorites. A shoo-in for the final four overnight dates."

Between his hand still on Kate's shoulder and the thought of her anywhere near Flynn, I need to get the hell out of here. "Did you want something, Miles? I have a meeting." I look at my watch and then to Kate pointedly. "In eight minutes."

"Be a few minutes late. I need to talk shop." Shop equals he needs something from me.

"I can't. It's an urgent deal I'm in the middle of. I need to tie it up this morning. Call Helen and get on my schedule." I turn to Kate and nod before stalking to the elevator bank.

"Kate Monroe is here to see you," Helen's voice flows through the intercom.

"Send her in. And hold my calls."

"I thought I was going to call you tonight so we could talk?" Kate says as she enters my office.

"Change of plans." I shut the door behind her and deadbolt it. The loud clank of the lock clicking shut captures her attention. She turns to look back at the door and then to me.

"Are you locking people out, or me in?" She arches an eyebrow.

"Both. Come here." I crook my finger.

"You really are bossy."

"Does that bother you?" I close the safe distance she's left between us.

"It depends."

"On what?" I brush the hair from her face.

"On what you're bossy about."

I lift her hand and kiss her knuckles. "Just about you."

"Just me?" The challenge in her voice softens as our eyes meet.

I nod. "Kiss me."

"Bossy."

"Difficult."

"I'm not diff ..." She doesn't get the chance to finish her protest before my mouth is sealed over hers.

"Wow," she says when I release her a full five minutes later, and it makes me smile. I noticed she's said it after each time I kissed her. Almost as if the effect it has on her takes her by surprise. "You're really good at that."

"No. We're just really good together," I say. "I can tell already."

I pull her to me and hold her tightly against my chest. Neither of us says a word for a few minutes.

"Cooper?" Her voice is quiet, but the simple two-syllable word tells me she's about to bestow news I don't want to hear. I tighten my hold on her.

"Hmmm?" I kiss the top of her forehead.

"We need to talk."

chapter eight

Kate

"I really like you. I do … but …"

Cooper holds up his hand. "Don't."

"Don't what?"

"Don't give me the I really like you speech."

Well, there goes what I spent half the night planning to say.

Cooper folds his arms across his chest. "Sit."

"Bossy," I mutter under my breath, but sit anyway.

"Is it the show?"

I nod.

Cooper paces while he speaks. "Is quitting an option?"

Regretfully, I shake my head.

"I'm not sure I want to hear the answer, but I'll ask anyway. Do you have feelings for *him?*" He rakes his fingers through his hair and says the word *him* with harried disdain.

"Who? Dickhead?"

Cooper's mouth twitches at the corners. "Yes, Dickhead."

"He's really nice." His jaw clenches. "But that's not it."

"You're locked into a contract?"

"Yes."

"I'll talk to Miles. He owes me one. Or a thousand and one. I've lost track."

"No. You can't."

"Why not?"

"Because I need to stay on the show."

"Do you want the exposure? I'll tell him you need to stay on the show, but that you aren't living up to whatever the terms his warped mind has conjured up."

"I don't want the exposure."

Cooper stops. "Then what is it?"

"I need to win."

"Why? If you don't want the prize?"

"It's not the bachelor that I need."

"There's a financial incentive?"

I nod. Suddenly, I feel like a whore.

The clock ticks by, long seconds where the silence hangs thick in the air, neither of us saying a word. Finally, I speak. "I can't see two men at once. I need to keep my focus, and I won't be able to do that if we keep this up."

When I see the disappointment in his face, my chest feels like someone stepped on it. "How long does the show have left?" he asks.

"Seven weeks, two days." Not that I'm counting.

He blows out a thick stream of air, nods, holds me tight before we say goodbye. When his grip on me loosens, it takes everything I have to walk out his door.

chapter nine

Kate

The more I get to know Flynn, the more I find there is to like. So why is it that I resist elevating things to the next level? He's a complete gentleman with me. Taking things slowly, not pushing, leaving it up to me to decide the next step. We've definitely connected, yet there's something holding me back from moving from friends to more. *Damn you, Cooper Montgomery.* It's been a week since I saw him, yet I still can't get him out of my mind.

"Earth to Kate." Flynn bumps shoulders with me.

"Sorry. I overslept and didn't get to have coffee yet."

"Well, we need to fix that. Al, can we pull over at the next Starbucks, please?" Flynn asks the bus driver.

I smile. "You don't have to do that."

"You're going to need it for today's challenge." He winks at me.

"You know what today's challenge is?"

"Yep. Not my favorite. You'll understand why soon. But I need you to wake up so you can win." The bus pulls into a strip mall parking lot. There's a Starbucks at the end. "Al, you wanna see if anyone else wants anything?"

I stand, ready to go inside to grab my coffee.

"Sit. I'll get it."

I smile, but not because of how sweet Flynn is. *Sit* reminds me of bossy Cooper.

Flynn returns with my coffee, and it's exactly how I take it, even though he didn't ask. The bus driver hands out everyone else's orders. You would think Flynn had handed me an engagement ring, rather than a cup of coffee, from the looks I get from some of the other girls.

"So, you going to give me a hint about the challenge today?" I whisper when Flynn sits next to me, arm slung casually over the back of my seat. His fingers gently rub the exposed skin on my shoulder.

"How about I give you three hints and you see if you can guess?"

"Deal." I turn, giving him my full attention.

"One. You're really good at it. But we haven't done it in a while and I miss it."

"Hmmm … I'm intrigued."

"Two. I hope no one wants yours today."

"You need to give better hints."

His eyes sparkle. "Three." He leans in and kisses me softly on the lips. It's an innocent kiss; his forehead rests tenderly against mine as the bus slows to a stop.

Everyone crowds to look outside the windows at where we are. Santa Monica Pier. A minute later, Miles hops on the bus and delivers today's challenge.

"Ladies. Welcome to Santa Monica Pier. Today's challenge may earn one lucky contestant immunity from going home this week. With only six women left, the winner will have only one more elimination ceremony before making it to the coveted final four. I'll let your boyfriend tell you all about what we're doing here at the pier."

Flynn stands. "You can bet this one wasn't picked by me." He catches my eye before continuing. "Your challenge today is to earn more money than me. We've each been assigned a booth and we're going to see who the best salesperson is."

"What are we selling?" Jessica asks from two rows behind me.

"You're selling you, Jessica. Each of us is manning a kissing booth today. One dollar buys a kiss. The winner has to earn more money than me and all of the other ladies."

"How are we supposed to sell more kisses than you? Look at you," Jessica coos.

"I have confidence you'll make a killing, Jess."

As we step off the bus, Miles hands us each a chapstick and flashes a leering grin.

"Is she serious?" Sadie motions to Jessica's booth, where the line is probably a hundred deep. We were each allowed to make one phone call and have a friend bring a single item to help us in our challenge today. Jessica received a bikini top from her friend—if you can call it that. Technically, I think "bikini top" is too generous; it's more like nipple covers. Me? I asked Sadie to bring me a box of Altoids. Not my most well-thought-out plan.

I kiss a young boy on the cheek and stuff his dollar into the box next to me. I actually have a pretty decent line, especially considering I'm wearing a tank top that covers my boobs. I look over to Jessica's booth. I gotta hand it to her, she certainly knows how to work it. Leaning over at the waist to reach each tongue-wagging guy, her ass cheeks hang out from her short shorts almost as much as her boobs flow over from her sad excuse for a top. Each guy gets a full pucker kiss on the lips. Even the fourteen-year-olds. There are going to be a lot of wet dreams in Santa Monica tonight.

Two hours later, the director calls for a fifteen-minute break so the crew and contestants can all use the bathroom.

"How's it going over there?" I ask Flynn as we meet in the hall walking out of our respective bathrooms.

"Aside from the sixty-year-old who stuck her tongue down my throat and the fifteen-year-old who left gum on my lips? Not bad. You?"

I laugh. "I had a seventy-year-old man who took a selfie of us kissing to send to his wife because she pissed him off this morning, and I've kissed the same thirteen-year-old boy on the cheek eleven times. He keeps going back on line and trying to turn his head to catch my lips with his."

"Kid's got good taste. I would've been on your line a couple of dozen times too at that age."

"Not Jessica's?" I tease.

"Nah. I'm more the girl-next-door type. I like to use my imagination to picture what's underneath the shirt." Flynn's eyes drop. He starts at my toes, his eyes lingering at my breasts, before his gaze locks with mine.

"Like what you're imagining?" I arch an eyebrow.

"More than you know." He winks.

chapter ten

Cooper

My car veers off the Pacific Coast Highway as if it has a mind of its own. I've kept away the last week, at least in person. Although it hasn't stopped me from obsessing over the dailies I make Helen have on my desk every morning by seven. I'm beginning to feel like a voyeur. Slowing down the parts where Kate's on screen, analyzing her every move when she's around Dickhead.

I've been with women who get possessive too early; it makes me cut ties quickly, deeming them a stalker when it slips they knew where I was the night before without my telling them. Yet here I am, pulling up to the Santa Monica Pier like the stalker I've become. I watched the dailies this morning, told myself I was just going to go for a drive, put the top down and clear my head. I'm even bullshitting myself.

There's a crowd off to the left. It's not hard to find the taping when I see a hoard of predominantly boys and men. *Kissing booth.* I want to kick Miles's ass. It's hard enough to think about Kate kissing Dickhead, let alone a few hundred in line. Thanks, Miles. Way to go, little brother.

"I guess this stunt is a success," I say disparagingly to Miles when I've finally made my way through the crowd of horny assholes.

"Free publicity. This shit will be all over the news tonight." My brother beams with pride.

"What's the winner get?"

"Immunity from going home this week."

"So they don't have to grovel at the asshole bachelor's feet to stay for a few more days?"

"What's your problem with Flynn? He's a good guy." Miles looks at me, finally peeling his eyes from his prized production.

"A good guy? What kind of a man goes on a television show to date twenty women?"

"Not everyone lives a golden life and has women throwing themselves at their feet, my brother."

I ignore him. My eyes focused on only one thing. Across the pier, Kate smiles and kisses a boy on the cheek, but he tries to turn his head and catch her lips. He almost manages to do it too. Kate leans in and whispers something to the boy and he beams. Two seconds later he runs to the back of the line again, digging a dollar from his pocket. I smile as she kisses a few teens innocently on the cheek. Then a muscle-head who must have escaped from Venice Beach saunters up to the table. My teeth clench so tight, I give myself an instant headache.

"Saw you pulling out of the parking lot with Kate in your car the other night." Miles turns to watch me.

I shrug, keeping my stare straight ahead and try to sound casual. "Found her with her hood open. Car problems. I gave her a lift."

"Camera loves her. But she seems to have lost some of her interest in Flynn. Think we need to script her to get back in the mood."

"It's disturbing the way you think you're a puppeteer, Miles." I turn to glare at my brother.

"Get off your high horse, Coop. We're a lot alike. We both hire people and expect them to perform for us. We make them into entertainment."

"I expect them to *act*, Miles. They know what they signed up for."

"So do these women. Do you really think any of them are naïve? Look at them." My brother looks around the pier. "They're all playing a game. No one is forcing any of them to be here. In fact, it looks like they're quite enjoying themselves. I see smiles behind those booths, not chains holding them there."

"Maybe they don't have a choice."

"I'm sure the street walker tells herself the same thing right before she bends over in the alley every night."

"Ten minutes left, everyone!" the director yells through a bullhorn.

"I'm going on line. Gotta put my dollar in for the one I want to stay."

"Whose line are you going on?"

"Jessica's." Miles nods toward her booth. She's wearing a strip of material as a top. Her breasts look like they're about to bust out of the ties that hold everything in place. The show may go from R-rated to X in a few seconds.

"Why don't you spend a buck? Maybe for two, one of them will let you cop a feel?" he says smiling, completely oblivious to the scowl on my face.

Ten minutes later, I'm almost to the front of the line. Kate and I have been playing cat-and-mouse with our eyes since hers landed on me. I wait patiently for the guy in front of me to stuff his dollar into the box and then it's finally my turn.

"Didn't take you for the kind of man to pay for a kiss," she teases.

"First time for everything."

"That will be one dollar, please, sir." Kate extends her open palm.

"So you don't have to make nice to Dickhead if you win?"

"The winner gets immunity from *Flynn* sending them home this week, if that's what you mean," she challenges.

"Is there a limit to how much a man can pay for a kiss?"

"I don't think so. But they're only a dollar."

I dig into my pocket and pull out a wad of hundreds, our eyes locked as I shove them in the box. "Now give me my money's worth." I lean in.

"Bossy," she breathes.

I seal my mouth over hers and don't stop until the director yells time's up.

I only made it worse going to see her today. Kissing her. In the moment it was worth it, feeling the way she melted into me and let me consume her, not pulling away, even though anyone could look over and see us. But the afterglow has worn dim and now I'm sitting home alone like a chick pining for some kid who won't give her the time of day. With all the women I've dated over the years, the one that decides to walk the other way makes me want to crawl after her to catch her.

The intercom buzzes. "A Damian Fry here to see you, Mr. Montgomery." The weariness in Lou's voice comes through loud and clear.

"Send him up." Damian Fry is definitely not the typical guy I invite over for a visit. I've only used him once before. An actor with a thousand-dollar-a-day coke problem wasn't showing up for a high-budget film we were shooting. Everyone knew he had a problem, but I needed the dirt in my hands to get out of his multi-million-dollar contract. Damian didn't just deliver the drug problem on video; he found out the actor was screwing the director's wife too. Damian could dig up dirt on a saint.

"Come in." It's nearly ninety outside, yet he's dressed in long sleeves and pants, head-to-toe black, and smells like day-old booze and cigarettes. No wonder Lou was suspicious.

"Nice place." Damian sizes up my net worth in thirty seconds. I'm sure my price just doubled. Should have met this fucker at my office.

"Thanks." I get straight to the point. "I have a job I need done. But it needs to be kept extremely quiet."

"Quiet is my specialty." He grins.

"Definitely not a word to my brother."

His grin widens to a sneer.

chapter eleven

Kate

"Wanna dance?" Flynn offers me his hand. I've been sitting on the couch since after dinner—*sulking* might best describe my temperament.

"Ummm ... there's no music?"

His boyish smile helps lighten my somber mood.

"Don't need it."

I take the hand he's offering and stand. "You dance without music often?"

"Ah. I didn't say there wouldn't be music. I only agreed there was none playing." Flynn wraps his arm around my waist and pulls me close to him for a slow dance. Leading my body perfectly, he sways to a soothing rhythm until my head rests on his chest. I think his lips might brush the top of my head, but I can't be sure.

His voice is whisper-soft when he starts singing a ballad. I've heard him sing rock before, knew he had a nice voice. But the way he croons the words to this beautiful song, it's absolutely breathtaking. The song is about a son who has to save his mom. Every word rings raw; it makes me certain he's talking about his own mother.

Do you know who I am?
When I see you today.

I'm still the same.

When I see you today.

Let me help you find your way.

You've given me plenty,

Now it's my turn.

Let me help you find your way.

When I see you today.

We keep swaying to the music long after he finishes singing. Eventually Flynn pulls back slightly, enough to look down at me, but our bodies still touching. I swallow, my mouth suddenly dry from the way he's looking at me. His eyes are half-mast, the heat in them unmistakable, when they drop to my mouth and linger for a long moment. He wets his lips and, I swear, my heart pounds so loudly I can hear the blood pumping through my ears. Ever so slowly, his head begins to drop, his eyes watching mine— silently seeking permission. Our faces are almost lined up when, like a needle scratching to a halt on a record, something comes over me and I effectively kill the moment when I speak.

"Do you think it's going to rain later?" Inwardly, I smack myself in the head for sounding like such a dim wit. I couldn't come up with something less obvious?

Flynn's eyes close, but then he rests his forehead against mine, and chuckles when he speaks. "Worried you didn't bring rain boots?"

A cameraman comes in and interrupts, asking us to move to a different area where the lighting is better. I'm grateful for the quick change in mood it brings.

"Wanna go for a walk on the beach?" Flynn asks, releasing me from his arms, but keeping his hand still meshed with mine.

"Sure."

"Do you want to go change?"

I look down at the gown I'm wearing. The salt will probably destroy it. "Nah, it's theirs, not mine."

Flynn smiles.

We walk along the shoreline for a half hour. The warm water occasionally reaching up and wetting our feet.

"So who is he?" he asks after a long, comfortable bout of silence.

I look around. There's no one else on the beach.

"The guy who you won't let go long enough to give me a real shot."

I turn to look for the winded cameraman that was following us. The boom can pick up our conversation a hundred feet away.

"He's sprawled out on the jetty a half mile back," Flynn says, reading my mind. "Probably still cursing us for making him do more exercise than he's done in ten years."

"Oh."

"So, who is he? Ex-boyfriend or fiancé?"

"Neither, actually."

"Damn." Flynn clutches at his chest. "You're killing me. At least pretend there's some great guy waiting in the wings." He smiles.

"It's not you. Really it's not."

"This conversation is getting worse by the minute. What comes next? 'It's me, not you'? Like I haven't thrown that one around before. You're ruining my self-esteem, here."

I laugh. "I think your self-esteem is just fine, rockstar."

"It was." He turns and walks backwards, holding both of my hands. "Until I met you."

"You're sweet. But you've had twenty women throwing themselves at you. I think you'll bounce back quickly."

"Nineteen," he corrects me. "But I'd really like to get the twentieth on board finally."

"You've had nineteen other women chasing you. Why do you need number twenty?"

"Number twenty is all I need. The other nineteen aren't for me, long-term."

"I think your ego is just looking for a little stroking."

"It's not my ego that wants you to stroke it." He wiggles his eyebrows suggestively.

The tide washes up, covering my feet. I splash a wall of water in Flynn's direction, catching him by surprise. He splashes back and before I know it, we're both drenched from head to toe. An hour later, we walk back into the house arm-in-arm—soaked, smiling and stirring a scandal we didn't know was brewing.

chapter twelve

Cooper

Tatiana Laroix is the *it girl* of Hollywood. But she still needs an appointment to make it past Helen. Thank god. I thought by now she'd be chasing someone equally as enthralled with seeing himself up on the big screen. No such luck.

"She said she's shooting the trailer edits in hangar three and needs to speak to you. She didn't look happy at being turned away. Again." Helen hands me a stack of messages. "James Cam is also in that pile, he said it's urgent he speaks to you this morning. I'm guessing the two may be related."

I groan. James Cam is the director of the movie Tatiana just wrapped for Montgomery Productions. The two didn't agree on anything. I thought I was finally done with the petty disputes when we closed down production, but then the trailer needed reshoots, so we had to bring them back for a few days.

I call James back. Apparently Tatiana is refusing to shoot what he wants, claiming it isn't the artistic vision she had in mind for the trailer. *Actresses.*

Two months ago, I made the mistake of taking Tatiana to a premiere. I knew by the end of the night it would be our only date. The way she spoke to people, her newfound fame had already gone to her head. At the after-party, her fingers crawled up my thigh under the table.

I ended the date early, by Hollywood standards anyway, and told her I needed to go home, get a good night's sleep. But she didn't take the hint. Instead, she tried to unbuckle my pants as I drove to her place.

There was no avoiding her at any of the film related parties when we finally completed production. She was always by my side, her hand wrapped possessively around my arm, even though the gesture wasn't returned.

I told her I was busy the next few times she called. Then she showed up at my apartment unannounced. She was near tears, upset about a fight with a director, so I let her in. It was a line I shouldn't have crossed. She was nicer when she wasn't in public putting on a show, but still not for me. She dropped by my place once more, twice now at the office.

"Helen, I'm going down to hangar three, call me if I'm not back in a half hour to help me exit."

She smiles. "Miles is next door in hangar two, shooting some promos. He asked if you could drop by. I'd told him you were packed for the day. But if you're down there ..."

The day just keeps getting better. I've avoided anything *Throb* related the last ten days. It still hasn't gotten Kate out of my head, but at least I can focus on work a little better.

"Can we just talk about it here?" I try not to sound as impatient as I feel. "I have a packed day today, Tatiana."

"You have to eat," she purrs, placing the palms of both her hands against my chest. *Yes, but I'd prefer to eat alone.*

"It's important and we"—she looks around the room at all of the waiting staff—"need to talk in private."

The room full of waiting gaffs and production staff is probably costing me two thousand an hour. I look at my watch. "A quick bite, I need these guys back to work."

She smiles victoriously. I open the door, allowing Tatiana to pass through first. I take four strides and walk directly into Kate.

And Dickhead.

We both freeze, staring at each other.

"Coop. I thought we were in a rush." Tatiana quickly moves to my side. She gives Kate the once-over, then wraps her hands possessively around my bicep.

"Kate." I nod, ignoring Tatiana.

"Cooper," she says softly. "Ummm ... this is Flynn."

"How's it going, man?" The longhaired dickhead is oblivious to my scowl.

"Cooper Montgomery." I nod and squeeze his hand a little too tight when we shake.

Kate looks to Tatiana, who I completely forgot is standing next to me. "This is Tatiana Laroix," I finally say.

The seconds that follow are awkward. Even more so when Dickhead slings his arm casually around Kate's shoulder and says, "We were just going to grab a bite to eat."

My eyes are glued to the arm touching her shoulder. It's difficult to contain the urge to physically remove it for him. "Us too." My jaw clenches. "Why don't you join us?" Kate's eyes go wide; Tatiana's grip tightens a little more.

"Sure." Dickhead shrugs, looking like he doesn't have a goddamned care in the world.

Lunch turns out to be less uncomfortable than I would have thought. Dickhead tells Tatiana he's a big fan and the two of them spend the next half hour talking about her favorite subject: Her.

"You should have thrown it the other way," I say to Kate. Her eyebrows draw together.

"Salt," I clarify. "You tried to do it discreetly, but I saw you throw it over your left shoulder a minute ago."

"Oh." She pauses. "But why would I throw it the other way?"

"It's to ward off the devil by throwing it in his eyes, right?"

She wrinkles her nose, still confused at what I'm insinuating.

I point my eyes to Mr. Rock and Roll.

She shakes her head, but stifles a laugh.

"I've missed you," I say quietly.

Her eyes dart to the other side of the table, to Tatiana and Dickhead. But neither one of them are paying attention. Tatiana is busy chewing his ear off about the similarities between filming movies and singing on stage.

"Me too," she whispers, forlorn in her tone. She forks her lunch around aimlessly on her plate.

"So, can you give us a hint who your favorites are?" Tatiana asks Flynn as the conversation turns to the reality show.

"Nope. Not allowed." He smiles and winks at Kate.

Knocking out a tooth from his Donny Osmond smile isn't really an option in a room full of people, so I take the path I much prefer. I slip my hand under the table and rest it on top of Kate's thigh. Her eyes bulge, but she quickly conceals her surprise. Thank god for skirts.

"Are you and Tatiana working on a project together?" Kate asks, her words falling quickly, nervously.

"We're almost wrapped. It's due out in October. *Perfect Sense*. Maybe you've heard of it?" Tatiana asks. You'd have to live under a rock to not have heard; the bestselling book is a widely anticipated blockbuster movie.

My hand inches up Kate's thigh.

"Sure. It looks great."

Another inch up. I'm midway between her knee and hip.

"How much longer do you have on your show?" I ask Kate.

"A little more than …" My hand slides up another inch and drops from the top of her thigh to the inside.

"Ummm …" She stares at me, then straightens in her seat and blinks a few times. "I'm sorry. What did you ask?"

I grin. And slide my hand up farther. I feel the heat resonate from between her legs now.

"I asked how much longer you have on your show." I grip the inside of her thigh and pull her legs wider apart. Her breath does a sharp intake that only I seem to notice.

"The show lasts another six weeks."

"That's almost as long as it takes to film a movie," Tatiana interjects.

My hand slides the rest of the way up, lightly skimming the lace edge of her panties. Kate's eyes close and she takes a deep breath.

My phone rings, forcing me to remove my hand. "Yeah, Helen?"

Helen reminds me I have a meeting this afternoon and that I've also requested she call to help me escape if I wasn't back in a half hour. "Thank you. I'll be up shortly."

Tatiana jumps on the opportunity. "Well, that's my cue. I want a little alone time with Coop before I lose him back to run an empire. I'm sure you understand how hard it is to get alone time around here." Tatiana winks at Flynn.

A flicker of something ignites in Kate's eyes. Jealousy?

Flynn stands. "It was nice meeting you both."

"You too." *Dickhead.*

"Kate. It was good to see you." I lean down, kiss her cheek and whisper, "My office, ten minutes."

chapter thirteen

Kate

"**K**ate." Miles catches my arm just as Flynn and I approach the entrance to the hangar, returning from lunch. "Joel needs to see you, Flynn. Kate and I have some things to discuss, she'll meet you inside in a bit." His tone is dismissive. "Why don't we go talk in my office?" He asks like it's a question, but he's already steering me down the hall.

Not surprisingly, Miles's office is nothing like his brother's. It's the same size and shape, even boasts a similar view, yet everything is exaggerated, rather than understated like Cooper's. The walls are lined with framed movie posters, shelves are filled with awards and accolades. A round meeting table has a dozen tall piles of manuscripts.

"Have a seat. Can I get you something to drink? A cocktail perhaps?"

I look over at the red couch Miles motions to. *Definitely a casting couch.* "No. I'm good. Thank you."

He pours himself one and joins me, sitting a bit too close. "How is everything going, Kate?"

"Umm ... good, I suppose." I'm not clear on exactly what he's referring to.

"Flynn really likes you." He sips his drink, then reaches out and brushes my hair behind my shoulder. "I can see why. You're a beautiful woman."

I force a smile, resisting the urge to smack his hand away from me. "Thank you."

"You seem a bit stressed lately. Things are a little off between you and Flynn. Is there anything I can do to help?" Miles's leg brushes up against mine and his hand grips my shoulder and rubs.

Instinctively, I lean the other direction, pulling my shoulder from his reach. "I'm fine. I don't need any help. But thank you."

Miles gulps from his glass, watching me over the brim as he drinks. His stare makes me uncomfortable, but I stand my ground, not looking away. The glimmer in his eyes changes, the flirty mock caring gone, he squints. "Let me get to the point then. This is scripted reality TV. You and Flynn will get ratings. I need you to be a little friendlier with him."

"A little friendlier?"

"You know what I mean."

"I'm not sure that I do."

"You're the gambler, Kate. How much do you think doing what I ask increases your odds of staying on the show?"

Standing, I offer an insincere smile. "Is there anything else?"

He leans back on the couch, swallows the remnants of his glass and grins at me. "I like a woman that knows how to play the game. That will be all."

Sitting in my Jeep, I inwardly debate one more time before turning the ignition key. It's been almost an hour since Cooper left lunch. No doubt he's growing impatient by now. But I just can't. His hand under the table was enough of a reminder of what that man makes me feel. What I haven't given Flynn a real chance to make me feel. I can't give winning my all while I'm anywhere near Cooper Montgomery. A reminder of why I'm doing this show is undoubtedly what I need right now.

The half hour drive does little to clear my head. I'm still thinking about the heat radiating from Cooper's hand on my thigh as I pull into Mom's driveway. I take a deep breath and shut my eyes for a full ten minutes before venturing inside.

"Hey, sweetheart." Mom stands and rolls her portable oxygen tank over to greet me.

"Hi, Mom." Her color is better, her step quicker; the new tank is definitely working. "You look good. How are you feeling?"

"I feel great." She'd say the same thing if her oxygen saturation level was below eighty and her organs were quietly shutting down. She never wants me to worry.

"For a change, I believe you." I grin and kiss her on the cheek. "Kyle at therapy?"

"Yes. He's doing great with it. There hasn't been any improvement yet physically. But his spirit is doing so much better. That clinical trial you got him into is the first hope I've seen in him since before the accident." My little brother Kyle and I were always close. Even as kids, when other siblings were busy fighting, we stuck together. But ever since the accident, our lives have bound together tighter. My happiness is no longer singular … it's codependent on his. Hearing that he is showing any sign of improvement, physical or mental, lifts my heart. I'm already glad I came.

I usually visit twice a week to check in on them, but with the show filming at odd hours, I haven't been by in ten days. They have almost round-the-clock aides, but I still need to see for myself they're okay. A friend of mine, Mark, has stopped in to check on them for me and called with reports. He's a year behind me in school.

"You know, Mark is very handsome. And single."

"Please tell me you weren't interrogating Mark again, Mom. We're just friends. You need to stop trying to fix us up."

"You need to make more time for a social life. I can't remember the last time you talked about a man." *An hour ago I was sitting next to a man I'm dating on national television and had another man's hand inching up my skirt.*

"I'm good, Mom, really. School keeps me busy." She has no idea I took a year off and decided to try to win the prize on *Throb*. Luckily, none of her friends watch reality TV.

"You find love when you least expect it. Sometimes at the most inconvenient times." *You can say that again.*

We sit and talk for a while, and inevitably the conversation turns to finances. It's been a consuming topic since Dad died and all of the ugly truths came out. "The bank sent an appraiser over." She sighs.

"What are you talking about?"

"Yesterday, a man came by to look at the house."

"How do you know the bank sent him?"

"Because he told me they did." Oh geez. Being married to one of the world's biggest card sharks for thirty years certainly didn't affect my mother the same as it did me. I'm always looking for the sleight of hand. Mom is way too trustworthy.

"Did he leave a card?" I have a power of attorney on file with her bank and mortgage company. They should have called me if they were sending someone over. Builders and potential investors have been snooping around since the house first went into foreclosure.

"No."

"What was his name?"

"I don't recall. It was something odd though. One of those names that has a dark ring to it." She shrugs and sips her tea. "But it went with what he looked like, I suppose."

"What did he look like?"

"He was tall, bald … wore all black. Looked tough. He was very nice though. Just looked a bit rough around the edges. At first, when he rang the doorbell, I was sure he was a friend of your father's. I'm surprised you don't know about it. He knew your name. I guess the bank must have given it to him."

We finish our tea and sit around talking for a while. I have such limited time with Mom that I make the decision not to spend it worrying about something I can't change right this minute. I make a mental note to call the bank tomorrow.

Spending the afternoon with my mother reinforced that I'm making the right choices, although it doesn't make it any easier to forget the feeling of being near Cooper today. My heart leaped just seeing him. Knowing how much he wants me made it that much more difficult. Remembering how it felt to have his hand on the inside of my thigh, inching it's way up to the heat between my legs, made it impossible. I have no willpower around that man. There is no choice but to keep away from him. And work on rekindling whatever sparks Flynn and I may have had before Cooper Montgomery walked into my life.

My phone buzzes as I turn onto the crowded Pacific Coast Highway. I press the button on the dashboard and the blaring music is replaced by the sound of a man's voice.

"Kid?" I've never talked to Frank Mars on the phone before, yet I know it's him with just that one simple word.

"Hi Frank."

"You busy tonight?"

"You're married, Frank. I can't go out with you."

"In my dreams, kid. In my dreams." I can tell he's smiling through the phone. "Listen, Grip can't make it tonight. The bum just called, something about Bernice's bursitis. We need a fourth. You free?"

I am, but I'm also wary of whom I'd be sitting next to. "Umm ... is Ben playing tonight?"

"You're killing me. You got a thing for Ben? If you like old men, I'll drop my wife faster than you can say 'don't let the door hit your fat ass on the way out, Sharon.'"

I laugh. "No worries. My heart belongs to you, Frank. I was just asking so I'd know if I should bring the cufflinks I won from him last time."

"Yeah. Bring 'em. But I'm betting he doesn't win them back. And you haven't met Carl yet either. We won't let on who you are. He can be your sucker tonight."

Disappointed, yet relieved Cooper isn't going to be one of the four, I agree to play. This morning I had two men who seemed interested, yet tonight I have no plans. Dating a man who has five other girlfriends makes for a very lonely Friday night.

chapter fourteen

Cooper

"**Y**our father would be proud right now, Cooper," Ben Seidman says, a stack of papers sitting in front of each of us. Red and green tabs stick out from the sides, indicating dozens of places we both need to sign to formalize the deal.

Ben's right—my father would be proud. Co-produced movies are a rarity in the film business, especially when the two production houses are the number one and number two producers in the world. But if any two companies can make it work, it's Diamond Entertainment and Montgomery Productions. My father's best friend is a formidable opponent, and will make an even better feature film partner.

"Fucking Grip," Ben grumbles as he reaches the bottom of the signing pile. "The old bastard was whipped before he retired, now he's all but hog tied to Bernice."

I'd forgotten it was card night. "You need a fourth?"

"Nah. Frank got someone. Don't you have a hot date or something better to do than sit around losing all your hard-earned money anyway?" He signs the last document and tosses his pen on the desk, leaning back in his chair. "Isn't anything sacred anymore? Jack and I, we never missed once in twenty-eight years."

I slide the paper he just signed across the desk to my side. One more signature and we'll be changing the film industry as we know it. I lift my Montblanc, thinking I'm putting this pen aside. The one Dad used to ink his first film deal is sitting in my top right hand desk drawer. This one should keep it company. "Who's filling in tonight?"

"That cute little card shark girl."

I put the pen down before signing on the last empty line. "Ben," I say, "there's one more condition to this deal ..."

Case of disgusting Budweiser in hand, I stroll into the studio, letting the loud slam of the door echo through the tall, open space. My eyes are already trained on Kate when she looks up. Eyes wide as saucers, sharp inhale—she's surprised to see me. Tonight is all about winning. I'm going to use the element of surprise to my advantage.

"I thought you were going to be Ben," Frank says.

"Change of plans. Ben's not coming," I respond to Frank, but my eyes don't leave Kate.

"Whadda you mean, Ben's not coming? He hasn't missed a night in twenty-five years."

"Twenty-eight," I correct him.

"Is he all right?"

"He's fine."

"What the hell was so important that he would miss? It's not like Ben."

"I'd tell you why he can't make it, but I wouldn't want to break the no-business-talk rule before I even sit down."

"Whatever," Frank grumbles and waves my comment off. "You remember Kate?"

"I do." I arch an eyebrow at Kate and nod.

"Carl hasn't played with Kate yet. I told him to take it easy on her." Frank winks, shuffling the deck.

Aggressive women were always a turn-off for me. But aggressive card-playing women—that's apparently a whole different ballgame. Kate folds the first two hands, Carl raking in the pot both times. Hand three, even I caught Carl's facial tic when he picked up his cards, indicating he thought he had a winner. I nearly laughed out loud when Kate took two cards and her eyes bulged from her head. Even a novice card player would cover up better than that. But Carl bought her shit—hook, line and sinker. And Frank and I quickly bowed out to enjoy the show.

On his raise, Carl pushes in a tall stack of chips. Kate actually nibbles on her lip a bit, pretending to debate whether she should go all in or not. The smile on Carl's face when she shrugs and pensively pushes her chips in is absolutely priceless. He turns over three queens, gloating, hands already reaching toward the center of the table.

"Does this beat three of a kind?" Kate asks innocently, laying a full house down on the table.

We let poor Carl lose his shirt, not letting him in on the joke until we take the usual bathroom break. "You guys are assholes," he mutters, throwing his cards down on the table before stalking off to the restroom. Frank follows him out, chanting, "You got beat by a girl. You got beat by a girl."

"You must have gotten lost on your way to my office after lunch this afternoon," I say when the door slams shut, leaving just the two of us. "Avoiding me won't solve the problem." The room is so quiet I can hear the distinct hitch in her breath, even though she tries to conceal the effect my words have on her.

"What will?" She busies herself collecting the cards from the table and speaks without looking at me.

"Working through it."

"Am I supposed to believe you're here by coincidence? If you want something, set it free, if it comes back to you, it was meant to be ... or something like that?"

"Do you believe in that stuff?"

She pauses for a moment, considering my question, and then begins shuffling again. "I think I do. Do you?"

"I'm more of the school of if you want something bad enough, pursue it aggressively until you wear it down and it gives in."

Her mouth twitches with suppressed amusement, but she still doesn't look up.

"You didn't push my hand away today," I say, my eyes never leaving her face.

"I didn't want to make a scene."

"You liked it there. The way my fingers traced the outline of the lace. I could feel the heat. You wanted me to dip my fingers inside and feel how wet you were as much as I did."

She closes her eyes.

I stand and step around the table.

"It made me insane to see his hand on you," I admit as I graze my knuckles lightly down her cheek. She still doesn't look up.

"Look at me," I say, quietly but firm.

Her eyes close again.

"I can't, Cooper." There's sadness in her voice. "I can't spend time around you and do what I need to do."

I take her chin in my hands and force her gaze to meet mine. "And I can't stop thinking about you."

"I'm sorry."

"Bet me."

"What?" Her brows furrow.

"If I win, give me tonight."

"That's crazy."

"Is it? Leave it up to fate. You just said you're a believer."

"Cooper," she warns uncertainly.

I kiss her lips. Sweetly this time, even though all I really want to do is grab her and pounce.

"Last hand," I breathe, hating to pull my lips from hers.

"I don't know …"

The door opens, and the boisterous sound of Frank still needling Carl interrupts us before I can get her to agree. A part of me wants to clear the room. Tell Frank and Carl I need them to leave so I can finish our conversation. But I don't. I respect the hell out of these guys, and when we leave work at the door, we leave me being the boss there too.

We play for two more hours. Frank peppers Kate with all kinds of questions about her family and plenty about her infamous father. I suspect he has a bit of a crush on Kate; my guess is she knows it too. She flirts playfully with him. It makes me smile almost as much as it does Frank.

"That's two in a row you lost to Frank. Are you letting him win or is your luck starting to turn?" Tipping my beer up, I eye Kate.

"My luck must be running out. I only let people win to build their confidence."

"Well, my confidence is dwindling here, maybe you should throw some charity my way." I motion to the sparse pile of chips in front of me.

"I don't think you've ever experienced a shortage in confidence, Mr. Montgomery."

Frank snickers. "You got this one pegged. Hard to be lacking in confidence when you're walking around with Ms. Laroix on your arm."

"She's beautiful. I saw you with her today. Is she your girlfriend?" Kate asks, a sly smirk on her face.

"No." I throw two chips into the pot, even though I have another shit hand.

"Looked cozy." She shrugs. "Friends with benefits?"

My eyebrows jump. "No. Not friends with benefits either."

"Ohhhhhh," she says, as if something dawns on her for the first time. Then says nothing more.

"What?" Eventually I take the bait.

"I didn't realize you played for the other team."

Cute. Really cute. I'll show you what team I play for. "No. I don't play for the other team. I actually just met someone."

She tosses her cards on the table, folding for the third time in a row.

"Looks like your luck really is running low," I say. "You know what, guys, I have an early morning tomorrow. What do you say we make next hand the last hand?" She knows exactly what I'm doing. Yet I don't have a damn clue what she's up to. For all I know, she can be playing us all. Folding three hands in a row and taking my mind off the game.

"You have those diamond four-leaf clover cufflinks your old man used to wear? I'd love to get my hands on them in a last-hand pot," Frank says.

"No. Wish I did. He lost them in a game. He swore it was the reason his luck changed." Kate's face saddens.

"Sorry, kid."

She forces a conciliatory smile.

Frank rakes in the final pot of chips for the night and everyone digs for their final ante. Frank tosses in a business card holder with my initials on it. I haven't seen that thing in ten years. Carl tosses in Frank's high school ring, and I throw a custom Montblanc platinum pen engraved with Ben's initials into the mix. Kate is busy in her purse.

Just like the first time we met, she tears a piece of paper. Grinning, she picks out the fifteen-hundred-dollar pen from the pot and scribbles something, her hand covering the content like a schoolgirl writing a note. She folds it a few times, concealing what she's offering to the winner.

Frank chuckles. "You know I already have your phone number?"

"Maybe it's not my phone number," she says cryptically, smiling at Frank fondly. But her eyes blaze when they turn to me.

Carl's the first one out. He hisses and pushes back from the table.

I eye the stack of chips in front of Kate and dig into my pocket. My eyes never leave hers when I toss a wad of hundreds into the pile—Tiffany money clip and all.

Frank bows out. "Too rich for my blood with the crap cards I got."

And then there's just the two of us again.

Kate and I stand off, her eyes gyrating through an assessment I've become familiar with. First she squints, looking deep into my eyes, then her eyes relax again. Her gaze drops to my lips and then slowly makes its way back to my eyes. An ever-so-slight uptick on the right side of her mouth is the only indication that she thinks she's got me.

She pushes all of her chips in.

I take a deep breath and turn over my cards.

Three kings.

And two tens. I haven't had a full house this high since, well … ever.

The guys whistle.

Kate's eyes sparkle. I hold my breath as her eyes drop down to read my cards and then quickly return to mine. She throws her cards into the pot. Face down. Defeated.

Laughter erupts in the room. Carl stands, grabbing his jacket. "Damn. That was intense. Nice job, Coop. Glad one of us didn't get beat by a girl. It was a pleasure, though," he says to Kate. Then he nods to Frank. "Come on, I'll help clean this up."

"Go ahead, guys. I got it."

"You sure, Coop?"

"No problem. Have a good night, gentlemen."

Frank slaps me on the back as he leaves. "If I can't have your old man around, you're the next best thing. You turned out good, kid. You turned out good."

The room goes quiet as the two men exit. Neither Kate nor I have moved from our seats. We stare intently at each other. I watch as her pupils dilate and the rise and fall of her chest seems to grow deeper with each breath. And then something happens. It hits me. And I realize playing the game really is all about reading people. So I reach into the ante pile and my hand hovers over the folded-up paper for a long count. Then I veer slightly to the left and flip over her cards.

Four of a kind.

Beats my full house by a mile.

Kate grins and arches an eyebrow. I don't bother to clean up. She grabs my hand and we head for the door, leaving her folded-up bet that reads *One Night* unopened.

chapter

fifteen

Kate

"I'll follow you," I say as we reach the warm summer air outside.

"No. I'll drive you."

"But I need my car to go home later."

"You aren't going home tonight."

"But ..."

Cooper stops in place. He takes my face into his hands and speaks. "I won one night. I get the full night."

"I don't have any clothes."

"You won't be needing them." He opens the door to his car and leads me in.

"But what about my toothbrush?" I grasp at something. I know it was my decision, but I need a minute to think about the consequences of what I've just done.

"You can use mine."

"But ..."

He interrupts me. "Buckle up."

I pull the seatbelt on and the engine roars to life. I give it one last college try. "I need ..."

Cooper cuts me off. Again. "I'm not giving you a chance to change your mind."

"How do you know I'll change my mind?"

"Because you already are."

"I'm n ..." I trail off.

He removes his hand from the gear shifter and turns to me. "Look at me."

"Bossy," I say under my breath, but he hears it.

"You haven't even begun to see bossy yet. Tonight I'm going to tell you to do things, and you're going to do them. When I tell you to open wider, or take my cock deeper, you're going to listen. You know why? Because since the moment we met, all I've wanted to do is make you feel good. Hell, I don't even need to get off physically. Because I'm going to get off watching you every minute. So, yeah, I'm going to be bossy. Now let's put the rest of this behind us. Do you want to be with me tonight?"

After that prelude, I nod my head fast. I'm no fool. Who wouldn't?

The short drive is enough to make me flip-flop twenty times. I've never wanted to be with another man more than I want to be with Cooper right now. But I'm being selfish—risking losing—a prize my family needs. With each elimination ceremony, my odds increase. I'm fooling myself by thinking tonight won't tilt the odds in the other direction. I could get caught. How will I look into the eyes of another man after giving another piece of myself to Cooper tonight? I know this is a bad idea. But then I look over at Cooper and my resolve weakens.

One night ... it's just one night. I can do this. *We* can do this.

Arriving at his sleek high-rise, Cooper nods to the doorman and whisks me past. His hand at the small of my back, he quickly steers me inside a waiting elevator.

I stare up at the numbers slowly lighting as the elevator painstakingly climbs the floors. Cooper stands quietly behind me, close but not touching—although I can still feel him. Panic sets in as the floors move to double-digit numbers. What the hell am I doing? I take a deep breath and speak low. "This isn't going to work, you know?"

He's quiet for a moment before he answers. "Why not?" His hand snakes around my hip, gripping it tightly.

"Because you're not the type of man who gives in easily."

He grips my hip tighter. "I'm not giving in."

The elevator slides to an abrupt stop and the doors slide open. An older couple smiles pleasantly and begins to step toward the car. Cooper says brusquely, "We're going up."

"That's okay. We'll take the ride up."

"If you don't mind, could you wait for the next one?" He pushes the button to the top floor, even though it's already lit.

"That was rude," I say as the doors slide closed on the confused couple.

Cooper turns me, searching my face. He ignores my comment, still completely focused on our conversation before the elevator dinged. "Is that what you think I'm doing? Giving in?"

In the dim, confined space, the green in his eyes look almost grey. The intensity of his stare scares me a little, but sucks me in at the same time. "You want more than one night, but you agreed to tonight only."

"That's not giving in, Kate."

"It's not?" I'm almost afraid to ask.

He shakes his head slowly. A sinister smile quirks at his sexy lips. His know-it-all attitude pisses me off, yet turns me on. But it's the pisses-me-off part that flows from my mouth. "You asked me out. I said no. We agreed to one night. Isn't that giving in?"

"No."

I take an exaggerated, frustrated breath and roll my eyes. "Okay then. Enlighten me. What do you call it?"

His eyes darken and his face lowers to align with mine. "This isn't giving in. This is staking my claim. I'll send you back to him tomorrow if that's what you want. But you won't be able to sit without thinking of me for a week. Every time your sexy ass touches down, you'll be reminded of what it feels like with me buried deep inside you. Your bones will ache from the relentless pounding I plan to deliver."

Despite my irritation at how full of himself he is, my mouth drops open and body buzzes at the visual he's planted in my head. Cocky arrogance or not, the man has a way of setting my body on fire.

"I'd rather not send you back tomorrow. But get one thing straight right now, Kate. I'm not giving in. I'm meeting you halfway. And you can be damn straight agreeing to one night won't stop me from trying to take the rest of what you don't give tonight."

The elevator car glides to a stop, reaching the top floor. The ease of his manners is so starkly different from the seduction of his voice. "Shall we?" The doors slide open and he leisurely extends his arm to the looming double doors marked *Penthouse*. I get the feeling that I'm about to step through the wardrobe. And the lion is right behind me.

"Would you like a drink?"

"A glass of wine would be good." Perhaps a bottle to calm my nerves.

He nods and gestures toward the bar stools on the other side of the kitchen island. The floor to ceiling windows in the adjoining living room catch my attention. Perched high on a cliff, the apartment's view of the sparkling lights of downtown LA almost appear fantasy like. It's amazing how a little distance between things can sometimes make you see a very different picture than the reality of being up close. "That's some view."

Cooper fills two crystal glasses and offers me one. He follows where my attention is fixed. "I don't think I've noticed it in years."

"Really?" I'm utterly perplexed at his statement. But he's serious. "Why?"

"I'm not here much."

"Where are you normally?"

"The office. The gym. A lot of work-related functions."

"What's your typical day like?" I sip my wine.

"Up at five. Gym at five thirty. Office by seven. Home by ten."

"Ten?"

"I work late a lot."

"Where do you eat?"

"At the office usually. Or at a function. I do a lot of business over meals."

"Sounds like you need to stop and look around every once in a while."

"You're right. I do." Cooper sips his wine, his eyes no longer admiring the view. Instead they're focused intently on me.

"Can we go out on the balcony?" I ask, not turning in his direction.

"Are you stalling?"

I smile at how astute he is in reading me. He's already figured me out better than the last guy I dated for six months. "Maybe. Is that a problem?"

"Not at all."

He leads me to the balcony. It's a beautiful night. Warm, breezy air wafts a hint of saltwater from off in the distance. The sky is so clear, not even the massive light pollution of LA can dim the twinkling stars. Standing behind me, one hand on either side of the railing, we quietly take in the view. Then his arm wraps around my waist and he buries his nose in my hair with a deep inhale. With his hard chest pressed tightly against my back and strong arms holding me, it's easy to let my head loll back and relax.

"This is nice," I say, exhaling a long cleansing breath that washes away some of my fears.

"It is."

We stay silent for long minutes, enjoying the view and relaxing. I probably should have stayed that way, but sometimes my mind wanders and pushes out words past my filter. "It's one night. Does that mean you'll be dating someone else by next week?"

"Will you?" he asks in a curt voice. Of course I will—he knows that. I'm going back to dating another man tomorrow. And possibly heading for an overnight date pretty soon.

"That's not an answer."

"What do you want me to say, Kate? That I'll stay celibate while I wait for you to finish dating another man?"

I turn to face him. The thought of Cooper being with another woman makes me crazy. So I channel everything I'm feeling and haul myself up on him, grabbing his neck and pulling him down for a kiss at the same time I lift and wrap my legs around his waist.

Our passion quickly ignites—turning angry, frustrated jealousy and confusion into a ball of fire that burns into a smoldering kiss. He pushes back as hard as I press, until our bodies meld together. He cups and squeezes my ass with one hand, the other maneuvering my head where he wants it so he can devour my mouth. I may have started the kiss, but there's no mistaking who controls it.

Movement into the apartment and down the long hallway to his bedroom doesn't even register until we finally break for air. "What was that for?" We're both breathing hard; his voice is hoarse with need.

"I don't want to waste any more time. I only have so many hours to wear you out enough so that you'll be useless to another woman for six weeks."

Cooper throws his head back, laughing. He finds me projecting his own superlative promises back at him entertaining. Reaching the bed, he leans forward and gently lays me down. The amusement dancing in his eyes quickly turns into something stormier as he stands and takes in the sight of me lying on his bed.

Lowering his body, one hand on either side of me supporting his weight, Cooper presses his lips gently to my exposed collarbone. He kisses his way up my neck, light nips alternating with whispery caresses. By the time he reaches my ear, the nips and kisses have escalated to bites and sucking.

His hand makes its way down my body, slowing to appreciate my curves before traveling lower. He lingers at the hem of my skirt before slipping beneath. A moan escapes from my lips when his fingers stroke me through the lace of my panties.

"You're so wet. I feel it without even putting my fingers inside." He finds my clit easily and massages up and down. "First I'm going to fuck you with my fingers. Because I want to watch you the first time I make you come." Oh lord. My body is halfway there just hearing him say *fuck you with my fingers*. Seriously, there's a pre-orgasm buzz pulsing through my body. I may not even make it until his fingers feign their first pump.

His hand slips under my panties. "Look at me." His voice is throaty and incredibly masculine. "And then, I'm going to lick you until you scream my name." He dips one finger inside of me. My eyes shut. It's been a long time. Too long, but I'm suddenly happy I've been on a self-imposed hiatus.

"You're so tight," he groans. "Jesus, Kate." He works me slowly, my wetness allowing him to glide in and out. Feeling my body surrender, he pulls almost all the way out and pushes back in with two fingers. A few pumps and my body greedily accepts him, my back arching off the bed as I climb closer to release.

Covering my clit with his thumb, he growls when I let out a shameless moan of pleasure. His eyes flare with desire and our gazes lock. It takes all of my willpower not to close my eyes as blissful waves of orgasm roll over me. My hips writhe to meet each wave, riding the rollercoaster from explosion to euphoria.

Cooper's hoarse voice mumbles something, but the words are incoherent over the sound of my heart beating wildly. What remains of my clothes are rapidly discarded, and it isn't until I feel him hauling me down the bed that I'm even aware of what he's doing.

Dropping to his knees, my ass hovering at the foot of the bed, he parts my shaky legs and his mouth is on me before I can object. A futile attempt to push him away is short lived when his tongue flutters over my clit. *Jesus. The man has me on the edge again within thirty seconds.*

Abandoning my efforts to stop him in favor of raveling my fingers through his hair and pulling him closer as he laps at me hungrily, I yield to his skilled mouth. My body trembles as his tongue dips inside me, luring an unabashed moan as my second orgasm threatens quickly. His hands push my thighs wider, his mouth licking and sucking, his tongue lashing furiously over my swollen clit until I explode again, this time gasping his name.

I think I may have lost a few moments in time, somewhere between orgasm number two and his repositioning me in the center of his heavenly king-sized bed. But then the lush green eyes filled with golden sunflowers are staring down at me, his rigid cock throbbing near my tender opening.

"Reach up," he says in a firm, yet strained, voice.

My heavily hooded eyes must display my confusion.

"Hold the headboard with both hands."

"But …"

"Do it, Kate."

I lift my arms, reaching over my head for the iron headboard. It's cold, but I wrap my heated palms around the rounded metal and squeeze tight.

Cooper raises his head slightly, admiring the full view—me, underneath him, looking glazed and vulnerable.

"Beautiful," he murmurs in my ear. "Don't let go."

I nod, unable to form words, his warm breath spreading heat throughout my body. He licks the shell of my ear, and then his tongue travels down my neck, making its way to my taut nipple. He sucks hard, then bites, his teeth not releasing me until I whimper. Then he lavishes sweet kisses on the swollen buds he just assaulted, making them more than better.

He spends time worshiping my body, the length of him frequently rubbing up against me, teasing me mercilessly. Even after two energy-draining orgasms, he's able to work me back into a frenzy. Eventually I can't take it anymore and I reach down, desperate to feel his thick, hard erection.

"Back on the headboard," he growls, stopping me before I'm able to touch.

"But I want—"

"Don't let go again," he warns, cutting me off and ignoring my plea.

Seriously? I'm pretty sure I'm not going to be able to keep my hands off of him. Every ridge of his ridiculously toned body is calling my name. His cock taunting me the loudest.

"I don't think I can."

My honesty is rewarded with a wicked grin. His already massive ego just shot up another stratosphere. One hand deftly rolls on a condom. Knowing my eyes are fixed on the way his fingers curl around his thickness, his hand lingers, stroking himself up and down leisurely. "Tell me what you need. I'll give it to you."

"I want to touch you."

"What do you want to touch, Kate?"

I'm laying spread-eagled beneath this man, yet I feel bashful saying the words. "You know." My face flushes.

"Why, Kate." His mouth is back at my ear, his hand working my breasts, kneading my sensitive nipple. Every tweak sends pleasure shooting through my nerves. I even feel it down in my toes. "Does my sharp-tongued woman not like to say naughty words?"

"You're trying to torture me."

"Tell me what you want."

"You." I buck underneath him.

"Say it. Say what you want. What you were reaching for."

He surprises me by pushing two fingers back inside me. My body clenches down, tightening around them. "Is this what you want? You want my fingers inside of you?" He strokes in and out, rubbing me close, but it doesn't satisfy the need I have. I need more.

I shake my head.

"Then tell me," he croons, his fingers pumping in and out faster.

"Please," I moan.

"Please what?" He sucks on the sensitive flesh beneath my ear.

"You know," I groan, breathless from his expert touch.

"Say it." His strained, throaty voice quivers at my ear. I'd pretty much say or do anything to get him to give me what I need.

"Your cock. Please. I want your cock inside of me."

A flash of virile male satisfaction crosses his face, but a shadow shudders over the ego, turning to a possessive darkness. His jaw clenches tight and he takes one of my hands white-knuckling the headboard above me and brings it to his mouth. Gently, he kisses my hand, then replaces it on the headboard to grab hold.

I gasp loudly when he rams deep inside of me, giving me what I desperately need. "Oh, god," I pant, my body convulsing at the rock-hard intrusion. He's so thick, it's almost a struggle to accommodate his girth. If I wasn't primed sodden, taking him in so deep might fall on the other side of the slim wall that separates pain and pleasure.

He lets my body adjust and then begins to move. Stroking places inside of me to find ecstasy like he's been doing it forever instead of it being just our first time. It doesn't take long for him to lure the orgasm from my hungry body. But after he does, he groans and his thrusts intensify to a deliciously ravenous pounding that my body longed to feel.

Sometime in the aftermath of our escapades, in between kisses that feel like so much more than just kisses, I realize why I feel such a remarkable sense of relief. It wasn't the hours of foreplay building to a crescendo. I'd been waiting for this moment since the first time I met him.

I wake to the distant sound of Cooper's voice coming from the other room. He's on the phone, so I only hear one side of the conversation. But it makes me smile nonetheless. He's barking orders at someone; his voice, full of authority, leaves no question as to who's the boss. There was certainly no question last night either. Without a doubt, the man takes charge, there's no mistaking he's an alpha male. Yet there's something different in him. Something other bossy men are missing that makes the world of difference. Cooper may *seem* like he takes control away from me, but he'd never take it unless I was giving it to him. I never realized letting someone else take the lead could be so empowering and yet freeing at the same time.

I pick the dress shirt he was wearing yesterday up from the floor, button it enough to cover me, and go searching for the voice.

"He can have until five tonight to decide. After that we're moving on and going with our second choice." Cooper is wearing lounge pants and no shirt, his back to me, but he turns, sensing me, even though I make no sound with my bare feet. His eyes sweep over me, taking their time as they crawl up my bare legs and linger finding the hint of breast peeking out of the scarcely closed shirt. I only fastened one button up from the navel. He crooks a finger at me with a grin. I roll my eyes dramatically, but walk to him anyway, quite enjoying the way he watches my every step intently.

"Just let me know by five." He hangs up the phone without even saying goodbye and tosses it on the granite.

"I like your shirt." He wraps me in his arms.

"Thanks. Coffee?"

"Already made." He kisses my forehead and leads me to the island to sit while he fixes me a steaming mug.

"Sleep well?" Leaning casually against the kitchen counter, he eyes me over his mug.

"Like a baby. I was really out."

"I know. I've been up for two hours."

"What time is it?"

"Eight."

"You sleep well?"

"Best night of sleep I've had in years." He smiles. It's a genuine smile, it makes him look so young.

"Working so early on a Saturday?" I sip my coffee.

"Had a few loose ends to tie up. Wanted to get them done before you woke. What time do you turn into a pumpkin?"

My smile fades. "I have to be on set at three."

"Finish your coffee." He drains his mug and walks closer. "You sore?"

"Not really." A little achy, but I keep that part to myself.

"Let's go fix that. I want you to feel me for six weeks."

chapter

sixteen

Cooper

The morning after a sleepover, I'm usually ready for a woman to leave. I'm not rude or brash about it, but I'll admit weekday sleepovers are more my thing. No leisure time the next day to spend making post-coital nice. It's not that I don't like a woman's company outside of the bedroom, I do, although I generally prefer that time to be *before* sex, rather than after.

"Lunch should be here any minute," I say as Kate comes from the bathroom. Wet hair and a makeup-free face; she grows more beautiful each time I look at her. I glance at the clock again, dreading the minutes ticking by so fast. Why is it that the first woman I want to spend the entire weekend with doing nothing is also the one running on a meter set to expire way too soon?

"Great." She looks at her watch and back to me. Her face shows as much dread over the ticking away of the moments as I feel.

"I'll drop you back at your car after lunch."

She bites her lip. "Would you mind dropping me home? I need to get my bag."

"Bag?"

"We're sequestered at the house for a few nights."

I fail miserably at letting her words roll off of me. My face hardens, jaw clenches down and I open and close my fists.

"Sorry," she offers apologetically. And it looks like she means it. Oddly, the anger doesn't make me want to walk away from her. Instead, I get the feral urge to fuck her long and hard again. I'm not oblivious. I do realize it's most likely the primal urge to mark my territory in the most glaring way I know how. But that doesn't make the urge any less real.

The intercom buzzes, saving me from myself. I walk to the door and press the button. Lou's voice booms through the loud speaker.

"You have a guest, Mr. Montgomery."

"I ordered lunch, you can send him up. Thanks, Lou."

"Ummm … it's not lunch. Well, not unless Ms. Laroix has it hidden in her bag."

Shit. The woman just refuses to take a hint. I glance back at Kate. She lifts her eyebrows, but says nothing.

"Can you please tell her she needs to call the office and get on my schedule?"

"Okay. But she doesn't like when I send her away."

That doesn't seem to stop her though. "Just do it, Lou." I release the intercom button with a huff.

"I can grab a cab if you have business to discuss," Kate says with a bit of suspicion in her tone.

"I don't have any business to discuss with her anymore."

"Oh," she says.

"I didn't mean her visit was personal. I don't know why she came, I meant."

Kate tries to shrug it off. "It's okay. It's none of my business."

"We just spent the night together and it's none of your business why she's here?" Fuck. I sound defensive.

"I'm sorry. I meant, well … I don't know what I meant. I guess I meant to say I don't have any right to question what you're doing, when I'm heading back to Flynn."

His name from her lips hurts me, but it comes off more like anger. "I'll get dressed to drive you *back to Flynn*." I slam the door to my bedroom a little too hard.

The silence screams loudly on the ride back to her apartment. I have plenty of things I'd like to say, but what's the point. Last night was what it was. One night. Six weeks is a long time and who knows where either of us will be then. I should be fine with a night of *just sex*. Hell, I probably needed one.

"Listen." We both start speaking at the same time as I pull into a parking spot at her building. "You go first," I offer.

"I was just going to apologize."

"Me too."

"I don't know what else to say. If things were different ..."

"It's okay.

She leans forward and kisses my cheek softly. "I had a great time last night."

"Me too. Hope you don't mind if I don't wish you luck on your show."

She smiles. I walk around the car and open the door, offering my hand to let her go, even though I want nothing but. I pull her close and hold her tight, neither of us saying a word.

"Can you be the one to let go of me? Please. I can't seem to do it." The strain in her voice is real. As much as I don't want to let her walk away, the urge to make it easier on her wins out. I kiss the top of her head and release her.

Not quite ready to let her disappear, I watch her walk away until she's out of sight. An irrational part of me wants to chase after her. Give her the money she needs, even though I have no idea why she needs it so badly.

Patience wearing thin, I call Damian Fry on the way home and bark at him—he has twenty-four hours to get the report I requested on my desk.

chapter

seventeen

Kate

I shift on the couch, leaning my weight to the right side, and inwardly smile thinking of Cooper. *This isn't giving in. This is staking my claim. I'll send you back to him tomorrow if that's what you want. But you won't be able to sit without thinking of me for a week. Every time you sit down, you'll be reminded of what it feels like with me buried deep inside you.* Goosebumps break out on my arms just thinking about the words he said.

It's been two days. He wasn't kidding when he said he'd make me think of him when I sat down for a week. My body aches, but it's a good ache, unlike the ache in my chest that keeps me perpetually glum.

"What gives?" Ava asks, plopping herself down next to me. I'm not sure I would still be here if it wasn't for her. With the selection of the final four looming in less than a week, things have turned from unfriendly to downright vicious. One of the girls actually slammed a shoulder into me this afternoon as I was coming out of the bathroom. She feigned it was an accident, but the glimpse of an evil smile on her face when I fell on my ass assured me it was absolutely intentional.

"Nothing. I'm just tired. Think I might be coming down with something."

"Well, you look more like someone killed your dog."

"Thanks. That's attractive."

"No problem. Anytime." She grins.

"At least Flynn won't have to look at you in the black box."

"Who thinks of these challenges anyway?" Tonight's challenge is a test of how *in tune* Flynn is with the contestants. In a little while, he'll be alone, seated on a chair, in an empty pitch-black room. Each contestant takes a turn at going in to visit with him for five minutes. No talking or sound of any kind is permitted by the contestant. He must identify them without hearing them. *Touching*, of course, is permitted. Any contestant who makes even the slightest noise is disqualified. The woman Flynn is able to identify in the least amount of time gets tomorrow's one-on-one date with him. I'm guessing Miles had a hand in conjuring up this challenge.

"How long do you think it takes for Jessica to make him feel her up?" Ava asks.

"Eighteen seconds."

Her eyebrows shoot up. "Eighteen seconds? That's pretty specific."

"I'm good at these things." I shrug. "Bet you?"

"I think you have a gambling problem." Ava smiles.

"Chicken?"

"What are we betting?"

"You have to wear my Chargers t-shirt."

"That's cruel. You better not stretch out my Raiders t-shirt if you lose."

I look down at her boobs and smirk. "Your t-shirt is the only one I could possibly stretch out in this house of breast friends."

We all gather in the viewing room to watch as the first contestant makes her way into the black box. The camera has infrared viewing, which makes Flynn's pale blue eyes look more like a jaguar's hunting its prey in the dead of night. He holds a small square box with buttons that will electronically record which woman he thinks is in the room, as well as the time it takes him to formulate his guess.

Mercedes, the first contestant, closes the door behind her. Crap, I never thought of props. She's wearing a naughty nurse costume. Her ass cheeks peek out from beneath the white one-piece zip-front uniform, a stethoscope around her neck and a pill-box nursing hat sitting atop a fully teased head of sexy hair.

Hearing the door click shut, Flynn's head turns in the direction of the sound. "I'm over here," he says. Mercedes struts in his direction, the clack of her five-inch heels echoing on the tile floor. She stops a few feet from him, unsure of where to go.

Flynn begins to hum softly, the sound of his voice her guiding light in the darkness. She continues toward him slowly until her legs bump into his knees and then he stands. A few minutes pass while we all gawk at the screen, riveted as he touches her. He bends and starts at the bottom. Leisurely running his hands from the tips of her toes to the top of her head. Somehow he avoids being too obscene, skipping over the front of her shirt and swell of her ass in favor of gliding down the curve of her side. The way he moves his hands is incredibly seductive. The breath of a few of the girls watching hitches in unison with Mercedes as he caresses her while humming a sexy rhythm. Eventually, before time is up, he stops and pushes a button. The door opens again and Mercedes is escorted from the dark room.

The last three contestants to go are Ava, Jessica, and then me. Ava comes back after her turn and fans herself a bit. "Seriously. That was incredibly erotic."

"Been a while since you've been felt up, huh?" I tease. But I would imagine she's right. It's pretty damn erotic to watch.

"I can't wait until you go. You'll see. Something happens when you walk into a silent room that is dark as night and a man's hands touch you. A man you *know* is sexy."

Our conversation trails off as we both gape at Jessica when the door opens. She's wearing a bikini. The same nipple cover she wore at the last challenge. Only this time, she has the matching g-string bottom on instead of cut-off shorts. She shuts the door and wastes no time making her way to Flynn when his voice dictates the direction she needs to move in.

Flynn stands, his hands reaching for her hips and he finds bare skin. Rather than start at the bottom, as he's done with all the other contestants, his hands slither to her back and he reaches around, finding a hand full of bare ass. Abruptly, he sits back down and pushes a button.

"You're going to look great in my t-shirt," I gloat quietly to Ava as I walk toward the door, where I'm being beckoned to prepare for my turn.

Tonight's cocktail hour is the usual mix of mean girls on one side of the room, Ava and me on the other. It's going to be pretty lonely for one of us when the other is sent home. We've been nothing but nice to Jessica and her clique, I'm not even sure what I've done to alienate them, but their animosity toward me seems to grow by the day.

"You ladies look gorgeous. As usual." Flynn brings two glasses of wine over to where Ava and I are huddled and offers them to us.

"Thank you. You look pretty good yourself. At least I can see what you look like now." I smile and sip my wine.

"I can always see what you look like, Kate. Even in the dark, it's up here." Flynn taps his finger to his temple with a mischievous grin. "So what do you ladies think? Any guesses on who wins?"

"Jessica," Ava and I respond in unison.

Flynn smiles, but the now familiar bell calls our attention. It's time for an announcement of some sort. The three of us make our way to the center of the room where the host, Ryan, is waiting. A television is rolled in once we're all gathered.

"Ladies. You all got to watch a little of the challenge today. But what you didn't get to see was your own time with Flynn. Tonight you will each get to watch your own replay. In private. With Flynn. We've added some things to the bottom of the screen for your viewing pleasure. On the lower left-hand side, you'll see a clock. The clock will continue to run until Flynn makes his guess as to which contestant is in the room. But you will have the opportunity to view the full five minutes that you spent with your boyfriend. You will not, however, find out if Flynn correctly identified you. Instead, after your video is viewed, you'll be given a card with your time to hold up at tonight's challenge ceremony. Flynn will then give out a flower to each contestant he correctly identified. The constant holding a flower with the lowest time will be the lucky winner of the *last*, and very romantic, one-on-one date tomorrow night."

Chatter erupts in the room. "Okay, ladies. Let's get started. Mercedes, why don't you join Flynn in the other room and be the first to watch your video."

Jessica squeals as she returns to the group after her viewing. She holds up her sign, waving it proudly over her head. Giant black bold typeface announces how easily identifiable she truly is, even in the dark. Eighteen seconds. *Damn, I'm good.* "Think I have a matching baseball cap for your t-shirt," I whisper to Ava before walking toward the viewing room for my turn.

Flynn kisses me on the cheek and pats the loveseat next to him. Even though he's probably done the same act four times before I walked through the door, he has a way of making me feel like the act is just for me.

Using a remote, he dims the lights in the room, slings his arm around my shoulder and snuggles me close to him as the video begins to play.

On screen, I'm hesitant as I shut the door. The utter darkness was difficult to adjust to, but that wasn't the reason for my uncertainty. I was more anxious about the man in the chair and what I would feel with his hands on me. His playful voice comforted me quickly with two simple words: "Wanna dance?" I remember thinking he couldn't possibly know it was me, yet the words made me feel like he did.

I watch the screen, feeling a bit voyeuristic even though it's me. I make my way to Flynn, his voice guiding me as he hums a song. The same song he sang to me the night he asked me to dance on the balcony. On screen, I smile and walk toward where he's sitting. Our knees bump lightly as I reach him, and I remember catching my balance as I began to lean forward, thinking I was going to wind up in his lap. But it's the next part I don't remember. Before ever touching me, Flynn smiles and presses a button. The clock stops at eighteen seconds.

I squirm a bit in my seat when Flynn's hands start at my ankles and slowly trace their path up my body. He's a gentleman, well, as much as anyone can be a gentleman while he feels up a woman in the dark while a camera records the entire thing. But my palms start to sweat when he reaches my hips. On screen, his hands glide over my waist and begin to travel higher. Reaching the side of my breast, the low song he'd been lightly humming suddenly stops. Just in time for the microphone to pick up the distinct hitch of my breath.

Flynn's eyes turn to watch me, watch us. He knows his touch affected me.

The tension in the room is palpable. I'm glad the ceremony isn't in the kitchen, because Jessica looks like she wouldn't mind slicing me into a Kate sandwich she could chew up and spit out. But then Flynn walks to the front of the room and the daggers in her eyes miraculously soften to reverence as she flips her flowing blond locks from her shoulder. The girl could be an actress.

"Ladies. I'm sorry to say that I did not get a perfect score on today's competition. There are two women who I failed to properly identify. And for that, I apologize to those women."

Ryan, the host, interrupts. "The flowers that Flynn is about to give out were chosen by Flynn specifically for each woman. Unfortunately, only four of the flowers will be given out." With all the dramatic flare he can muster, Ryan removes two flowers from the table—a traditional solemn red rose and a cheerful Gerber daisy.

Handing out the first three flowers, Flynn explains his reason for selecting each one as he slips the flower behind each contestant's ear. Only a white calla lily remains to be handed out, even though there are three contestants not yet decorated—me, Ava and Jessica. Jessica and I have the lowest time, so if either of us receives the flower, we will win the date.

"The calla lily symbolizes purity and innocence, which is why it's frequently used to celebrate weddings," Flynn begins. "While I wouldn't necessarily call this beautiful lady innocent, I thought of her as soon as I saw the flower." He pauses for a moment. "Kate—this flower is for you."

There'll be no avoiding alone time tomorrow on our one-on-one date.

chapter eighteen

Cooper

Stephen Blake is a Hollywood super-agent. He's the guy who turns down clients who command five million a film just because he doesn't like the actor's personality. If actually liking an actor was a requirement for Hollywood agents, I'm pretty sure most of this town would be unrepresented.

"Miriam. It's good to see you. You still doing all the work and letting Stephen take the credit?" I lean down and kiss Miriam Blake on the cheek as I reach the table the two are already seated at. I immediately notice four place settings before I even sit.

"He still refuses to put my name on the letterhead, even though I closed more deals than he did last year." Miriam rolls her eyes at her husband. I've been stirring the same pot with these two since as far back as I can remember.

"Your name *is* on the letterhead. *Blake.* That's your name, isn't it?"

"The Stephen Blake Agency is *not* my name. It should be Blake and Blake. Right, Cooper?"

"Of course, Miriam." Stephen waves his hand at me, dismissing my encouragement of his wife. The two have been business partners for thirty years, married for twenty-nine. Miriam was also my mother's cousin.

"So … I invited a friend to join us."

Of course she did. She always does. No matter how many times I decline her matchmaking services. "A friend?"

"One of the female persuasion," Miriam says, as if I might not be aware she was going to bring a woman tonight. She's so focused on marrying me off, I'm honestly not sure if my father told her to see that I marry well or if she just uses that excuse so I don't decline. Either way, it's impossible to tell Miriam Blake no, even when you actually say no.

A few minutes later, a woman apprehensively joins our table. "Alexandra, sweetheart," Miriam greets her as we all stand. She's stunning. Hair a rich shade of mahogany, flawless porcelain skin, straight nose, full lips and eyes so pale I have to look twice to see if they're real or contacts.

"Cooper, this is Alexandra Sawyer. She's just signed with our firm. Another one of *my* brilliant finds." Stephen ignores her jab, instead holding up his glass, clanking the lonely ice around in the direction of a passing waiter.

"Nice to meet you, Alexandra." I pull out her chair for her.

Miriam skips the normal gratuitous small talk in favor of going in for the kill. She dives right into Alexandra's resume with a hard sell—she moved to California from Greece, speaks four languages fluently, graduated from the prestigious Guildhall School in London ..."And she's *single*. Imagine that?" Miriam's an agent; beating around the bush isn't her strong point. She winks at both of us.

Alexandra definitely hasn't been in this town long enough. She actually blushes when she catches on to what Miriam is none too subtly hinting at. I've grown so accustomed to the bluntness of this town, sometimes I forget how tactless it can be. But her blush makes her seem like a real person. "Ignore her, she has the subtlety of a jackhammer," I whisper when Miriam excuses herself to take a call. "Would you like a glass of wine? You're probably going to need it with these two."

We talk over dinner and drinks for more than two hours. Miriam has tried to fix me up dozens of times, but never with a woman like this. Alexandra is smart, beautiful, poised ... the adjectives to describe her are endless. So why is it I'm more interested in talking shop with Stephen than getting to know the stunning—and available—woman?

"You know, Alexandra just accepted a deal with Fox as a correspondent," Miriam says in an attempt to break up the business discussion Stephen and I have going.

"That's great. What show?" I say. I'd actually assumed she was an actress.

"Entertainment Fashion Files. I'm doing their nightly style report."

"Congratulations."

"It's not exactly my dream job. But it's a foot in the door."

"We had three networks that wanted her. We took a short contract. We know she's destined for bigger things," Miriam adds proudly.

I nod and smile politely. The conversation falls awkwardly silent for a moment, so I try to feign interest, even though I really want to grab the check when the next waiter passes by. "What was your project before this one?"

"I was on a reality show," she replies sheepishly.

"Which one?"

"Mr. Right."

"Is that one of Miles's?" I look to Miriam. I can't keep track of all his reality programs anymore. Well, except for one I may or may not have a bit of a small obsession with.

"No. It was on cable."

"Was the bachelor a nice guy?" Curiosity gets the best of me.

"Well. He was on the show. Or at least I thought he was."

"But he wasn't?" See. I knew my first instinct was right. Flynn is a dickhead.

"It's just really hard to see a person for who they are in that environment. You see what they want you to see."

"What did they want you to see?"

"A great guy."

"Was it a show where the women are eliminated?"

"Aren't they all?" She smiles resignedly.

"I suppose." The waiter interrupts and I finally get the chance to ask for the check, but this conversation has definitely captured my attention. "How long did you last on the show?"

"Until the end."

"You were the winner?"

"If you can call it that."

"How long until you split up?"

"I found out he was sleeping with the wardrobe person the day after the finale."

"Sorry."

"Thanks. But it's okay. It opened doors for me. I'm just a little embarrassed I couldn't see the forest for the trees. The producers make it impossible to not get caught up in the moment. They create a fairytale. The problem is, the prince turns into a pumpkin instead of Prince Charming."

An hour later I'm back home. I didn't even bother to ask for Alexandra's number. It made for an awkward departure, but leading people on was never my thing. She's beautiful, yet it's not her face I keep replaying in my mind from tonight. *The producers make it impossible to not get caught up in the moment.* Her words echo in my head, over and over.

I can't stop myself from picking up the DVD. It's been sitting on the dining room table since the doorman handed it to me on the way back from my run this morning. I woke up thinking about Kate, thought the run would help me clear my mind. No such luck.

Now the damned thing is taunting me. The labeled jewel case is like a magnet to my eyes. I stalk through my apartment to find something to busy myself with, but it's no use. My eyes constantly flicker back and forth. Settling in on the couch after a shower, I grab the paper and force my mind into the business section. The table is in sight from the corner of my eye. Like a child unable to control himself, I actually have to raise the newspaper so the case is out of view. I read the same paragraph three times anyway.

Goddamn it. I should tell Miles to stop sending the dailies. But I won't. Because I'm pussy-whipped obsessed with a woman who is dating another man.

I curse myself as I angrily swipe the case from the table and head to my laptop.

Dickhead comes on screen first. He's being interviewed by the host alone.

"So, Flynn, you've got a pretty big decision coming up. The final four—overnight dates. You've got to have some strong feelings for these ladies to pick them at this point. Tell me, are you struggling with your choices? What's going on in that head of yours right now?"

"Well, Ryan. You're right, I am struggling, but probably not for the reasons you think. I do have some strong feelings, but some of the ladies, well, one in particular, I can't read where her head is at."

"You don't think your feelings are being reciprocated?"

"I'm not sure. It's hard to tell. She's incredible, but I feel like she's still holding back."

"And why do you think that is?"

"That's the struggle. Sometimes I feel like I haven't penetrated her heart the same way she has mine. But then there's these other times … when she opens up and we have these incredible moments and I think she feels it too. Those times, I wonder if the camera is what's holding her back." *It's not the camera, Dickhead.*

"Tough choice. So how do you decide if she should be in the final four?"

"Oh. That's the only one I'm sure about. There's no doubt I'm picking her to go to the final four. There are no cameras in the overnight suite. A night alone is *exactly* what the two of us need."

I slam my laptop shut so hard, the screen cracks.

chapter

nineteen

Kate

Downward dog is usually my favorite yoga pose. Hands and feet against the floor to form an upside down v, it should decrease tension by elongating the cervical spine. But it doesn't. It reminds me of three mornings ago and Cooper bending me over in the shower while he defiled my body, mercilessly pounding into me with unrelenting focus.

"Your ass looks good. No wonder two men want to tap that thing," Sadie says from behind me. And not quietly.

"Shhh." Through my legs I look back at my friend, who is out of proper position. Instead of her head looking at her feet, it's bent forward to look at my ass in front of her.

The cute instructor comes by, shaking his head at Sadie and raising his finger to his lips to ask her to keep it down. He stands behind me and splays his hand on my lower back, applying light pressure to nudge my heels further down into the stretch. "Great, Kate. Perfect," he says before moving on.

"Even the yogi wants to hit that ass," Sadie whispers, or at least tries to.

We finish our hot yoga class, both drenched from sweat as we start our half-mile walk back to our apartment. "So tonight's the big night. Last one-on-one date. One step closer to the final four. Make it through and you'll have enough to catch the bills up."

"Making the final four, and getting the first round of prize money, will give me some breathing room, although I don't really have a plan for how I'm going to fix things long term."

"When you win the show, the prize money will go a long way."

"I'm not going to win the show."

"Why not?"

"Because our relationship hasn't moved in that direction. We're more like buddies."

"Didn't you tell me he felt you up the other day?"

"Yes, but that was in a competition."

"Did your heart race increase when he had his hands on you?"

"That's not the point."

"It is the point. You like this guy. If it wasn't for meeting Cooper, you'd probably be into him."

I sigh. "Maybe. But I just can't be with two guys at the same time."

"You're not with Cooper."

"I slept with him."

"I slept with our Chem professor in college. Didn't mean I wanted to be with him."

"You slept with Professor Mulch?" I stop in my tracks.

"Did I forget to tell you that?"

"Umm ... yes, I would have remembered if you slept with Massive Mulch."

"The curiosity finally got to me. We stared at that anaconda bulging from his pants for ten weeks. I had to see it."

"He was gross."

"I didn't look at his face."

"So ..."

"So what?" she asks coyly.

"Was it as big as the outline we stared at for months?"

"Bigger."

"He was still gross."

"He ruined me for petite-penised men everywhere."

I laugh. "I totally forgot what we were talking about. How did our conversation turn to Professor Mulch?"

"I was making a point. Just because you slept with someone doesn't mean you're committed to them."

"I know, but it just doesn't feel right."

"It doesn't feel right because you can't play ding dong ditch."

"The kids game?"

"The adult version. Where you play with his ding dong and then ditch him."

"You need help."

"I need to play ding dong ditch," she teases. "But seriously, Kate. I know you have feelings for Cooper. You know where I stand on that one. It's time you put yourself first and find a little happiness. Yet we both know you won't do that.... not when you see it as being at the expense of your mom and Kyle. So if you're not going to give Cooper a real chance, then really jump back into the show. The last thing you need is to be heartbroken and not be able to help your family."

I heave a heavy sigh. "I know you're right"

"Aren't I always?" She bumps my shoulder.

We step off the elevator and I'm surprised to find a man at our door. "Flynn … what are you doing here? I thought our date wasn't until tonight."

"Maybe he's playing ding dong ditch," Sadie mumbles so only I can hear her.

Flynn smiles at me, eyes doing a quick sweep up and down. I'm wearing a tummy-baring yoga top and second-skin yoga pants. But I'm also a sweaty mess. "Thought I'd see if you wanted to go on a pre-date date?" He leans in and kisses me on the cheek.

"A pre-date date?"

"A date before our date."

"I thought we were off until five today."

"We are. I was hoping to take you out, without the cameras, before our date tonight."

"Umm ... I'm supposed to help Sadie at her office today. This is Sadie, by the way." I motion to my best friend. She has that gleam of excitement in her eyes that always got us in trouble growing up.

"Don't be silly. We can do it another day." She turns her attention to Flynn. "Nice to meet you. You're even hotter in person."

Flynn's smiles, amused at her forwardness. "We're all set then."

"But ..."

Sadie interrupts me. "No buts. Go, have a good time."

Flynn looks to Sadie, the two of them exchanging more than just a glance. "You should listen to your friend."

"I'm a mess."

"I like the way you look."

"And I smell."

"I like the way you smell too," he says with a lopsided grin.

"Can I take a quick shower?" I finally concede, ignoring his comment.

"Sure."

"Flynn and I will get to know each other," Sadie says, unlocking the door.

That, I'm a little afraid of.

Forty-five minutes later I'm freshly showered and ready. I hear the tail end of Sadie and Flynn's conversation as I walk into the living room. "The fire department had to come and take apart the machines."

"Please tell me you aren't telling that story again."

"It's a good story."

"It isn't a good story. And I was nine. How much more play do you think you can get out of it?"

"You were fourteen."

"I was *not* fourteen. I was twelve."

"You said nine. I had to go with fourteen to get you to admit the truth."

I roll my eyes. "I was reaching for something I dropped."

"A Justin Timberlake sticker in one of those little see-through plastic gumball containers that are impossible to open."

"It was a collectible sticker," I defend my action, what else can I do at this point? As if getting your head stuck between gumball machines in the front of a busy supermarket on a Saturday morning isn't bad enough. Admitting you had to be rescued by the fire department because you were trying to reach for a Justin Timberlake sticker just makes it that much more embarrassing.

Flynn stands. "Wanna know what I got from that story?"

"Not really," I say.

He walks toward me. "That you have a thing for musicians." He takes my hand, weaving his fingers through mine, and raises our joined hands to his lips. "Means there's hope for me after all."

"You're not going to tell me where we're going?"

"Nope."

"Why not? It can't be against the rules if we aren't on a show-sanctioned date."

"It's against my rules." He glances at me and smiles, eyes quickly returning to the road.

The radio plays a familiar voice. "Is that ... ?"

"Yep," Flynn says proudly.

"Wow. You're on the radio. Turn it up!"

"I'd come off pretty full of myself if I blasted my own song on the radio, don't you think?"

"It's the first time I've heard you on the radio."

"Me too."

"Are you serious?"

"I knew our manger pushed out the single early to a few stations. But I've never actually heard it played."

I blast the radio as loud as it can go. Flynn taps his fingers on the wheel as he drives, the smile never leaving his face.

"That's very cool. I can't believe we just listened to your song on the radio for the first time together," I say as I lower the volume back down.

His normally cocky attitude turns humble. "I'm glad I was with you."

A short drive more and then we pull into the parking lot at Qualcomm Stadium. "Are we going to the Chargers game?" I ask excitedly. My Dad and I spent many Sundays watching football when I was a kid. I hadn't yet caught on that he was betting the games back then.

"We are."

"I'm a huge Chargers fan."

"I know."

"You do?"

"Sweetheart, the way you wear that t-shirt, the lightning bolt stretched tightly across your chest, I may very well have to turn in my lifelong Raiders fan-club card."

"You're a Raiders fan?"

"I'm a Kate fan."

Good answer.

The fifty-yard line is so close, some of the players on the sidelines may very well hear my screaming. It's a tied game at half-time and we decide to get a bite to eat.

"Hot dog?" he asks as we move to the front of the line.

"And a beer."

"Girl after my own heart."

There's a crowd milling around the beer station; a small group of girls of about eighteen or nineteen are staring in our direction. Eventually, they make their way over to us. "Aren't you Flynn Beckham?" one eyelash-batting girl asks.

Flynn's arm wraps around my waist. "I am."

The small gaggle of girls squeal. "I've seen you at Stardust a dozen times!"

"Well, thank you for coming. We'll be back on the road soon."

"Would you sign an autograph for me?"

"Sure."

The smiling girls dig into their handbags, one of them pulling out a red felt-tip marker. She pulls up her shirt, revealing a lacy red bra overflowing with more cleavage than a push-up bra could ever offer me, and thrusts them in Flynn's direction. "Sign over my heart," she says.

"That's very sweet of you. But that wouldn't be very respectful to my girlfriend here." He motions in my direction. It might be the first time they even notice I'm standing next to him.

The girl looks annoyed at my presence and doesn't lower her shirt right away. But Flynn handles it with grace. Grabbing a napkin from a nearby dispenser, he begins to scribble, asking the girl's name. "Jenny," she says. He writes her a quick note, complete with a few sketches of music notes, and signs his name.

His hand on the small of my back, he leads me away. "I hear the game starting. You ladies enjoy the rest of the afternoon."

"Nicely done, Rockstar," I bump shoulders with Flynn as we make our way back to our seats. "By the way, I think your *girlfriend* would have been okay with you signing some skin. It doesn't seem so risqué since you're dating four other women."

Flynn stops and unexpectedly pulls me close to him. "That's all for the show. But today, when it's my choice, I'm here with you only."

Our evening date is nothing like the way we spent our day. Gone is the casual, fun atmosphere as Flynn takes my hand to board the beautiful catamaran for a sunset cruise.

"You look beautiful. I can't decide if I like you better in a Chargers t-shirt or a dress." He looks me up and down approvingly.

"Thank you. You clean up pretty well, yourself." His dress shirt and suit are both dark, but his tie is the perfect shade of pale blue to match the sparkle in his eyes. Even though he's dressed more formally than this afternoon, there's still an air of casualness about him. A laidback vibe that I can't help but notice is so distinctly different than what Cooper Montgomery throws off. The way that man comes off is anything but causal. I feel guilty thinking of Cooper when Flynn has been nothing short of perfect today. In fact, I can't seem to think of a single thing Flynn's done to sour me to him since the day I met him.

We find a quiet spot on the bow and the catamaran sets sail. The uniformed waiter brings us drinks and hors d'oeuvres and quickly makes himself scarce. It's almost easy to forget we're being watched by the prying eye of a camera hidden somewhere discreet. The beautiful boat glides smoothly through the harbor, the front slicing tranquilly through gleaming waters as the sun begins to set in the distance.

"Come here." Flynn wraps his arm around my shoulders and hauls me close against him. It's nice. Peaceful almost. I really do enjoy his company. I lean back, allowing myself to relax as he locks both arms around me.

"I had a good time today," he says, his chin resting on the top of my head.

"Me too," I exhale.

"I always have a good time when I'm with you."

"Me too."

"Kate …"

I turn when he doesn't say more. "I like you," he rasps, meeting my gaze.

"I like you too."

"A lot."

Oh. I have no idea what to say. I really do like him. Sort of a lot too. But something keeps holding me back. Or more correctly, some*one* keeps holding me back. If Cooper Montgomery hadn't barreled into my life, Flynn and I would most likely be in a very different place right now. I need to focus—keep the memory of the kiss we shared before I met Cooper in the forefront of my mind. It was nice. Passionate even. There was a spark, I know there was. I just need to get back to that place. Yet I tense up when he moves in closer.

"Is it the cameras?" he whispers in my ear.

I have no idea how to answer, so I tell him the truth. Well, mostly the truth. It was difficult for me to forget the cameras even before I met Cooper. "Maybe a little."

A member of the *Throb* crew comes out from nowhere. "Sorry to interrupt, guys. But can you speak a little louder? We can't pick up your voices out here too easily."

Flynn sighs loudly. "Yeah. No problem." He smiles and leans his forehead to mine, intentionally whispering to avoid the mics. "I get it. I like that you're more comfortable when we're alone. Real life won't have cameras." He kisses my cheek and his sweet smile turns flirty again. "Well, unless you want cameras. I'd be into that too if it's just for our eyes."

chapter twenty

Cooper

"Coop. You got a minute?" Miles pops his head into my office.

Not really. "Sure. What's up Miles?"

"The ratings on *Throb* are climbing every week. Most reality TV shows drop as they go. We're heading in the other direction." He beams, but I stiffen, waiting for the other shoe to drop. He's not here to only share good news.

"That's great." *I wish the damn show would end already.*

"The final four are going to be picked tomorrow night. I can't wait to film the overnight dates."

"What do you need, Miles?" Exasperation and anger shine through loud and clear.

"We rented a wing of the Four Seasons in Barbados to shoot the overnight date shows in. But it's expensive. Between putting up the crew and closing off a section of the hotel to shoot for two weeks, it will eat away at a lot of cash. Cash that can be better used for more advertising."

"So you want another loan?"

"No. I was hoping to use the house in Barbados to shoot."

"*My* house?" *Yeah. I'd like nothing better than to have Kate fuck Dickhead in my bedroom. Awesome idea.* "I don't think so, Miles." The house was our father's; I bought Miles out when we settled the estate. "Do you want to shoot them *fucking* in our father's room?"

Miles shoves his hands in his pocket nervously. At least he has the decency to look embarrassed for asking. "What about if the crew stayed in the main house? And the contestant stayed in the guesthouse. Alone. We can keep the honeymoon suite at the Four Seasons and shoot there, but at least it would save me a fortune putting everyone up." He pauses for a moment. "Dad used to give the keys to the crew sometimes after they worked hard on a film, as a bonus. I don't think he'd mind the crew staying there."

"I don't know, Miles, let me think about it." *How the hell did I get so involved in his crap?*

"That's great." He perks up and smiles like I've just agreed to something.

"Don't look so happy, I didn't say yes yet."

"No, but you will."

"I have a meeting."

"Thanks, Coop. I have to cancel the hotel by tomorrow … if you could let me know by then." Miles walks toward the door and looks back. "Oh. I almost forgot." He reaches inside his suit jacket pocket and pulls out a DVD. "Today's daily. The last one-on-one date. Women are going to eat this shit up. He actually sings to his date under the moonlight in the back of a catamaran."

"Who was his date?"

"Kate."

The contents of the large envelope I finally tore open are scattered all over my desk. I'd hired Damian Fry to dig up dirt on Kate right after she told me she was doing the show because she needed the prize money. The envelope arrived the morning after we'd spent the night together. But by then, I'd flip-flopped back and forth a million times between needing to know and feeling like I was invading her privacy reading through what she was obviously not ready to tell me. Forcing myself to ignore the report, I'd shoved it into the back of my drawer, unopened. Until an hour ago.

The visual Miles left me of Kate and Dickhead under the moonlight this morning has left me unable to focus. Again. Everyone has some skeletons in their closet—I needed to harden my heart by learning Kate's. I thought whatever was inside the envelope might help me.

I stare at the mess of papers—the dirt Damian Fry dug up on Kate. Well, not really on Kate—she's squeaky clean. Which is actually pretty amazing considering the man she was raised by. It's her father who got her into the mess she's in today. Leaving her sick mother with enough debt to drown her. And her brother. Damn it. I'll never be able to think straight in a day full of jam-packed meetings.

Sitting around the boardroom table, I vaguely hear the voices of each department head drone on with their project updates. My mind is somewhere else. A vision of Kate beneath me fills my head, her smiling up at me, eyes shining with emotion. But then just as quickly as it came, the vision is gone, replaced by *him* singing to her. She looks up at him with the same emotion in her eyes.

I thought not seeing it on the screen would save me from another day of picturing her in his arms. Damn, was I wrong. My brain has gotten more creative, deciding to play a scene for me to watch, even though it has no idea what really is on the video.

I make no effort to participate in the meeting. It's a waste of my time and that of a dozen other high-priced people on my payroll. "Thank you for coming. See you next week," I mutter, standing abruptly, and walk out of the room, leaving faces full of confusion in my wake.

Irritated with myself for my lack of focus, I decide to feed my obsession, even though I know it's a bad idea. I walk into my office and head straight for my laptop. Helen follows me in, looking concerned. "Is everything okay? It's only eleven and your meeting usually goes until at least one."

"It's fine. I cut it early. I have some pressing things I need to take care of today." *Yeah, like stalking.*

I open the jewel case and slip in the DVD just as Helen begins to walk back to her desk. "Do you have Miles's show schedule for today?"

"Yes."

"Can you tell me when they're shooting?"

"Sure." She heads to her computer and comes back a minute later with a printout. "He's shooting a commercial up at the rental house." She looks at her watch. "It's scheduled to start right about now."

My jacket is on before she finishes the sentence. "Reschedule my afternoon meetings."

"Really?" The surprise in her voice matches her face. I don't go off schedule.

"Push them until tomorrow. I may not be back this afternoon," I yell back over my shoulder, already halfway out the door.

My foot leans on the accelerator harder as my anxiety builds. The needle on the speedometer ratchets up to eighty, although I don't even notice. My hands grip the wheel tightly as I weave in and out of traffic.

Her beat-up blue Jeep is parked in the circular driveway, jammed in with twenty other cars. I catch my reflection in the window—jaw tight, eyes set with determination, mouth in a taut line. The same way I look when a deal I've been salivating over for months is about to go south. I take a deep cleansing breath before walking inside.

"How's it going today, Joel?" The director turns, surprised to see me again.

"Cooper. Twice in as many weeks. You must have a big investment in the show." *You could say that. And it has nothing to do with the one-point-two I loaned my brother.*

"What are you shooting now?"

"Some footage for commercials. We're going one woman at a time. Still waiting for the first one to come out of makeup. This one's a bit of a prima donna."

"Which one?"

"Name's Jessica."

"What's the scene?"

"A kiss. Rough life this Flynn has. Has to kiss five beautiful women today."

"Where's Miles?"

"Last I saw him, he was giving one of the women a lecture on what her kiss should look like."

I pass by the makeup and wardrobe room. Jessica's in a chair, a team of frayed-looking assistants primping and priming as she berates them. I stop a stagehand walking down the hall. "Kate?"

"Bathroom, I think," he says, pointing in the direction he just came from.

I knock gently on the door. Her voice hits me like a ton of bricks. "I'll be out in a minute."

I wait, eyes anxiously patrolling the empty halls. Finally the doorknob begins to turn and I see Kate before she sees me. I guide her back into the bathroom and close the door quickly, successfully avoiding being caught by anyone.

"Cooper!" Her eyes go wide. "What are you doing here?"

"I needed to see you."

"Here? What's the matter?"

"Why did you let me win?"

"What are you talking about?"

"Cards. Why did you let me win?"

"You know why."

"No, tell me." I move in closer.

"I wanted to be with you."

"And now?"

"Now I'm here. You knew I had to come back."

"Have you slept with him?"

"Did you seriously just come here and push me into a bathroom to ask me that?"

"Answer the question."

"No."

"Answer the damn question, Kate." I grip her hip tightly.

"It's none of your business."

"It is." My other hand combs through her hair and I wrap the back length around my fingers.

"We agreed to one night."

"I lied."

"But—"

I interrupt her. "I'm going out of my mind. Just tell me. Did you sleep with him? Answer the question." I sound desperate and I hate myself for sounding that way. "I need to know, Kate."

We hold each other in an intense stare-off before she finally responds. "No, I didn't."

I let go of any hesitation I'm restraining and my mouth crashes down on hers fiercely. It takes less than a heartbeat for her to join me. We claw at each other, desperation and longing mixing together into a combustible spark that leads into a slow burning to be inside of her. Now.

We tear at each other's clothes. It's a testament to our need that we can't even wait until we're both fully unclothed. I grab her ass and lift her to the sink. It's the perfect height. Her hands clench my ass, and before I even realize what's happening I'm poised at her opening.

"Fuck." My body trembles as I pause. "You want this?" I push the desire that's fueling me aside, needing to hear I'm not forcing her into something she doesn't want to do.

She responds by lifting her legs from the floor and wrapping them around my waist. "God, yes. I've missed you." Her voice is raw and needy and it's all I need to hear.

I sink inside of her with one thrust of my hips, burying myself as deep as I can. The feeling overwhelms me. It's raw and carnal and I can't even try to fight the urge to fill her body like an animal claiming his mate.

I fuck her hard. Starved for the feel of her perfect body taking every inch of me inside of her. It's a ferocious race to make her scream my name. *My* name. One hand wraps around both her wrists holding them behind her back, subduing her as I pound into her without mercy. She trembles as she climbs higher and higher, until I feel what's left of her resolve flee from her body, finally surrendering to me completely.

"I've been going crazy thinking of you here." My lips worship her neck. Sucking and kissing and biting along the pulsating heartbeat running from her ear to her collarbone. "I can't think of anything else but you," I rasp. Both of our breaths are ragged, fast, erratic.

A juddering moan falls from her lips. "I'm … I'm …"

"That's it, beautiful." My hips slam into her harder and harder until I feel her body tighten and then go limp. Her eyes roll into the back of her head and shut as her pussy convulses around the length of me. It takes everything I have to hold back my own orgasm. But I do, until her gaze finds mine again, then I look deep into those sated blues and come inside of her. Erupting long and hard and deep.

chapter

twenty-one

Kate

My reflection stares back at me, looking like what I am—thoroughly fucked. Lips swollen, hair disheveled, face completely flushed, I respond to the third knock on the bathroom door. "I'll be out in a minute."

The production assistant sighs from the other side of the door. He probably thinks I'm busy dolling myself up before I go on camera. Although for all I know, the whole place may know what I was doing in here fifteen minutes ago. I try hard to remember if we were loud, but all I can seem to recall is the incredible feeling of having Cooper inside my body once again. Everything else faded into the oblivion.

Five minutes ago he slipped out the door after the second knock came. I could tell he wanted to fling open the door and give whoever was on the other side a piece of his mind. But he didn't—he held back and let me answer. I told the assistant sent to beckon me for my turn at filming that I wasn't feeling well, that I needed some time.

The minutes that followed after orgasm are a haze. Sated and in Cooper's arms, nothing, it seemed, could go wrong. But with every moment that ticks by, the haze clears and the trouble brewing rings so loud in my ears, I can barely hear.

I do my best to fix myself, the disheveled exterior anyway. A few minutes later another knock comes. "Kate, it's Flynn."

Shit.

"Are you okay?" he asks when I don't respond.

"Yes. I just don't feel that great."

"Can I come in?"

I want to say no. I don't want to see anyone right now. "I just need another minute." *Or year. Year would be better.*

"I'll wait."

Two minutes later I take a deep breath and open the door. Flynn steps in and closes the door behind him. "Are you okay? You look flushed."

"Yeah. Just not feeling so hot, I guess."

The look on his face is concern. He reaches out and feels my forehead. "You're not warm." I look down—I can't possibly look into his eyes. I was just in the arms of another man and this sweet guy is concerned that my freshly fucked flush might be a fever. I'm a horrible human being.

"Come here." He pulls me to him. I want to run away, not let him touch me, but instead I freeze in place, unsure of how to react. He wraps his arms around me. "I think you're just nervous about the shoot. The camera really makes you anxious, doesn't it?" One of his hands moves to my shoulder. "You're a ball of stress. Let me work my magic fingers on you for a few minutes to help it disappear."

Nervous, I walk to the set next to Flynn, thankful he doesn't try to hold my hand. There's no sign of Cooper anywhere, but I know he's here somewhere. He's giving me space because I need it to get through this shoot, but Cooper Montgomery is *not* the type of man to stay in the shadows for very long.

The camera crew quickly arranges Flynn and me where they need us to stand. "Facing each other," one of the production assistants says, "Kate's palms flat on your upper chest. Talk for a minute or two. We'll yell 'ready' when it's time for Flynn to lean in for a kiss."

Even when I'm situated in my assigned position, palms flat on chest, I avoid Flynn's eyes. I can't bear to look at him; surely he'll see what a complete fraud I am.

"Kate," Flynn says gently.

I still don't look up at him.

"Kate," he repeats. When I still don't look up his hand gently cups my chin, lifting my face so my eyes meet his gaze. "You look gorgeous. Nervous and flushed is a good look for you." He flashes a boyish smile and speaks quietly. He's trying to put me at ease.

"Thank you." God, I'm an utterly disgusting person. I'm not even sure what I feel guiltier about at the moment—my hands touching another man not twenty minutes after Cooper was inside of me, or the disrespect I'm showing Flynn.

"Ready!" The director yells, queuing us for a kiss.

Flynn and I stare at each other, I'm lost somewhere in outer space, and he tries diligently to find me. His eyes fall to my lips and then back to meet mine. I must look like a deer in the headlights, because he shows mercy, swerving to avoid a near disaster. Leaning down, he avoids my quivering mouth, instead pressing his lip to my temple. "I'll deal with them. I'd never make you do anything you don't want to do," he whispers as a tear falls from my eye.

Flynn and Miles have a nearby heated exchange. And then Flynn returns, his victorious smile fading when he sees me.

"My kisses really aren't that bad. I promise. I might have even heard a rumor that I was good at it." He laces our fingers together and lifts my hand to kiss the top.

"I'm sorry. I feel terrible. It's not you." They might be the first truthful words I've said to this man today. It really isn't him.

"Think you can handle a dance with me?"

The confusion on my face is evident.

"They're going to shoot us slow-dancing. It's what I worked out instead of a steamy kiss."

My chest tightens. I'm not really even up to a dance, but how can I tell him that without making him think he doesn't repulse me?

"Thank you. That would be great."

"Don't thank me. I might have been a little selfish suggesting it. I may not be getting a kiss, but I'm still getting your body pressed close to mine."

Cooper's classic Porsche is parked out front of my building when I finally return home. I pretty much expected him to appear at every turn today, but he didn't. The anticipation of when he might appear only made the day that much more unbearable.

I pull into the spot next to him. He's outside, leaning against his car, when I park.

"I wasn't sure where you went," I say.

"I couldn't stay there any longer."

"When did you leave?"

"About two seconds after the director yelled 'Ready.'" He tugs his fingers harshly through his locks. It looks like he's done quite a bit of that since earlier today, his mussed hair having bore the brunt of his stress. Yet I still can't help noticing how sexy it makes him look.

"I couldn't watch another man put his lips on you." Cooper maintains the safe distance between us as he speaks.

"He didn't," I say softly.

"He didn't what?" His hopeful gaze blazes into me.

"Kiss me."

He steps closer, narrowing the gap between us until my back is up against my car. Positioning one hand on either side of my head against my Jeep, his eyes search mine. "Are you just telling me that because it's what I want to hear?"

I shake my head. His eyes close with relief.

"Come home with me." His voice is gentle, raw.

I thought not physically being around Cooper would free me to jump back into the game. Rekindle a spark that I'd once felt with Flynn. But that spark has been extinguished. And physically keeping away from Cooper doesn't work because, unlike whatever I felt with Flynn, things with Cooper are more than physical. I nod and let him lead me to his car without bothering to get any of my things.

Cooper finally breaks the silence as we make our way onto the highway. "I'm glad he's a fool."

"He's not a fool."

"Don't defend him." His eyes flash to me. "Give me that much at least."

"Okay. But he was just trying to be respectful."

"Respect or not, given the chance to kiss you, I'm taking it every damn time."

Inside his apartment, Cooper opens a wine fridge and lifts a bottle of wine, offering it to me for approval. "When do you have to be back?"

I nod. "Tomorrow night. We have a selection ceremony and then a week off. That's if I make it to the final four."

"I need you to stay tonight."

"Okay."

"Okay?" He hands me a crystal glass and pushes the hair from my face.

I nod. "I want you to hold me. I know you had to leave today, but I felt it when you were gone."

He responds by wrapping me tightly in his arms and buries his nose in my hair, inhaling deeply. We stay that way until what amounts to a sigh rolls through my body.

"I need to wash off all this makeup they put on me."

"Why don't you go take a shower?"

"Okay."

"I could also use a shower," he says, running his hand down my arm and leaving a trail of goosebumps. "Although we're only going to need another one after we get all sweaty."

He leads me into a bathroom I didn't see last time I was here and pushes a few buttons on a nearby panel. It's a walk in shower bigger than my first apartment. Built for more than one, water shoots out of jets from three sides, the top an indulgent oversized rain shower.

"Fancy shower."

"Hmmm." He slips off my shirt, his focus shifting from conversation to undressing me.

"Looks like it's made for more than one." The hand reaching for my pant zipper freezes and he glances up at me.

"Never took a shower with anyone in here." I catch that he says *in here* and it makes my mind start to wonder if that's why he's brought me into this bathroom. It shouldn't matter; I'm no virgin either.

"Or in the other shower," he says directly into my eyes.

"I didn't say anything."

"Yes, but you were thinking it."

I ignore his comment, although I reach for the buttons on his shirt a little happier. "So now you know what I'm thinking?"

"This time. Yes." He draws down my pants and kneels down, tapping my calf for me to step out. "It would make my day a lot more productive if I knew what you were thinking more often."

"Are you blaming me for your unproductiveness?"

He unfastens the back of my bra with one hand. The extent of his dexterity removing lingerie doesn't go unnoticed. "Yes. I'm blaming you for my unproductiveness." The finger stroking the side of my breast pauses. "I've been near idle since I met you." He looks up at me.

In the moment, I fall a little bit harder for him. The domineering, sexy, authoritative man, who takes command of a room just by walking into it, just admitted I was his kryptonite. I'm barely able to stop myself from launching at him. Instead, I kiss him fiercely. Hard and long, until I'm so lost in his arms that I don't even realize he's carried me into the shower.

I love the way we kiss, as if we've been starved for each other for weeks, when it was only a matter of hours since he was buried inside of me. We grope and pull, scratch and claw. He bites my lip so hard when I go to pull away for air that it hurts. But it's a pain that shoots down to the sensitive flesh between my legs, inciting a fire deep inside of me. My hands go to his hair, pulling, wrenching, clenching—needing him closer. I can't get enough.

One of his hands drops to my ass and he grabs a handful, squeezing hard before he lifts and guides my legs to wrap around his waist. My back hits the cold tile wall, his hand behind my head protecting me from the full extent of the harshness of our actions.

My entire body aches for him. In a way I've never experienced. A savage need rumbles in the pit of my stomach that leaves me desperate to feed it. I moan, feeling the full length of his hardness pushed up firmly against my belly. "I want you," I breathe out against our pressed lips.

"Patience," he mumbles back.

I arch my back and use the wall to leverage myself, forcing my body lower in an attempt to bring what I want closer. I *need* him inside of me. He pulls his head back, amused, his mouth curving to a wicked grin. "That will only make it longer until I give you what you want." He drops his head and sucks my nipple in.

Somewhere between agonizing torture and blissful euphoria he finally concedes. My head falls back, thudding against the tile, and I whimper as he pushes into me. He drives deep, filling me completely, and then stills, claiming my eyes under the same control that he possesses my body before he begins to move. Satisfied with our gaze locked, he sets an unrelenting pace, pulling almost all the way out each time before slamming back into the hollows of my body. The intensity of each stroke is heightened by the emotions I see in his eyes as he watches me, focused keenly on satisfying my needs before his own.

My body wilts as I come, but the way he says my name with a jagged edge as he fills me, never breaking our gaze, leaves me in awe of the passion we are able to ignite. *Together.* I'd heard the phrase a million times but never really thought it had any truth until this moment. Cooper Montgomery *just ruined me for all other men.*

chapter twenty-two

Cooper

"My dad died last year. He left my mother and brother drowning in debt. My mom is sick and my brother is disabled." We're lying in bed, the room dark, her head snuggled in the crook of my shoulder as her finger traces light circles on my pec. "My brother and I were in an accident a few years ago. I was the only one who walked away." Her voice cracks with a sadness that wraps around my heart and squeezes. "I applied to the show because of the prize. I didn't really give it much thought. I guess I never thought they'd pick me as a contestant."

I already know everything she's confessing, but it means a lot that she decides to share it with me. I kiss the top of her forehead. "I'm sorry. How bad is it?"

"The house is mortgaged for more than it's worth and there was barely any life insurance after they deducted the loans my father had taken. He was an all-or-nothing type of man. Didn't do things halfway. It was great when he was on a winning streak. But when he was losing, he didn't stop until he had nothing left but the shirt on his back. He was missing the in-between gene."

"And your brother?"

"He's doing okay, health-wise at least, right now. We don't burden him with any of the financial stuff. He's already been burdened more than any other teenager should have to be."

"Will the prize money get them out of debt, or is it just a temporary fix?"

"It depends."

"On what?"

"On if I make it to the final four or the end. The final four is a Band-Aid. The end makes the problem go away."

"I see the way he looks at you. You're definitely making the final four."

"I thought you didn't stay to watch today?" She lifts, perching her head up on her elbow, and looks down at me.

Time for a little of my own confessions. "I've been sort of watching the dailies of the show every morning."

"Sort of?"

"Maybe 'sort of' isn't the right term."

"What would be the right term?"

"'Religiously' might work."

"You've been religiously watching the dailies of the show every morning?"

"Hence the unproductiveness I mentioned earlier."

We're both quiet for a while, and then I say what I've been thinking about since Damian Fry delivered the background report on Kate and her family. "Let me help you."

"What do you mean?"

I shift, easing her to her back, and sift my fingers through her loose hair. "I'll give you the money you need."

"That's sweet. But I can't do that."

"Why not?"

"I can't take money from you, Cooper."

"Then consider it a loan. You can pay me back someday."

"I'll never be able to pay you back. The bank was right in turning down my application. My student loans will strangle me for the next ten years."

"I can't watch you with him, Kate."

"So stop watching."

"You act like I have a choice."

"You do. It's easy. Don't press play. Plus, there hasn't been anything happening worth watching."

"He's in love with you."

"He is not. But even if he was, it wouldn't matter."

"It matters to me. Were you telling me the truth when you said you haven't slept with him?"

"Is that what you think of me? I'm lying here in bed with you. Do you think I'd be doing that if I was sleeping with him?"

"I can't think straight anymore, Kate." I yank through my hair.

"That's why this wasn't a good idea." She rolls away from me and sits up. "I shouldn't have come."

Like a fool, I say nothing, instead only watch as she goes to the bathroom and comes out dressed. "I called a cab," she says quietly, her eyes purposefully avoiding mine. "But then I realized I don't know your address."

"Come back to bed."

"Just tell me your address so I can go."

"No."

"No?"

"If you really want to go home, I'll take you. But you're going to listen first."

She doesn't agree, but she doesn't make any attempt to move to the bed either. So I move to her, not bothering to put on any clothes or cover up. It throws her off guard. "Kiss me."

"What? No."

"Damn it, Kate." I cup her head and seal my mouth over hers. Her flimsy attempt to protest is quickly swallowed by a moan as her body sags into my arms. My heart is raging in my chest as I lift her and carry her back to bed.

"Cooper …"

I cut her off. "Shhh … tomorrow. We'll figure it out tomorrow."

chapter twenty-three

Kate

Stubble. If I thought Cooper Montgomery was a god cleanly shaven, wearing a custom-tailored suit, it was only because I've never seen him in ripped jeans, a dark t-shirt and stubble. Jesus. The man does things to me. Seeing him standing at the stove, suddenly the speech I'd rehearsed in my mind has escaped me.

"Morning." He grins at me and eyes my stealing his dress shirt again with approval.

"Coffee?"

"Kiss first." He crooks his finger in my direction with a steely gaze.

I roll my eyes like it's the ultimate sacrifice as I lazily shuffle over to him.

He grabs my ass with one hand and directs my head to where he wants it with the other. The hand on my backside swats with a hard smack when he releases my mouth.

"What was that for?" I rub the stinging cheek of my ass.

"For rolling your eyes at me." Strangely, I think to myself that I'll need to remember to roll my eyes more often.

"I thought you didn't cook?" I peer at the three burners he has going.

"I don't."

"Looks like you know what you're doing."

"I said I didn't cook. I never said I didn't know how. Sit. I'll pour your coffee."

"Bossy," I mumble under my breath, but take the seat he points to on the other side of the counter.

"You must be difficult to work for."

Cooper cocks one eyebrow. "And why is that?"

"Because you're so bossy."

"My employees don't tend to be as difficult as you." He slides a mug over to me.

"Is that so?"

"It is."

"Do you have a lot of female employees?"

"Would it bother you if I did?"

"I'm not sure." I shrug and consider it. "It might. But that's not why I asked."

"Okay. Well about half of my department heads are women."

"And do you find any of them bossy?"

A wry grin crosses his perfectly masculine face. "You think I have an issue with women in general?"

"Maybe." I sip my coffee.

Cooper plates breakfast and walks around the island to join me at the stools. He leans down, sweeps the hair from my shoulder and tenderly kisses my neck. His words vibrate on my skin. "You're the only woman I have an issue with."

Belly full, I fork the remnants of breakfast around my plate, delaying the inevitable. The conversation is bound to come. "I seem to overeat when I'm with you," I say, finishing the last of the bacon.

"That's good. I like to watch you eat."

"Well if I ate like this often, I'd gain ten pounds in a month."

"Not with lots of exercise."

"I'm not really great about getting to the gym. Twice-a-week yoga if I'm being good."

"There are plenty of other ways to burn calories I think you might enjoy better." Cooper kisses my mouth and takes my plate to the sink.

He turns around, leaning against the counter and folds his arms. "You ready to have that talk?"

"Not really."

"Oh. But I have an idea to make things interesting." He turns, opens a drawer, pulls out a pack of cards, and tosses them on the counter.

"We're going to play cards?" I furrow my brow.

"Yep. I have some ideas. But you may not like a few of them. So we're going to play a hand to decide our stalemates. You in?"

"You do know I'm pretty good at playing, right?"

Cooper grins. "I do. But I plan to throw off your game by distracting you."

"And how will you do that?"

"We're going to play naked."

I look up at him with raised eyebrows. "Confident your nakedness will throw me off, are you?"

Cooper draws down his pants, his semi-hard erection springing free. Damn. Commando. He leisurely strokes his cock a few times. My eager eyes follow the slide of his hand up and down. My mouth salivates when a tiny drop glistens at the tip of the wide crown.

"Kate." My eye leap to his, but he keeps stroking and my gaze falls victim to the ever-growing swell. "If your concentration isn't rattled enough, I'm going to use my mouth on your sweet pussy until you can't see the cards straight."

"Oh." I try to force my thoughts out of the gutter and focus.

"You ready?"

"Do I have a choice?"

He grins. "Not really."

"I think your real plan was to get me out of my clothes so I couldn't run away after you told me that."

"It was a light investigation. I do more on my employees."

"And you run background checks on women you date too?"

"So we're dating?"

"You know what I meant."

"If we were dating, maybe I wouldn't have had to figure out what was going on myself. Maybe you would have shared it with me."

"I did share it with you."

"Last night."

"So?"

"I needed to know what I was up against before that."

"So you invaded my priva …" I trail off, my eyes getting caught in his web of actions again. He's sitting against the headboard, naked as a jaybird, with me between his legs, facing him—wearing a matching outfit. And he starts stroking again just as I'm about to yell at him.

"I know what you're doing," I swallow and say.

"And do you like watching me do it?" His mouth curves to an impish smile. This is going to be more difficult than I thought.

"I'll start."

"Okay," I say with trepidation.

"I want to be with you. Do you want to be with me?"

"Yes … but …"

He holds up his hand. "Let's take baby steps. I've thought this through all morning."

"Okay."

"So we've got the most important thing established. We want to be together. The rest will take some negotiation."

"I think you've figured out something we both already knew. The hard part is how to get through the next five weeks."

"I'd like you to quit the show today. I understand you want to help your family. I find it noble actually. But my first preference is to pay off the debt for you. I have the money and it would make me happy to help."

"I can't do that, Cooper." It's tempting, truly it is. Even the thought of having a little of the load I shoulder lifted, makes me feel like someday I really will have my own life back again. But I need to take care of my family before that can happen.

"That's an impasse. We'll play a hand for that decision." Cooper removes the cards from their box.

I squint my eyes, watching him. Something in the way his jaw flexes lights the bulb over my head. "I'll shuffle and deal," I say, extending my hand.

"Are you concerned I might cheat if given the opportunity?"

I don't respond verbally. Instead I deal out five cards each, suits facing up. Cooper's hand miraculously has four queens. "Did you think four aces would be to obvious?"

The corner of his mouth twitches. "Maybe."

I scoop up the cards. "You want to settle things this way. We'll do it, but we'll do it fair and square." I shuffle the cards with one hand like a pro.

Cooper loses the first hand. "You even beat me without your lucky chip."

"You're probably one of the few people I *can* beat without my lucky chip."

"You really believe in superstition that much?"

"No, you're just that bad."

"Maybe your brand of superstition just doesn't work for me."

"You prefer blowing on dice to a lucky chip?"

"Dice is *definitely* not what I prefer you blowing on." Cooper's hand drops and my eyes follow the firm stroke of his hard on.

"Stop that," I scold.

"Fine. But we need rules then. If you're going back to the show."

"What kind of rules."

"Rule one—No sex with anyone but me. That's a given."

"Done," I say. Easy decision there.

"No kissing."

"But at the ceremony ... we always have to kiss him when we get picked."

"So I can stick my tongue in Tatiana's mouth?"

"Has it been there before?"

"That's not the point. If you're okay with kissing, you won't mind if I say hello to Tatiana with my tongue."

"Rule two—no tongue kissing," I grumble.

"You make it through to the final four, collect the prize money, then quit. I'll loan you the money to pay off your mother's debt, and you can pay it back after your student loans are paid off."

"That's ten years."

"I'm not worried about it."

"Impasse." I hold out the cards. "Can I trust you to deal this time?"

"Maybe you should deal. My hands have better things to do." He strokes himself, then reaches out and pinches my nipple.

"It's not going to work." *It's totally working.*

I deal quickly.

I win again. I would never have guessed I'd be happy to win paying off my own student loans.

"Miles wants to use our family home in Barbados to house the contestants the last two weeks. I'm going to let him. The contestants will stay in the guesthouse. I want you to be comfortable; there's a room I want you to stay in there. Dickhead will stay at a hotel."

"I'd love that."

"There's more."

His face is apprehensive. I feel like I'm on a roller coaster. One minute I'm riding high, packing my imaginary bags for a week in Barbados. The next minute, I'm perched at the top, my stomach hurling to a nervous drop as I wait for the free-fall that's about to come.

"You took your brother out of therapy."

I quirk an eyebrow. "A *light* background investigation, huh?"

"The investigator might have gotten carried away."

Sure, the *investigator* got carried away. "The therapy is still considered experimental. The insurance doesn't cover it."

"I want to pay for the therapy."

"I can't let you do that. But it's sweet of you to offer. Really."

"Impasse."

"This doesn't even have to do with me or the show."

"Does it cause you stress that he's not going to therapy?"

"Yes."

"Then it's related. Deal."

Not even the best players can win every hand. I try in earnest, but lose.

"Good thing I won that one."

"Why is that?"

"Because I paid the therapist over the phone before you got out of bed this morning."

chapter
twenty-four

Cooper

I've never understood why people slow and stare at a bad car accident. They know they're going to witness something horrible, something the mind won't be able to rewind and unsee. Yet the more gore, the bigger the traffic backup. I've always been the guy to curse the idiots in front of me riding their brake lights as they passed the mangled pile of steel. I refuse to let unbridled curiosity get the best of me, never allowing my head to turn despite the powerful pull of the wreckage.

Yet here I am, sitting in my car, staring at the front door, knowing there's an accident waiting to happen right on the other side. But there's not a goddamn thing I can do to stop myself from going in. She made me promise not to watch the taped show tomorrow. Technically I'm not breaking the promise—I never said I wouldn't come to watch the live filming tonight. Each morning I have to restrain myself from hurling the laptop across the room. I can't imagine it won't be a million times harder to stop myself from walking through the door and knocking Dickhead on his ass. A string of curses litters the air as I stomp from my car to the house.

"Coop! I didn't know you were coming." Miles actually looks happy to see me. Unfortunately, the sentiment isn't returned, although my scowl actually has nothing to do with my little brother for a change.

"Miles." I nod.

"You came at a good time. The ladies are sufficiently loose. We plied them with liquor, now it's time to unleash the bachelor and watch the horns start to rise from their pretty little heads." He rubs his hands together like a child unable to contain his excitement. "I'm going to go check in on Flynn. Have a drink—we just brought out one of the two rolling bars from the shoot." He slaps me on the shoulder. "Your favorite scotch is in there, although it's half gone. You and Flynn have similar tastes."

I stroll straight to the bar, ignoring the cameraman who starts speaking to me, and pull out the Macallan single malt. The bottle is less than half full. *Dickhead.* Gulping back two fingers worth, I slam the tumbler down.

"Bad day?" Joel Blick, the director, reaches over the bar and grabs a glass. He pours himself a double and tips the bottle to me asking if I want a refill. I slide my glass in his direction.

"You could say that." I nod my glass to him before drinking.

"Well, maybe a little girl-on-girl catfight will cheer you up. There's a storm brewing amongst the contestants tonight."

"What's it about?"

"The bachelor." He finishes his drink. "What else?"

"Which girls?"

"All the camera's favorites. Jessica, Mercedes and Kate. They were going at it pretty good. Got heated. But now, after the alcohol and bringing Flynn into the game ... I wouldn't be surprised if the early rumbling leads to a big explosion."

"You have the argument in the can?"

"I do." I stare at him and wait. "You want a replay?"

Who can resist watching a car accident waiting to happen?

"You think you're better than everyone here?" Jessica seethes, her normally pretty face contorted.

"I don't even know you. You've had something against me since the first night and I have no idea why," Kate replies in a dismissive tone. It only serves to anger Jessica more that she doesn't get a sufficient rile out of her.

"You walk around thinking Flynn is wrapped around your little pinky finger."

I know it's irrational. But just hearing Kate in an argument that has anything to do with Dickhead brings my already heated blood to a boil.

"I think you've had too much to drink," Kate says, then pivots to walk away.

But Jessica grabs her shoulder. "I know the game you're playing," she warns.

Kate turns and glares at her. For a long moment, the two stare off—neither of them backing down. Then a familiar look on Kate's face appears, and she calls her opponent's bluff. "We're all playing a game, aren't we?" She dusts Jessica's hand off her shoulder and walks away.

The camera fades out. "What was that all about?" I ask.

"Got me. But something's up and Miles is busy trying to stoke the fire."

The live feed monitor captures everything happening on the other side of the wall, even though they're not filming at the moment. Kate looks beautiful in a curve-hugging dark blue cocktail dress. The expansive living room is filled with women who are unquestionably knockouts. Yet Kate stands out, even though her assets aren't on full display. The crew is setting up lighting and she laughs and smiles with them. A short young intern is struggling to set up a high camera boom and Kate, in her five-inch heels, walks over and helps her. They spend five minutes talking afterward. The other women don't even notice the crew, they're too busy waiting for someone more important to walk in the room.

For a few minutes, I stand and watch her, the mounting stress that had been building all day slowly beginning to ebb.

The green live-filming light flashes, then *he* walks in the room.

Dickhead.

He makes a beeline for Kate, not even seeing the other women who are right in front of him. *Tunnel vision. He wants her bad.* Where have I seen the look on his face before? Oh, yeah. *In the mirror.*

He kisses her on the cheek. There's a cocky smile on his face as his eyes roam all over her body. *My fucking body.* I'm not sure if it's a good thing or a bad thing that I can't rewind. I'm desperate to know what he just whispered to her, but if I knew, I'm not sure I'd be able to keep myself from marching in and punching him square in the face.

Eventually Jessica pulls him away, a phony plastic smile shining at Kate as she hooks her arm into Flynn and leads him outside onto the deck.

"Do you like my dress?" Jessica asks coyly, looking down. Her eyes lead his to follow hers down to the tits overflowing from her scarlet red gown.

Any thought of Kate seems to disappear quickly as Dickhead licks his lips and leans in to whisper something in her ear. Jessica takes his hands and wraps them around her waist, pushing what he's salivating over against his chest. Kate should see this. Know just how loyal Dickhead is to her.

"Make Kate walk out on the balcony while those two are locked together," I bark at Joel.

He ponders my suggestion for a second. "That's not a bad idea. Might finally get the claws to come out on Kate." Joel picks up his walkie-talkie and orders a stagehand to direct Kate to walk outside.

The timing couldn't be more perfect. Arms wrapped around each other, Dickhead's head is buried at Jessica's ear, when Kate steps out onto the balcony. She stops, catching sight of them locked in an intimate embrace. Dickhead's back is to her, but Jessica tags Kate the minute she walks out. And it only fuels her performance. The hands around his neck jump to his head and she ravels her fingers in his hair in what comes off as a familiar sexual touch.

The camera pans in close, catching Jessica smile at Kate smugly before planting her lips on Flynn's neck. Kate bows her head and walks away gracefully. She doesn't see Flynn pull out of Jessica's claws and rebuff her attempt at a kiss a minute later.

"Great eye. Maybe you'll find a career in reality TV with your brother after all," Joel says as I stand, ready for a refill.

"Don't count on it."

chapter

twenty-five

Kate

"You never asked me if I made it to the final four last night," I say as Cooper presses his lips to the curve of my neck. He'd ravaged me the minute I walked in the door at midnight. Barely uttering more than four words before my back was pushed up against the wall, there was urgency to his need. I knew my being anywhere in the vicinity of Flynn was hard for him, so I didn't question what prompted his appetite. Instead I yielded immediately, letting him feed off how quickly I'd come to submit to him.

"I didn't have to ask." Grabbing a fistful of my hair, he tugs, giving him better access to lick and nip his way up to my ear.

"Why is that?"

Cooper stops abruptly and draws his head back. His light green eyes are the same darkened green they were last night—there's a wildness to them that is more than arousal. "I told you, I see the way he looks at you. Now can we not talk about *him* in my bed."

I hadn't thought about it that way. Bringing up another woman as I kissed him would most definitely have upset me. "Sorry." I wrap my arms around his neck and pull his mouth to mine for a kiss. He obliges, kissing me with the same fierceness that I'd felt between us last night. An urgency that makes me feel like he needs to be reminded that I'm only his.

Our kiss breaks and I slip out from underneath him. "Where are you going?" he growls.

I lift to my feet and stand on the plush area rug next to the bed, waiting until our gaze locks. Then I sink to my knees.

"Christ, Kate," he exhales deeply. "I won't last. You have no idea what seeing that does to me." He rakes his hands through his hair as he comes to stand before me.

With painstaking slowness and deliberation to his movement, he winds the full length of my hair tightly around his hand until his fist is against my scalp. "Look up at me while you take it."

My lips slide over his thick crown and I suck gently, fluttering my tongue in a circle. I wrap my hand around the thick base of him and slide up and down the full length a few times as I increase the suction.

"More," he groans. "Take more of it." The strain in his voice heightens my own arousal and my body swells in response. Jesus. I might be able to come without him even touching me.

I swallow more of him, falling short of taking him in fully, but enough so that the tip of him hits my throat. I flatten my tongue and run it along the underside, tracing his pulse on the thick vein that throbs as he grows even more hard and swollen.

"All of it. Take my cock down your throat," he rasps, our gaze intense and locked. My eyes flutter closed as I open my throat as wide as I can and swallow the length of him down. My jaw strains wide and my breathing shallows as I struggle to catch my breath through my nose.

"Ah. Kate." He swallows and makes a sound that borders on pain. "You on your knees ... my cock down your throat ..." his voice trails off.

Fueled by the effect I have on him, I can't get enough. I feel greedy, my head furiously bobbing up and down as I suck hard, until I feel the change in him.

"Fuck ... your mouth." His hands fisting my hair still my head and then Cooper takes over. Ferociously thrusting into my mouth. Pumping hard and deep, each time hitting the back of my throat as I struggle to keep up with his primal need.

With a groan that roars, he wrenches from my mouth as his grip on my head loosens. "I'm going to come." He attempts to dislodge and pull out, but I sink my nails into his ass and tug him back.

The words he mumbles as he releases into my mouth are inaudible. His body trembles as he empties into me and I struggle to swallow. It's amazing how he can still remain semi hard even after such a powerful orgasm.

He stills, his breath finally slowing and then he reaches down and gently lifts me, cradling me in his arms as he returns to bed. There's something so tender about the way he holds me only minutes after his actions were rough. Yet oddly, they both warm me the same.

The sight of Cooper Montgomery dressed in a crisp white shirt tucked into navy trousers that hang delectably from his narrow waist makes my mouth water.

"Stop looking at me like that." He lifts the starched white collar and slides the tie around his neck, fastening a perfect knot with dexterous fingers.

"Like what?"

"Like you want to eat me?"

"I thought I already did."

His eyebrows raise and he walks around the kitchen counter. I'm still only wearing his shirt from yesterday, even though he's fully dressed. Grabbing my ass, he hauls me to the edge of my seat as he stands between my legs.

"This is a good height." He pushes his bulge further between my legs. "Helen is going to call paramedics if I don't show up to the office soon. It's not like me to cancel a meeting."

"Are you saying I'm a bad influence?" I pout.

"I'm saying you're impossible to walk away from." He tugs at my shirt, exposing my shoulder, and plants a wet kiss. "What are your plans for today?"

"I have to go to wardrobe to try on things. They want everything done before we get our filming break."

His jaw flexes, but he nods.

He's still never asked for confirmation that Flynn picked me to advance to the final four. We're not in bed anymore, so I broach the subject again. "You don't seem surprised I need clothes for the show." I catch his gaze.

He looks away for a second, but it's enough to tell me he already knew for sure I was picked. "How did you know? And don't tell me from the way Flynn looks at me."

His face hardens. "Can you not say his name?"

I'm not letting him change the subject this time. He promised he wouldn't watch the DVDs and I'm curious how he already knew. "How did you know *Dickhead* picked me for the final four?" I say.

He sighs and then wraps his hands around my waist. He thinks I'll storm off once he tells me. I brace myself for his response.

"I went to the taping last night."

My eyes bulge. "You promised you wouldn't watch it."

"I promised I wouldn't watch the dailies. I never said I wouldn't watch the live taping."

"That's splitting hairs." I squint. "And you know it."

He exhales a frustrated breath. "Can we pretend the show doesn't exist for the next week? You're off for a week and I want you all to myself. No talk of the show, *Dickhead* or my brother. I just want you and me."

I swallow hard. "Okay. I'll go to wardrobe and then no talking about the show for the entire week-long hiatus."

"Thank you." He plants a chaste kiss on my lips, fishes into his pocket and hands me a set of keys. "Black Mercedes parked next to the Porsche. Don't worry about anyone recognizing it at the studio. It's never made it there yet. Keys to the apartment are on there too. I'll meet you back here at five."

"Bossy," I mutter, taking the key ring.

He shakes his head and grins, kissing me one last time before taking off. "I tell you what, I'll let you pick what we do tonight to show you how amicable I can be."

chapter twenty-six

Cooper

Even two hours late to the office, I get more accomplished in a half day than I have in weeks. Helen delivers lunch along with the jewel case I'm usually tapping my finger waiting for.

"Throw the DVD in the shredder."

"Pardon?" Helen is confused at my sudden change of heart.

"I'm swearing off reality TV for a week. I want that thing out of my sight."

"Whatever you say."

I sit through three meetings, have two telephone conferences and sign a half dozen contracts that have been sitting on my desk waiting for my attention for more than a week.

Mid afternoon my phone chimes, indicating a new text. A rarity for me. I prefer in-person conversations. Yet another thing I learned from my father. I use my phone to read the news and make calls. But seeing Kate's name on the screen makes me smile.

> *What's your favorite color?*
>
> *Blue.*

I expect more to come, but it doesn't.

> *Why?*

Just asking.

Just randomly decided to ask my favorite color in the middle of the day?
Maybe.

Where are you?
Lingerie store

Then can I change my answer?
LOL. Sure.

Black. Lace. Thong. Garters.
That's more than a color.

Buy it or now I'll have to stop on the way home.
Bossy.

Maybe texting isn't so bad after all.

I clear as much of my calendar as I can, rescheduling the meetings that can't be changed from in-person to telephone conferences. The corporate travel department has everything I need on my desk by four thirty and I'm out the door ready, even though I still haven't asked her yet.

I'm anxious to get home. Women never frequented my apartment, and I certainly never offered anyone a key. Yet strangely, it didn't seem like a monumental occasion to hand over the keys to everything I owned. It seemed … normal.

Kate's in a floor-length silk robe when I enter. I head straight for her, my fingers going straight for the dangling belt tie. She stops my hands. "What are you doing?"

"I want to see what's underneath here."

"No 'Honey, how was your day even?'"

"How was your day?" I say, uninterested, as I tug crudely at the belt, ignoring her hands trying to stop mine. Her robe opens, revealing a sight I haven't been able to stop thinking about all day. Only, the actual vision is even better than the one I'd conjured up in my mind.

"Take off the robe."

She looks up, sees my face, and lets it slip gently from her shoulders. It pools at her stiletto-clad feet. She's wearing a black lace corset, tied together snuggly by a half dozen black silk bows. A present I can't wait to unwrap.

"Turn around." I want to see how well she followed my directions.

Slowly, she pivots on the ball of her foot and turns. Pale flesh, soft skin covering round hard globes, only a sliver of fabric runs up her sexy ass. Garters hold up sheer stockings. My request, followed to a tee.

I'm instantly hard, my hands groping her breasts as I push up against her ass from behind. "I'm going to fuck you leaning over the footboard. None of it comes off. Not even the shoes." I growl into her ear, allowing my warm breath to linger before I kiss down her neck.

"You like it?" she whispers.

"What do you think?" I grind my erection further into her ass.

"I'm glad." She turns in my arms. "But hold that thought. You told me I could decide what we do tonight. I want to take you somewhere first."

chapter
twenty-seven

Kate

He's still scowling ten minutes into our drive. "Are you going to pout all night?" I ask.

"No. But I'm going to make you pay for that little stunt later when we get back home." He flashes me a sinful grin and I cross my legs to quell the ache his threat incites.

"I did exactly as you instructed."

"You gave me a present, but didn't let me unwrap it."

"Good things come to those who wait." I smile. "Get off at the next exit."

"I'm going to get off at the next exit and pull you over my knee, you keep playing with me like that."

"I might like that."

"Kate …" he warns.

"What? I promise I'll make it up to you later."

"I promise you won't be able to walk when I'm done with you tonight."

Maybe it wasn't such a great idea to poke a lion and then take him where we're headed.

"Left on Alan Street."

"Where are we going?"

"Umm …" Suddenly I question my choice of destinations for the evening. "To my mother's house." He glances to me, then back at the road, then back to me.

"You're not kidding, are you?"

"Nope."

I watch his face, curious at the reaction I'll get. Especially considering I just left him sexually frustrated. At first, his brows knit together and he's not sure what to make of it. Then he reaches over and takes my hand. And for the first time since the accident and my Dad's death, I feel like I'm not in this alone anymore.

My grip on our laced fingers tightens as we walk up the driveway at my mom's house. She has no idea we're coming, which only seems fair since Cooper had no notice either. That he never complained or asked me why we're going makes me fall a little deeper for this man.

"Mom?" I let myself in with a key.

"Kate, is that you?"

"Yes, Mom."

She's walking to greet me before I can tell her to stay put. "What a nice surprise. And you brought company." She smiles.

"Why don't you have your oxygen on, Mom?" I rush to the living room and grab her portable tank. The one she's supposed to have on at all times.

"It was only off for a few minutes." Mom rolls her eyes as I wrap the flexible plastic tubing that delivers her air back around her face.

"Well, aren't you handsome," she says to Cooper.

He smiles amused and walks to her. "Thank you, Mrs. Monroe. It's nice to meet you."

Typical Mom. No filter between her thoughts and her mouth. Although she can sometimes embarrass the hell out of me, it's one of the things that I love about her most. "Mom, this is Cooper Montgomery. This is my mother, Lena Monroe."

"Call me Lena," she smiles at Cooper and he nods. "Are you a friend of Kate's, Cooper?"

"I am." Cooper looks at me, squints slightly, then adds. "Boyfriend."

"Well, I'm glad Kate brought you around then. You must be pretty special. Kate doesn't bring many men around." My plan was to show Cooper why I'm doing what I'm doing, so it would be easier for him to understand as I head into the last few weeks of the show. I forgot Mom would alternate between interrogating Cooper and sharing embarrassing stories.

"What do you do for a living, Cooper?"

"Mom," I politely warn. "We just got here. Why don't you give Cooper at least ten minutes before you interrogate him? And where's Kyle?"

"It's fine. I don't mind at all. I make movies. I own a production company."

"He's in his room taking a nap. He gets tired after his therapy." She turns to Cooper. "Are they adult films?"

Cooper chuckles. "No, ma'am. Regular mainstream movies. No adult films."

"Do you have any children?"

"No children yet."

"Do you play cards?"

"Once in while with some old friends."

"Well, don't play with my daughter. She's a shark. Just like her father."

"I could have used that advice a few weeks ago." Cooper smiles.

"Are you superstitious?"

"No. I don't think I am."

"Mom," I warn because I know what's coming next. "I'm not superstitious either."

"Hmm … mmm," she responds patronizingly to me, but leans in to whisper to Cooper, though I can hear every word. "If I was a betting woman, I'd bet there was a four-leaf clover still tucked behind her license in her wallet. And a lucky penny hidden somewhere too."

I shake my head and roll my eyes, but never deny my mother's accusation. She peppers Cooper with questions for another fifteen minutes until Kyle yells from his room. I excuse myself and go to help my brother into his chair.

Kyle is a quadriplegic. Five years ago I picked him up from a soccer game on a sunny Friday afternoon in May. His team had won, Dad was on a winning streak, and I was about to move into my first apartment with Sadie. Life was good, the future was looking even better. Driving down the highway that connects Malibu to Santa Monica, the radio was blaring and Kyle laughed at my attempt to sing along in tune with Gwen Stefani. His smile is the last thing I remember from the thirteenth of May.

Later that night, a policeman explained to me what happened. A surfboard dislodged from the top of a Volkswagen Rabbit and went sailing into the windshield of the car behind it. The driver swerved, lost control of the car, and veered into oncoming traffic. And head on into us. Somehow I walked away with only a broken arm and a few cuts and bruises. My brother wasn't so lucky—he never walked again—paralyzed from the neck down.

The first few years were really rough. Kyle was a 14 year old trapped inside a cage of a body that would never set him free. I, on the other hand, was free to move about, while my mind was caged with guilt over being the one who got to walk away. I was the driver, what if I had swerved faster? Did the blaring music distract me? No matter what the witnesses said, I needed to replay that night over and over in my mind in order to know for sure it wasn't my fault. But I couldn't remember a thing. Every time I tried, I saw my smiling face singing. Then I woke up in the hospital. Being told the news of Kyle's condition replayed over and over in my head, taking the place of what I couldn't remember.

Until recently there was no prospect of recovery … but a new drug running in a clinical trial has given him a modicum of hope. Some early studies have shown that certain rehabilitation programs increase the effectiveness of the drug. I spend a few minutes with Kyle before helping him into his chair and we both return to the living room.

"My sister either thinks you're superman or she doesn't like you very much … leaving you alone with Mom," my brother says as Cooper walks over to meet him.

"My cape's in the car." Cooper smiles. "Nice to meet you, Kyle."

"You too."

"Check this out." Kyle's eyes point toward his feet. Two toes wiggle. It's not much, but we're able to see it.

"Oh my god, Kyle! That's amazing! What did the doctor say?"

"They said not to get my hopes up. I can see their advice is lost on deaf ears with you too." He grins.

"Do it again." I say and he does. He moves his toes again on command. My brother tries hard to act like it's not that big of a deal, but we both know it's huge.

"What do you think?"

"I think it's the most beautiful thing I've seen since the day your fat head came into this world." Bending down, I plant a kiss on my brother's forehead.

"Dude." My brother looks to Cooper for help. "You gotta make her stop kissing me."

Cooper smiles. "Not sure I'm much help there. I like when she kisses me."

"Gross."

We all sit around and talk for an hour. Cooper talks sports with Kyle, and Mom and I catch up on her updates from Kyle's doctors. The conversation between the two men grows a bit heated when Cooper mentions he's a Raiders fan, rather than a Chargers enthusiast. Sitting back in my chair, I silently watch as the two argue over statistics and players. Most people are uncomfortable around Kyle. They don't want to upset him—pity stops them from disagreeing with anything he is saying, even if he's dead wrong.

But not Cooper, he treats Kyle like a regular nineteen-year-old kid. I didn't bring him here with the intent of observing his interaction with my brother, yet the simplicity of what I see speaks volumes about the complexity of this amazing man.

I lose track of time, spending hours more than I'd planned. Cooper's quiet in the car on the way back. "My brother liked you."

"Don't think he liked my taste in sports teams."

"Well, your taste sort of does suck."

"I've been reconsidering my loyalties anyway."

"Why is that?"

"Didn't really see the appeal of the Chargers before you."

"And now you do?" I eye him suspiciously.

"First time I met you, you were wearing a Chargers t-shirt."

"I was?"

"Pink, with a gold lightning bolt. Jeans with a tear at the left knee and right thigh. Black flip-flops."

Inwardly, my peacock feathers fan that he remembers so many details, but I don't let him know it. "Not sure we want such an easy-to-flip fan on our side of the bleachers."

"That didn't take long." I hear the smile in his voice, but his eyes stay on the road. "You're back to being difficult I see."

I ignore his comment. "My mom liked you too."

"Mothers love me."

"You're so full of yourself."

"I'd much rather be filling you." He winks at me and shifts the gear into fourth as he merges onto the highway. Even the way the man handles the gear shifter hints at how good he is in bed. He controls the car like he does everything else in his life. With unwavering authority.

"You have a one-track mind."

"All Kate, all the time," he says and it warms me. Although it's a different warm than I get watching the man exert his power over simple things. I'm starting to realize there's more than one way he causes a rise in my body temperature.

I put my hand over his on the shifter. "Thank you for coming with me."

He nods. "Thank you for taking me."

I sit atop the long marble double sink countertop in the bathroom swinging my legs, watching him get ready. "Did you play sports in high school? Seeing him with my brother made me imagine what he was like in high school.

"Yes. You?"

"Soccer."

"Football."

"Was your girlfriend a cheerleader?"

He smiles. "Cliché, huh?"

"I might've tried out to be a cheerleader instead of playing soccer if you were at my school."

"I wouldn't have went out with the cheerleaders if you were at my school."

"Ssss," I make a hissing sound and he furrows his brow. "You said cheerleaders, not cheerleader … as in, you went out with more than one."

He finishes brushing his teeth and kisses me chastely on the lips. "Let's not have this conversation."

"Why not? It's harmless. We're talking about high school."

"Yes, but I'd rather not talk about either one of us dating anyone else right now." He lifts me from the sink and I oblige him, wrapping my legs around his waist. I flip off the light switch as we pass through to his bedroom.

"Cooper," I whisper as he rests me gently on the bed and buries his face in my neck. He pulls his head back to look at me. "Make love to me."

His eyes roam my face and he kisses me softly. Then he slowly makes love to me with the same domineering possessiveness that he always has. Only, this time it's sweet and filled with heartfelt emotion.

It's almost one in the morning by the time we've both quenched our desire. "Do you know why I wanted to bring you there tonight? To meet Mom and Kyle?" I say as I snuggle into the crook of his arm, fully sated.

"To show me why you're doing the show?"

I should have known Cooper would see right through my thinly veiled plan to remind him why he needs to have patience with me when things get harder during the taping of the final four. "Did it work?"

"I already knew why you were doing the show."

"I thought maybe it would make it easier to see the reason. Telling you what I'm working for doesn't have the same effect. Making it to the end will go a long way for them. I would be able to almost fully pay off my mother's mortgage and cover Kyle's therapy while I finish school."

"I can certainly appreciate your determination more. But if we're being honest, nothing is going to make it easier to see you going out on romantic dates with another man." He kisses the top of my head. "Although it means a lot that you tried."

There's a long silence and I start to think he's fallen asleep. "Go away with me while you're on hiatus?"

The question is unexpected. "Where?"

"My house in Barbados."

"The house we're going to stay at when we film?"

"I want you all to myself until then. Plus, I need to have you all over the island so there isn't one place that you could sit with *him* and not remember me coaxing an orgasm from your body."

I certainly don't object to a marathon of orgasms on a tropical island. "I have to work tonight. But then I'm all yours."

"Good. We leave tomorrow morning."

I laugh. "You've already made the plans before asking me, haven't you?"

"I did."

"What would have happened if I would have said no?"

"You didn't, did you?"

"That's not the point."

"I suppose I would have had to change your mind."

"Let me guess, you'd screw me into submission."

"You make it sound like it's a bad thing."

"It's not a *bad* thing. It's not a thing at all. You couldn't make me change my mind by having sex with me if I really didn't want to do something."

"Then I'd have to use my mouth on you if my cock didn't work."

"You're totally not getting what I'm trying to say."

"Let's try out your theory, shall we?" My exhausted body shudders at the challenge in his voice.

"I'm too tired."

"Are you?" He flips me on my back and is above me, his mouth sucking my nipple in deeply, before I can even object. I am exhausted, but my traitorous body reacts anyway.

Forty-five minutes and two orgasms later, I drift off, thinking I might need to say no more often, just to get him to change my mind.

chapter twenty-eight

Cooper

The first thing I notice as I step foot into the casino is the costume the dealers are wearing. It's basically little more than lingerie. In their red corsets and short black skirts, they look more like they belong at Hugh Heffner's mansion than at a casino about to deal cards. I follow the sign to the high-stakes room with renewed purpose in my step.

It's six in the morning, so the only people still playing cards are the degenerate gamblers and the drunks. Both appear to be at Kate's table as I approach.

She watches me intently as I take a seat and pull my billfold from my pocket.

"Cash in." She lays out my ten one-hundred-dollar bills on the felt table and turns to a suit, who nods.

"What can I get for you this morning, sir?" She arches an eyebrow and, just like the first time I met her, my damn dick twitches in my pants.

"Whatever you want to give me." No one at the table notices our exchange. There's four players, an old guy wearing a thick gold bracelet and four different diamond rings, and a group of three drunk young people who may have gotten in using fake IDs.

She pushes a stack of chips in my direction and smiles. "Good luck, *sir*." Another damn twitch.

She deals the first hand and I win. "Looks like you're lucky this morning."

"Maybe it's the dealer bringing me luck."

She deals another hand. "Hmmm ... well you better hope not. I'm off in twenty minutes."

I win again, but the old guy loses his last stack of chips. He throws down his cards and leaves the table, muttering something about assholes and luck.

"So are you going to say yes if he proposes?" The tall blonde sways as she takes a drink from the waitress. She hasn't anted up yet and Kate is holding the next deal to give her time to pile her chips in the circle.

Kate's eyes flash quickly to me and then back to Swaying Blonde. Laying her hand on the table next to the empty circle, Kate politely asks, "Will you be sitting this one out?"

Drunk Guy pipes in, "Shut up about the bachelor asshole already and play cards. She already told you an hour ago she can't talk about the show." *I prefer Dickhead, but asshole works too.*

Swaying Blonde stacks a pile of black chips, not even flinching when she loses a thousand-dollar hand. I'd bet my bank balance it's Daddy's money. "She said she can't *talk* about it. But maybe she can nod or something."

"I don't get your obsession with that guy anyway. He's a scrawny poser."

"He is *not* a scrawny poser."

Drunk Guy shrugs. "Whatever. Ante up and pay attention to your cards."

The table falls silent and I win another two hands. Five in a row, it has to be a record for me. Kate smiles as she pays the last win. "Looks like your luck keeps getting better today."

"I hope so. I'm hoping to get lucky trying my hand at something new this afternoon," I say cryptically.

Unfortunately, Swaying Blonde was just taking a few moments to gather her idol-worshiping thoughts. She continues, "I knew the first time he kissed you that you two would wind up together in the end."

Kate ignores her comment and keeps dealing, but Swaying Blonde doesn't take a hint. "That episode where he sings to you and you slow dance together." She clutches her chest. "It's like watching an old movie. You build a friendship, but behind it there's so much passion." She sighs. "You two were just made for each other."

Jaw tight, I watch Kate's face as she deals the final face-up cards, but she doesn't look up. Not until she leans toward me to sweep the double stack of chips. "Looks like my luck just changed." I toss my cards, stand and walk toward the door without looking back.

Fifteen minutes later she opens the passenger car door outside of the casino—where I *should* have waited, rather than surprising her early. My whole mood has changed and I know I'm acting like a jerk for taking it out on her, yet I can't seem to bring color to my own self-induced grey mood.

"Sorry about that."

"It's not your fault," I say as I navigate the large circular casino driveway, although I'm not sure I really mean the words. Deep down I think I *do* blame her, maybe not for how the words were delivered tonight, but for not being able to give us a clean start. It's selfish, I know it is, I've seen the reasons she's doing what she's doing, but I want her without any qualifiers. Sneaking around, hiding something I feel the urge to publicly claim as mine, isn't in me.

Kate puts her hand over mine on the gear shifter and we drive in uncomfortable silence.

"Long-term parking is in Concourse B," she says as I pass the sign.

"Not going to long-term parking. The private jet terminal has its own parking lot."

"We're flying on a private plane?"

"Montgomery Productions and Diamond Entertainment co-own it. We use it mostly for films. I know you don't want to be seen in public with me." The last sentence comes out with a bite.

Neither of us says much as we exit the car on the tarmac and go through a quick and pain-free security check. The taxiing and takeoff are smooth, yet there's turbulence in the hollow of my gut. Kate yawns, reminding me that even though I just woke up, she's coming off a ten-hour shift on her feet.

"There's a cabin in the back. The captain should give us the all-clear to get up soon. You should get some sleep, it's a long flight."

She nods. "Are you going to join me?"

"Maybe later. I have some work to do."

A few minutes later the plane hits its cruising altitude and the captain makes an announcement that we are free to move about. I encourage Kate to go. "First door on the right. There are extra pillows in the cabinet below the bed. Just push the button over the end table if you need anything."

She offers me a weak, forced smile and a nod before retiring. I take out my laptop to read the weekly summary of pitch recommendations. The first pitch is for a film that already has a huge buzz. It's one of the most successful indie books being pitched for a highly anticipated film. I read the first page and lose interest, although it has nothing to do with the story. My eyes wander to the closed cabin door in the back. I open a new pitch, hoping it will focus my attention. It doesn't.

Five minutes later, I guzzle a glass of juice and unbuckle with frustration, my body bringing me to where my mind already is.

The door creaks as I slip inside. It's pitch black and quiet, the only sound the rhythmic deep inhales and exhales of Kate's breath. I remove my shoes and make my way to the bed in the darkness, lifting the covers and easing in beside her.

"Took you long enough," she whispers, catching me off guard with the sound of her voice. I thought she was sleeping.

"Sometimes I just can't get out of my own way." I reach out for her, hand falling on her hip in the absolute darkness. My hand meets skin, not shirt or pants. So I slide my hand gently up until I reach her ribs, then back down to her thigh. *Skin.*

"You're naked."

"I am."

"You knew I'd come in after you."

"Maybe. Maybe I always sleep naked."

"Do you?"

"Not usually."

I chuckle, feeling a bit of relief. "I'm sorry for being an ass. I just find myself feeling ... frustrated by things between us sometimes."

"I know," she whispers softly. Then her hand reaches up to my face, her fingers feeling the ridges of my jaw, my nose, my eyes. "That's why I'm naked. Thought maybe it would help you alleviate some of that frustration I saw in your face."

"It might take a while." I take her hand on my face and pull it down to my mouth to kiss each finger. "I'm *really* frustrated." I add and surprise her by hauling her from next to me to on top of me. She giggles and my frustration starts to ebb already.

"I'm dedicated to the cause. I'm willing to work hard." *Hard* pretty much describes me just from having her naked body near mine.

The captain announces we have twenty minutes until landing. I hate to wake her. She looks so peaceful and I took an hour and a half of her nap for other things before she fell asleep. I clean up and brush my teeth in the small *en suite* bathroom and she wakes when I climb back into bed.

"Good nap?" I say before gently kissing her lips.

"You smell good." She snuggles up against me, pressing her warm sexy body to my already clothed one.

"It's time to get up. We're going to land soon."

She stretches and pouts. "But I'm so comfy."

I swat her ass. "You can be comfy for almost a week in my bed. In fact, I intend to spend an inordinate amount of time in my bed, making you comfy. But right now you need to get up and get dressed so we can land."

Begrudgingly she gets up. She walks her naked self to the bathroom. "Ummm. Cooper."

"Yes."

"Is this a, a.... hickey?"

"Where?" I pretend not to know what she's talking about as I walk up behind her in the bathroom and our gaze meets in the mirror.

"Right here." She points to her right breast, where there's an unmistakable bright red mark.

"Hmmm." I cup her breast from behind. "It might be. I guess I didn't realize how much frustration I had to let go of."

"Hmm ... mmm." She eyes me suspiciously.

"I'm glad it's there though. Because this week, you're all mine and we don't have to worry about any cameras catching you since no one knows where we are."

chapter twenty-nine

Kate

I'm not sure if it was the sex or the nap, or maybe even the Caribbean sunshine warming us as we step onto the tarmac in Barbados, but Cooper's a different man than the one I boarded the plane with.

"What do you want to do first?" he asks as he laces our fingers together. It feels odd to walk in public with him like this. We've basically been in hiding since we met.

"Hmmm … what are my choices?"

"We could have sex in the yard, by the pool. Or at the beach. The master bedroom has a Jacuzzi if you prefer that."

"Do all my choices include sex?"

"They all begin and end with sex. How you'd like to fill the hours in between, I'm happy to oblige whatever suits your fancy."

"How very generous of you, Mr. Montgomery."

"I thought so." He kisses my lips and gives me a carefree smile that makes him look younger than his years. His face is relaxed. It's a look I haven't seen in a while and he wears it well.

A uniformed officer comes to meet us as we reach the building and does a quick check and stamps our passports. "What about our bags?" I ask as we enter the airport terminal.

"They'll be brought to the car that we'll meet out front of baggage claim. It's a small airport, so there isn't a special area for private planes.

197

We've already cleared customs, so we can just walk through the airport and exit where everyone else does."

The airport is busy, but Cooper navigates us through swiftly. As we walk through the baggage claim area, I spot a uniformed man holding a sign that reads *Montgomery*.

"I guess that's us?" I say, but Cooper doesn't hear me. He's preoccupied looking off in another direction.

"Cooper?" He still doesn't respond, so I trace his line of sight. I don't see anything unusual. Mostly it's just a group of tourists in Hawaiian shirts and straw hats anxious to get their luggage. Then I notice a man in the group who stands out. He's grabbing a bag from the conveyor belt, but that's not what makes him different. Dressed in a long-sleeved shirt and pants—head to toe in black, his bald head is the only thing that shines from his otherwise dark façade.

"Cooper?" I call again. "Do you see someone you know?"

"Hmm?" He turns to me, having heard my voice, but still not hearing my words.

"I asked if you saw someone you knew. You seemed distracted."

"Actually ... give me a minute, I'll be right back." He deposits me next to the man holding the Montgomery sign and takes off in the direction of the baggage claim he was staring at. The man I thought he was looking at is already gone, but I watch as Cooper surveys the surrounding area.

"Everything okay?" I ask wearily when he returns.

"Fine," he responds and we walk to the waiting limousine. "I thought I saw someone I knew, but my mind must be playing tricks on me since you robbed me from the nap I was planning on taking." He kisses me chastely, then waves off the driver so he can open the door for me himself.

A woman is waiting at the top of the driveway when we pull up to the house—if you would call where we arrive at a house. Mansion, estate, perhaps just *paradise* might most deftly describe the vision that looms in front of me.

Up until now, everything about Cooper Montgomery seemed to match the man—a sleek penthouse suite, expensive-yet-old classic car. His assets are clearly luxurious, yet they have an understated quality about them. Like he doesn't need to show off the grandness to appreciate its value. But this—there is no mistaking the brazen grandeur of this home.

Flooded in white except for the massive dark-wood double front doors, the home stretches out far and wide amid lush tropical plantings.

"Welcome home, Mr. Montgomery, Ms. Monroe. Sugar Rose is ready for your arrival." The woman greets us with a thick island accent and broad smile.

"Thank you, Marguerite. It's good to see you." I hear Cooper have a short conversation with the woman, but I'm too busy looking around in awe to pay much attention.

"You like it?"

"It's stunning. I can't believe how big it is."

"That's not the first time I've heard you say that," he leans downs and whispers to me as we walk to the entrance with Marguerite in tow.

I shake my head. Before me is the man I first met—smiling, playful and full of himself. It's nice to have him back.

As Cooper talks to Marguerite, I walk slowly through the spacious home. The massive two-story living room is framed with a wall of glass that leads out to an equally impressive manicured yard. An oversized infinity pool makes it difficult to tell where the yard ends and the ocean beyond it begins.

A warm ocean breeze blows on my skin as I walk outside, bringing the smell and taste of the ocean to my lips.

"What do you think?" Cooper comes up behind me and wraps his arms around my waist.

"It's paradise."

He kisses my shoulder. "I'm glad you like it."

"It's amazing. Although it's not what I expected."

"Is that good or bad?" His lips at the nape of my neck vibrate against the skin.

"Actually, I don't think it's either. It's beautiful. It just doesn't seem like your style."

"It's not. My father built it for my mother." He kisses his way up to my ear. "Sugar Rose. My mother was Rose, but my father called her Sugar."

"That's so sweet."

"Inside or outside?" he asks.

"What I like better?"

"No, where you want me to fuck you first."

"No beating around the bush with you, is there?"

"Not when it comes to you, love." His hand tugs at my skirt to lift it. I'm lightheaded from the feel of him hardening against me from behind, but it's the way he just called me love that makes my knees weak.

"What about Marguerite?"

"Gone. No one for miles except for me and you."

I turn and face him. He wastes no time in taking my mouth. There's a hunger in his kiss that would never reveal he'd just been inside me only a few hours ago on the plane.

"Pool," I whisper against his lips when we break for air. At first his brows dip, but then he realizes what I'm saying. "The edge, where it looks out to the ocean."

I take his hand and begin to lead him in that direction. But he scoops me up off my feet and carries me instead. I love that he gives me choices, but then takes control back almost immediately. It's like he *wants* to please me, but he *needs* to do it in his own way.

He stops to undress us both before walking into the pool with me in his arms. Reaching the edge, he sets me on my feet and spreads my arms wide along the tile hidden just below the surface. His erection pushes against my back as he moves closer. "You should probably hold on," he says in a raspy voice. "I want to fuck you deep."

A shiver runs through me even though the water is warm and the sun beating down on my exposed body is even warmer. I barely have time to set my grip when Cooper drives deep inside of me. He was right, I need to hold on, the weightlessness of my body in the water makes it easy for him to maneuver me, but the tile is still hard along the walls of the pool.

"Kate," he groans, pulling out and then slamming back into me. A whimper escapes me and he lifts me up slightly, giving him an angle that allows him to pull me down on him even deeper. He lifts me and pulls me back down onto him to meet each thrust. The way he uses my body to feed his makes me feel empowered, even though he's clearly the one in physical control. I love that I bring such raw, unrestrained desire from a man who seems to keep everything else in his life so meticulously organized.

His fingers move to my swollen clit as the speed of his thrusts intensifies. I can tell he's close, racing to bring me to climax with him, as he relentlessly drives into me over and over. He groans my name again and his teeth sink into my shoulder. A wail of a moan shakes the air, leading my climax as it rushes from my body. I cry out as it takes me under, my moans echoing even though there are no walls to catch them.

Hours later, even after a much-needed nap, I'm still withered and unable to move. Cooper, on the other hand, walks around like he just started the day fresh, rather than having traveled six hours on the plane, and twice led our bodies to energy-draining climaxes after heavy cardio-induced sexual escapes.

I pull the sheet over my head when he walks to where I'm sleeping on the big comfy couch.

"You know I saw you were awake already, right?" I know he's smiling even though I can't see his face.

"I'm still sleeping," I groan.

"You haven't eaten anything today." He pulls down the sheet. "You're probably tired from lack of vitamin B and zero calorie consumption."

My stomach growls on cue.

"See, I told you. You need to eat to get your energy up. I have lots of plans, so you need to put some fuel in the tank." He pulls the sheet the rest of the way off of me and smacks my bare ass.

"What plans? I thought we didn't have plans to go anywhere."

"We don't. But I told you I plan to have you in a few dozen places around the property."

"Fiend."

Cooper's lip twitches in response. Then he scoops me up in his arms and heads toward the bathroom. "Shower. Then I'll take you out for something to eat."

He sets me down on the bathroom vanity so he can regulate the shower water temperature. "Although I do love the just-fucked look on you. You wear it so well." He kisses my lips and runs his fingers through my hair. "But I am looking forward to taking you out in public tonight. Showing the world you belong to me. Even if none of the people here know who we are."

Bay Street at night is a world away from the quiet seclusion of Sugar Rose. I'm quickly distracted as we weave our way through throngs of people inside and cross over to the beach extravaganza going on outside. Although I love to dance, clubbing was never my thing. When I lived at home, most of my free time was spent helping out with Kyle or studying. I occasionally went to clubs with Sadie after we first moved in together, but I wasn't a regular anywhere by any means.

We approach a bar on the back deck, the level before the sand, which is crammed with people. "What do you want to drink?"

I shrug. Not being a big drinker, wine is usually my thing, it's simple to order and it avoids a concoction whose taste is subjective based upon the mood of the bartender. But this isn't the kind of place that you order wine. "I'll have something with an umbrella in it."

Cooper smiles and yells our orders to the bartender. He hands me a large red drink with not one, but two colorful umbrellas and holds up his small glass filled with amber liquid.

"To showing off my woman in public," he says, clinking his drink to mine then tipping his head back.

Watching his throat work as he swallows, for a minute I wish we had stayed in. My fruity drink goes down smoothly, the effects heightening the blissful state I'm already in. "I love that smile." Cooper runs his finger along my bottom lip. "Your smile is always beautiful, but when you let yourself go and really relax, it's the most incredible thing I've ever seen."

I didn't realize there was a difference on the outside, but he's right on how I feel inside. The last five years have been tough, the past two even more so. I'm happy, although it's always tempered with something else—a weight that keeps me grounded. The happy that Cooper makes me feel is like floating. I don't know how he does it, but when I'm with him, it's okay to let it all go.

"Do you dance?" I ask, wrapping my hands around his neck. The music changes from island steel drum to something slow and sultry with a heavy rhythm that pulses through the crowd.

He pulls me flush against him, sliding a knee between mine, and begins to sway to the music. Of course the man can dance, I should have known from the way he moves his body in bed.

We dance close, his arms wrapped possessively around me, holding me tight for three or four songs. Eventually he pulls back to meet my eyes.

"I want this all the time. Dance with you, have you on my arm at events, that carefree smile on your face. I didn't even realize it was what I was missing, until I found you. I want this. I *need* this."

"Me too." Our eyes meet. I've never wanted anything more in my life. "Soon. I promise."

chapter thirty

Cooper

The bed has always been a place for two things—sleeping and fucking. If I wasn't actively doing one or the other, I saw no purpose in wasting time lying around. Yet waking with Kate's head nestled into my shoulder, listening to the sound of her rhythmic, peaceful breathing leaves me content to stay put the entire day.

She stirs for a while in her sleep before her eyes eventually flutter open. "Morning," she says with a lopsided smile when she finds me already awake.

"Morning." I smile and kiss her forehead. "Blanket hog."

Her sleepy eyes go wide. "I am not a ..." She begins to defend herself and then looks down. Both the sheet and duvet are wrapped around her body like she just lost a battle with a white boa constrictor. I, on the other hand, am completely exposed. "Sorry."

"It's alright." I pull her body on top of mine. "I'll use you as a blanket."

She giggles and the sound makes me smile. *Shit. I've gone soft.*

"What do you want to do today?" Kate props her head up in her hands.

"You."

"You've already done that a half dozen times. Don't you want to do something else? I don't want you to get bored."

"Bored of being inside of you? Never."

She smiles. "Okay. Well how should we fill the hours between you inside of me this morning and you inside of me later tonight?"

I brush my fingers along her cheek. Something about hearing her say *you inside of me,* already has my morning semi erection swelling to a full-blown hard on. "However you want."

She rests her head over my heart. "You said you came here all the time growing up, right?"

"Twice a year."

"Well what was your favorite thing to do back then?"

I think for a moment. "An afternoon trip on the Jolly Roger. It was a big party boat done up like a pirate's ship. It sailed out into clear water and Miles and I would swing on a rope and jump off. We'd make each other walk the plank, and snorkel with turtles. It was owned by Marguerite's family. My Dad would sit on the top dock drinking beer with her uncle while we played for hours."

"That sounds like fun. Is it still operating?"

"Not sure. I can call Marguerite."

"Can I ask you something?"

"You woke up filled with questions this morning, didn't you? Maybe I should fill you with something else to give your mouth a rest."

She playfully smacks at my abs. "Seriously." Gripping her lower lip between her teeth, she studies me for a moment. "What happened between you and Miles?"

It's a question I'm not expecting. And, in all honesty, I'm not even sure it's a question I know the answer to. "I don't know. As we got older, he sort of just pulled away. Some people see the glass as half full, he sees the glass as half empty. And thinks it's half empty because I *drank it all* on him."

"When did you stop getting along?" She pushes up onto one elbow.

"When Miles was in middle school." I still remember the first time he lashed out at me as clear as day. "There was a boy that was picking on him. Miles was smaller than the kid, but that didn't stop him from running his mouth. The kid challenged him to a fight after school. By the time I got there, Miles already had a bloody nose and black eye. I stepped in front of Miles, caught the kid's punch, twisted his arm, and brought him to the ground. The kid was out of shape and I was five years older … it didn't take much."

"And Miles got upset with you for stepping in?"

"He thought I did it to make him look bad to our dad. He actually accused me of arranging the whole thing with the kid who was kicking his ass when I showed up."

"Why would he think that? It sounds like a perfectly normal event. A brother stepping in for another brother in a fight. At least it was in my school."

"I have no idea. But that was when it started."

"Do you think …"

I cut her off. "I think you've had your fill of questions. Time to fill you with something else." I pull her naked body up mine, lifting her until her neck is within reach. I nuzzle her, cupping her breasts as I tighten my hold.

She moans. "That's not fair. I have more questions."

"There'll be more question and answer time later if you're good. I want my cock filling you now." I suck my way up to her ear and nibble on her lobe, something I've come to learn makes the sexiest tremble run though her. I grin when I feel it seconds later and then spend the next hour not answering any more questions.

The pool, the beach, the dining room table … hell, the bathroom yesterday on the Jolly Rogers. I wasn't kidding when I said I was leaving no room for her not to think of us when she comes back to Barbados with the show. Today is the guesthouse. It's where the four remaining contestants will be staying. I've already warned Miles that the main house is off limits for anything intimate, feigning respect for our father's home. The same home I've spent four days claiming Kate in as many places as humanly possible.

"It's beautiful. It's so cozy in here. Not that the main house isn't magnificent, but this house ..." She looks around. "It just feels homey for some reason."

I smile, remembering Dad telling me the story of the first time he brought my mother here. He'd bought the place as a surprise and had it completely gutted and remodeled, putting only the best of everything into the main house. When he told her to pick which room she wanted to furnish as the master bedroom, she picked the yellow room in the guesthouse, instead of one of the grand rooms he'd spent a small fortune having redone in the main house.

"You should take this room when you come back," I say without explaining why as I show her the bedroom with the yellow painted walls.

"It's the prettiest room in the house."

I continue with the short tour of the inside and then walk her onto the back deck. There are a few people lingering on the beach in the distance to the west. This portion of the estate is the end of the public property line; the *No Trespassing* signs just before the beach that aligns with the main house warn that this is private property.

The large deck off the back of the house leads to a long and narrow boardwalk that trails over the sand dunes and down to the beach.

I sit on the padded lounge chair and watch as she looks out to the beach with a dreamy smile. I wish today wasn't our last day here.

"It may not have the pool, but the view is just as beautiful," she says.

"You're right. It is." I fold my hands behind my head and take in every last drop of beauty before me. We've been here for four days and I intend to enjoy the last twenty-four hours doing my favorite thing in Barbados. *Her.*

"Take off your clothes," I say.

"You just want to christen the house." She turns from the water to set her gaze on me.

I shake my head.

"No?" She squints suspiciously.

"I want you right out here."

She turns back to look at the beach. It's empty now, but people wander into this area once in a while. "What if someone comes?"

"Isn't that the point?"

"You know what I mean." She rolls her eyes.

"Take off your clothes," I repeat, this time with more of an edge to my voice.

She looks back at the beach again, then to me. "Bossy." She slips the loose bathing suit cover-up she's wearing from her shoulders and lets it fall to the ground.

"Untie the top."

She hesitates—there's a conflicted look in her eyes—but then she does that thing that almost made me lose my mind the first time I met her. She squares her shoulders, squints to assess me and, with a devilish grin tempting at her lips, she slowly reaches around and unties her top.

I slip my hand into my board shorts and expose my already hard cock. Her eyes follow my hand as I firmly grip at the base, then stroke the full length leisurely up and down. She's ten feet away but I can feel her touching me just by the intensity of her stare. Watching her watch me is insanely erotic.

"Take off the bottom," I say as firmly as I can muster, my voice already showing signs of strain.

This time she moves with less hesitation. She shimmies her bikini bottom down her sexy tanned legs and steps out boldly. *Jesus Christ.* I'd hoped to give her a vision she wouldn't soon forget, but the vision before me will certainly be scorched into my memory for a long time to come. The sun at her back highlights her silhouette, leaving an angelic glow around her.

I watch as her eyes momentarily break from following my stroke to meeting my stare. She holds my gaze, her blue-green eyes darken with lust, and then I almost lose it when her tongue hungrily licks her painted lips.

"Come here. I want you to ride me. Face the ocean. Eyes open. Ride my cock until your vision goes blurry."

Her breath audibly hitches, but she comes to me. I take her mouth in a kiss before turning her and directing her legs to straddle me. Her perfect heart-shaped ass facing me, her legs shake as she hovers, ready to take me inside of her.

My fingers curl into her sides as I grip her waist to guide her onto me. She lowers herself slowly, taking me inside of her a little at a time, inch by inch until her ass is pressed firmly against me. She doesn't even have to move—the tightness of her pussy clenching me, the vision of her shapely ass and the sound of her labored breathing has me on edge instantly. The urge to fill her and mark her skin is so intense I can barely see.

"I need to come inside of you," I grunt out and lift her, taking over the rhythm she's set. I slam her back down on me hard and grip her hair when she moans.

"C. .C ... Coop ..." she whimpers. "Please."

"I love being inside of you," I groan, pumping up into her with full hard thrusts that meet her each time I guide her down. Harder and harder. Her hips circle and gyrate, taking in every inch that I give her until we're both no longer able to hold back and we release together, her chanting my name over and over until she has no voice left to give.

Sated, we lie naked, wrapped in each other's arms until it's time to get ready for dinner. I watch from the doorway as she turns back and takes one last look out at the ocean. I hope this afternoon is what she remembers when she's back here.

"You ready to go?" I stand behind her and kiss her shoulder. The white strapless sundress she's wearing exposes her glowing tanned skin, it's hard to keep my mouth off of her.

"Definitely." She turns to face me and kisses my lips. "That guy out there gives me the creeps."

"What guy?" I scan the beach but see no one in sight.

Kate turns to look back and shrugs. "Guess he's gone. Who goes to the beach fully clothed in the afternoon anyway?"

chapter
thirty-one

Kate

I'm afraid to open the door. I'm not worried about what *I* feel changing, it's everything around us that changes once I step outside again. Five days of bliss. It isn't just my body that I gave over to the man sitting beside me, somehow he's managed to steal a little piece of my heart. And *stolen* would be right word—since it isn't supposed to be available.

"Don't go in," Cooper says with a strained voice. We're in the underground parking garage at the studio. Miles is already here. His car is parked two over from us.

"I wish it were that simple."

"Doesn't need to be difficult."

I exhale a deep breath. We've had this argument already, the last time only yesterday on the plane ride home. It doesn't end well, and I hate to walk away from him feeling unsettled. He's been up front since we met, he doesn't want me to return to the show. I know he's serious when he says he'll take care of everything. But I can't let him do that. It's my family, my mess, my responsibility. My father lived his life borrowing from one person to pay another. It was a vicious cycle that needs to be broken once and for all. I'm certain what I'm doing is right for my family, yet it doesn't make it any easier for me to open the cocoon we've ensconced ourselves in the last week.

"I'm afraid returning to reality is going to change things between us." My voice is low and I can't hide the crack of worry that shadows my words.

"Are you returning to reality or about to leave it?"

Our first day back starts with one of Miles's production meetings in the conference room we've met in dozens of times before. I take a deep breath as I cross the threshold into the brightly lit room, my eyes combing over the full cast of characters already mingling. With Ava sent home before hiatus, I'll likely be keeping to myself a lot over the next two weeks.

Flynn is in the far corner of the room, chatting with Jessica. She's leaning toward him, her hand pressed to his chest, fluttering her long thick eyelashes. He spots me the minute I enter and smiles, quickly excusing himself from the conversation.

Jessica turns to find the distraction that has lured Flynn's attention away, and our eyes meet. *If looks could kill.*

"There you are." Flynn kisses me on the cheek. "I was starting to wonder if you were coming back." *That makes two of us.*

"I think some people might be happy if I didn't." I smile and discreetly tilt my head in Jessica's direction.

"Well, certainly not me." He takes both my hands and pulls back to look at me. "You look incredible. I guess you got to relax a bit on the break finally."

"Umm. Yes. How was your break?" Feeling guilty already, I change the subject.

"Good. Except ..." He leans in to whisper in my ear. "I missed you like crazy."

"All right everyone, let's get started," Miles's booming voice saves me from having to respond.

Everyone takes a seat around the table. Flynn chooses the seat next to me. So, naturally, Jessica saunters over and grabs the seat on the other side of him.

Miles steeples his fingers as he begins to speak in the front of the room, reminding me of Mr. Burns from the Simpsons. I study his face while he speaks, looking for signs of Cooper in his profile and mannerisms. He's nice looking, physically fit, there's definitely a physical resemblance. But it's the way he commands authority that is vastly different. His is through intimidation and fear, whereas people seem to defer to Cooper out of respect and admiration.

After a fifteen-minute lecture, Miles walks around the room, distributing two-inch-thick packets containing information on our shooting schedule for the next two weeks. He stops and makes small talk with some of the contestants as he hands out the binders.

"What a beautiful tan you have, Kate. It looks like you've already spent a week on a tropical island."

I swallow the water I'm drinking down the wrong pipe and choke. "Umm … thank you."

"You okay?" he asks, although I don't find true concern on his face. Instead I could swear I see something sinister in his eyes. Here comes the paranoia I'd forgotten all about.

"You okay?" Flynn asks, with something different in his eyes than Miles—sincerity.

"I'm fine," I wheeze, my eyes watering. Miles has already moved on and is busy talking to Jessica's cleavage.

"If you need mouth-to-mouth, I got you covered," Flynn whispers, adding a smile that reveals his killer dimples.

His playfulness, along with his flirtatious charm, actually puts me at ease a little bit. Flynn and I spend the next two hours alternating between playing tic-tac-toe and hangman as Miles spews his vision for the next segment of the show. I seriously could have summed up the two-hour lecture in less than thirty seconds. Flaunt it if you got it, kiss the bachelor frequently *with lots of tongue,* and the camera loves catfights.

We break for lunch and, surprisingly, I feel a lot better than when I came in this morning. I'd forgotten how at ease I feel around Flynn. He's a great guy, he really is. If I weren't crazy about Cooper, a relationship with Flynn wouldn't be such a stretch. Even though he's pretty much the polar opposite of Cooper. He's free spirited and easygoing, where Cooper is intense and driven. Even his look is everything Cooper isn't—tattooed, long hair, tattered jeans and tall and lanky. Couple the whole package with a voice that can make women from seven to seventy swoon, and it's no wonder the women vie so heavily for time alone with the bachelor.

"Wanna grab a bite?" Flynn asks close behind me as I exit the door.

"Sure, but there'll probably be a tack on my seat when I get back, courtesy of our castmates."

"No worries. I'd be happy to sweep the seat to protect your delicate ass from damage."

The afternoon session is even more painful than the morning. Miles spends the entire time coaching us on "how to seduce the camera." Halfway through, Flynn and I decided we should start a little drinking game—where every time Miles says the word "intimate," we'd drink. I stopped counting at sixteen, figuring I'd have alcohol poisoning by then anyway.

Toward the end of the day, Miles announces we will be having one more group date before we leave for Barbados the day after tomorrow. We're all going to the Film Critics Awards Banquet. Flynn and the four contestants are going to announce the nominees and winner for best supporting actor.

Flynn and I are the last ones to leave. Outside, the parking lot is nearly empty, and he insists on waiting with me for Sadie, who, of course, is late picking me up. We kill the time laughing as he entertains me by singing a rhyme he made up to mock Miles's coaching advice.

"I'll see you tomorrow. Thank you for making a waste-of-time day totally bearable," I say to Flynn as Sadie finally pulls up.

"No problem. Anytime I can put a smile on that beautiful face isn't a waste of time for me." Flynn leans down to kiss my lips and it takes me a minute to realize what's about to happen. *Shit. We haven't even been put in a private romantic situation yet.* I panic, feeling silly for doing so when the kiss feels almost innocent, but I turn my head just in time as Flynn's lips come down to find mine. Flynn catches the corner of my mouth. I, on the other hand, turn my head and catch the glare of Cooper Montgomery.

chapter thirty-two

Kate

I'm sorry. I shot off a text as soon as I buckled into Sadie's car. I wasn't surprised Cooper didn't respond right away. But it's hours later now and he's still silent. I visualize the moment over and over in my head. The almost-kiss on the lips, turning my head to find Cooper standing right there—eyes tempered with hurt. His curt nod and rapid departure leave me feeling unsettled.

Anxiously, I check my phone every five minutes until the minutes turn into hours and it becomes painfully obvious I won't be getting a response. I attempt to clear my head with a rare trip to the gym, followed by two glasses of wine. But all it does is blur my thoughts and leave me wondering if everything I was so sure would work out when we were in Barbados was even real.

Maybe if there would have been a scene I'd be able to sleep, but the unknown is killing me. I stare at the television, waiting for something to take my mind off what his lack of response means. It doesn't work. Around one in the morning, my lack of self-control wins out and I shoot off another text. *Can't sleep. The bed is empty without you next to me.*

My phone rings ten seconds later.

"Hey," I answer, uncertain as to what to expect.

"It's intolerable," he says with a breath of frustration.

"Sleeping alone?"

"Seeing him touch you."

A few seconds of silence pass as I internally debate how to respond.

"I'm sorry."

"You looked happy."

There's an ache in my chest. "I am happy. *You* make me happy."

"Then *I* should be the one on the receiving end of your smile."

"You are."

"I wasn't this afternoon."

There's no way to get through this conversation without a few bumps and bruises. "He's a nice guy. I like him … as a friend. Even if we weren't in this situation, I have guy friends—ones I'd occasionally share a smile with."

"Maybe. But I'd be able to wrap my arm around your waist and pull you close to me when I'm near you and see you sharing that smile with another man. I wouldn't have to walk away like you didn't belong to me."

"I'm sorry." And we're back to where we started. I have no idea how to make him feel better. "I really only think of him as a friend."

"That's not how he thinks of you."

How do I argue with what I suspect to be the truth? "I'm sorry." I'm starting to sound like a broken record.

"I can't wait until this is over."

"Soon."

"There'll be no mistaking who you belong to when this charade is over," he says with an edge to his voice that wakens my libido.

"I look forward to it," I say while sporting the first smile I've felt since this afternoon.

"Stay with me tomorrow night. I'll be at a work event until late. But I want you in my bed when I get home."

"Okay. But Miles added another event shoot to the schedule and we're going to some awards ceremony tomorrow night. So I might be late."

"What awards ceremony?"

"The Film Critics Awards Banquet."

"Great. More watching Dickhead paw you and not being able to do anything about it."

"You promised not to watch the dailies anymore."

"I won't have to watch the dailies. Miles's table is next to mine."

Miles catches my eyes as they linger on the empty seat at the next table for what must be the tenth time in the last hour. He forces a smile and I watch his eyes dart to the table I'm fixated on and back to me. No doubt he thinks I'm star struck looking at Tatiana Laroix or Benjamin Parker. I'm pretty sure the whole place is staring at one of the two of them.

There's no denying that Tatiana Laroix is a beautiful woman. But tonight she's beyond stunning—men and women both can't stop staring. Her hair is done in that Roaring Twenties-era finger wave that is feminine and dramatic, yet somehow still appears slightly understated. The exact opposite of her dress. The daring cleavage-baring nude gown is cut to her navel, leaving the men in the room fixated on the effectiveness of double-sided tape. Knowing the empty seat is where Cooper will eventually sit, I find myself jealous even though he hasn't stepped foot in the room yet.

Benjamin Parker costarred along side Tatiana in *Perfect Sense,* the upcoming film produced by Montgomery Productions. He's young, handsome and has a penchant for jogging all over LA shirtless. The media eats up his every step. I've stolen glances at the interaction between the two, secretly wishing I'd find sexual tension. But all I've caught is Tatiana scanning the door and watching her watch.

I don't need to turn around to know the moment Cooper walks into the room. I'd like to say it's because I feel it in my heart, in my bones, a whisper touch alerting my skin to his arrival. But that's not why at all. It's the way Tatiana changes—her face lights up, eyes sparkle with devilish lust and the thrust of her already obvious overflowing breasts strain forward to show off even more. He's not even near her yet and I'm spoon-fed a taste of the medicine Cooper was forced to swallow yesterday. Tonight is going to suck.

Cooper makes his rounds at the table, eventually coming to the only empty seat, next to Tatiana, just as the lights begin to flash, signaling the show is about to start. He never looks my way.

Twenty minutes later the cast from the show is ushered backstage to prepare for announcing the category we're assigned. After seeing the size of the room and all of the famous faces, my nerves kick in on high. I'm grateful they picked Jessica and Flynn for the scripted banter and all I need to do is stand there and not pass out. Although right now I'm feeling even that may be a challenge.

"You okay?" Flynn sees my face and his turns concerned.

"I'm a little nervous. Can you tell?"

"Not really." He grins, letting me know he's lying.

I take a deep breath. "How do you do this all the time? Get up in front of a crowd and sing?"

He shrugs. "You get used to it."

"Were you nervous when you first started?"

"Yep." He smiles like he's thinking back to a fond memory.

"What did you do to calm yourself?"

"Got shitfaced."

"How'd that go?"

"I fell off the stage and had to get seven stitches in my head."

"Think I'll try some deep cleansing breaths instead." I smile. "I just hope I don't trip."

The host announces our names over the loudspeaker, and a frantic woman with not one, but two headsets on barks orders into a walkie-talkie and shouts stage directions at us, and then we're on. In the moment, I'm thankful that Flynn grabs my hand and walks me on stage, because my legs are wobbly with fear.

Jessica and Flynn ham it up for the cameras and, luckily, our five minutes of fame is over in less than three.

"You did great."

"I stood there."

"You didn't fall."

"Because you held my hand."

"You're cute when you're nervous." Flynn kisses my nose and flashes his dimples. Twenty minutes later we're escorted back to our seats during an intermission.

People are up and mingling, Cooper is talking to the director right behind my seat.

"Hey," Flynn says with a friendly smile and extends his hand toward Cooper. "Flynn Beckham. We met at the …"

"I remember." Cooper dismisses him and turns to me.

"Kate." He nods and tosses back the contents of his short glass in one large gulp.

"Cooper." I follow his lead, mimicking his distant greeting.

Tatiana slinks up beside Cooper and hooks her arms through his. "Hey, lovebirds. How's the show going?"

Flynn casually wraps his arm around my waist and smiles. "Can't tell you any secrets." He looks at me, then back to Tatiana and winks. "But it's going great."

If eyes could shoot daggers, poor Flynn would look like Swiss cheese. Cooper's piercing glare complements the angry flex in jaw.

"I need another drink, Cooper," Tatiana whines with a faux pout.

"Maybe you should slow down," he responds without looking at her.

"Another drink might lower my inhibitions," she says in a voice aimed at being seductive. To my ears it's like nails scraping on a blackboard.

"You should take it easy," he warns.

"But I thought you liked it hard."

"Excuse me, Flynn. I need to use the ladies' room." I storm off without looking at Cooper or waiting for a response.

"Not so fast," Cooper warns in a low raspy voice as he grabs my elbow, steering me in the opposite direction of the bathroom.

"Don't, Cooper," I shoot back. But I should know better than to bother to protest. He's not a man easily deterred.

"Leave." He approaches a uniformed young man standing at the coat closet. The man's brows knit, but he quickly catches on when Cooper reaches into his pocket, pulls out a wad of cash, and stuffs half of it into the man's hand. "Fifteen minutes. I don't care if the place is on fire. The door doesn't open."

The man nods.

Cooper locks the door behind us.

"This isn't a good idea, Cooper." I finally look up and take the whole man in. Tension radiates off of him.

"There's nobody but you, Kate." He takes a step closer. His eyes watch me, study me, pin me in place. "Whatever happened with her was in the past. Everything is in my past now. Can you say the same?"

"I'm sorry." My words trail off. "It's just hard … watching her try to seduce you."

"How do you think I feel? He held your hand on stage. I couldn't even watch. It fucking kills me."

"I'm sorry."

"We can end this right now. My offer is still good. In fact, nothing would make me happier than to take care of your family and leave with you right now."

"I can't, Cooper. I just can't. I wish it was that easy."

"You make it harder than it needs to be."

"I need to take care of my own family. It's a lot of money and it's *my* responsibility."

"I don't care about the money. I need to take care of *you*."

My eyes close. It would be so much easier to give in. Not worry about the house, Kyle's therapy, leading Flynn on. "I'm sorry." I hold back the tears, but my voice cracks.

Cooper's hands reach up and cup my face, his thumb runs along my bottom lip. "I want to be the one holding your hand in public. I want to be the one to wrap my arm around your waist when another man comes near." His lips brush against mine.

"We shouldn't …" I weakly attempt to protest. Undone by the possessive rawness of his strained words, I stop trying to push him away and join him, chasing something we both need in the moment more than the air that we breathe.

"You feeling better?" Flynn asks when I return to my seat. "You got some color in your cheeks back."

"Ummm … yes. Thank you." I'm grateful it's dark because my *color* has just deepened to a lovely shame of crimson.

Out of the corner of my eye, I catch Cooper return to his seat. I had to make him promise to wait five minutes before coming back, I wouldn't have put it past him to follow right behind me, zipper intentionally open. As if she's a magnet and he's metal, Tatiana leans toward him the moment he sits.

I force my eyes away from his table and let them drift over the crowd. When they fall upon the man sitting directly across from me, I'm startled at what I find. Miles is seething, nostrils flaring, his unblinking eyes fixed on me in an angry stare.

chapter thirty-three

Cooper

Daylight has barely dawned as I make my way to the office. Leaving Kate lying in my bed, her hair splayed across a pillow and naked body beneath the sheets, was virtually impossible to do. But I'm meeting with my lawyers at seven to go over the terms of the union negotiation before I sit at the table and shake hands on the final deal.

My face is speckled with day-old stubble I had every intention of shaving until I walked into the bedroom and caught a glimpse of her bare ass peeking out. The decision to use the little time I had for other things was an easy one, especially when she mentioned she liked my five o'clock shadow right before I sunk into her.

I find myself thinking about what it would be like to wake up to her beside me everyday. To fall asleep to the sound of her light breaths and vision of her sweet mouth twitching up at the sides as she escapes into dreamland. The realization hits me when I least expect it: I'm in love with Kate Monroe.

The office is empty this early in the morning. I grab coffee, dig out my notes, and start to head to the conference room. Miles's appearance in my doorway surprises me. "I don't have time. I have a meeting with my attorneys in five minutes."

"Make time," he says with an angry bite.

"Not now, Miles," I warn.

He ignores me and sits on the couch.

I blow out a frustrated breath, prepared to leave him in my office. Whatever he wants can wait. "What do you need?"

"I need you to keep away from Kate," he says with an icy tone and a glare to match.

"Excuse me?"

"You heard me right."

I stare at him. There's an eerie flatness to his voice, cold and loathsome. I freeze.

A slow smile spreads across his face. "I finally have your attention."

"What game are we playing, Miles?"

He taps his fingers on a jewel case and then looks up to me. "You can have any woman in the world you want. Women fucking throw themselves at you."

I stay quiet. He needs to show his hand before one of us raises the stakes.

"I let you have your fun. Fucking strolling though Barbados without a care in the world. Without a concern for *me*. But last night ..." His fists ball at his sides. "Fucking that *whore* in a coat closet."

Impetuously, I grab him by his shirt with two hands. "Don't fucking call her that."

"You're ruining my show!" he growls in my face.

"It's a stupid fucking show. She's playing along for the camera. It's not ruining anything."

"You're a selfish asshole. Dad's not here anymore. Yet you still need to prove you're better than me every day ... purposely sabotaging my show just to prove something to a dead man."

"You're delusional. I'm not sabotaging anything."

"Ratings are flat. People are tired of watching America's Sweetheart refute Flynn's advances. They want to see the action, need to believe she sucks his dick behind closed doors."

"Shut your fucking mouth," I spit, tightening my grip. My veins pulse with seething rage.

"Break it off."

"Screw you."

"My show is going to get ratings, one way or the other. We can do it the easy way or the hard way. You decide." Miles breaks free from my grip and heads toward the door. He stops and tosses an envelope and DVD on the couch. "I don't suspect the video of you two fucking outside of the guest house will sway you. You're so goddamn full of yourself, you'd probably secretly like seeing your big dick flashed on every news network." He pauses. "I knew something was going on when Damian told me you came to him for an investigation on Kate. Did you really think he wouldn't play us against each other for a bigger payout?"

He takes a few steps and grips the doorway, turning back to drive his final stake into my heart. "I have my *life* invested in this show. Now you will too," he seethes. "She lied on her character affidavit to get her brother into that clinical trial he's in. One anonymously sent document and he'll be out. And I'm sure the medical licensing board will frown on giving sworn testimony to fraudulently obtain medicine. Maybe they'll let her practice physical therapy in Mexico someday." He pauses. "You have until we leave tomorrow to decide how it plays out." Miles walks out without looking back.

My phone buzzes on my desk again. *Everything okay?* It's the third text she's sent today that I haven't responded to. I fail at my attempt to sidestep the mess of papers strewn all over the floor as I stagger to the bottle for yet another refill. My unsteady hand spills the amber liquid on the table, the floor … everywhere but in my glass. Frustrated, I knock over all the glasses with one angry sweep of my arm. The sound of glass breaking sends Helen running in.

She looks around at the mess I've spent all day making, but says nothing.

"Go home, Helen," I mumble, slurring my words.

"I … I don't want to leave you like this."

"Go home!" I yell angrily and she jumps.

"Is there anything I can do? Do you want me to call Miles?"

Maniacal laughter emerges from my chest. With all the crystal tumblers broken, I grab an unopened bottle and stumble back to my desk. "My little brother has done quite enough for the day. Go home, Helen," I say, the sadness in my angry voice poking through.

She nods and disappears.

I squint to clear my vision through my drunken haze. I wish I had some glimmer of hope that the documents were fake, but Miles's face was all the verification I needed. I reread the Emergency Room report for the hundredth time.

> *Diagnosis—Alcohol-induced poisoning. Positive for marijuana consumption.*

And then …

> *Patient brought in by—Sister, Kate Monroe.*

Neither one of them could have known what the ramifications for taking a typical teenage partying junket a little too far would mean. Two weeks after that trip to the Emergency Room, Kyle was paralyzed in an accident Kate feels responsible for, even though it wasn't her fault. Both Kate and Kyle signed character affidavits to get Kyle into the clinical trial that gave them the first glimpse of hope either of them have had since the accident.

> *To your knowledge, has the applicant participated in the illegal use of drugs? No.*

To your knowledge, has the applicant ever abused alcohol? No.

I probably would have done the same thing—even for my brother. Nineteen years old and unable to move from the neck down. Life can be cruel sometimes. But Kate chose to put her brother first … putting herself at risk by lying for him. She'd give anything to make her brother well enough to walk again. *Even her own happiness.*

Unwittingly, she's about to sacrifice that too. I take another swig from the bottle. And so am I. There's no escaping what I need to do.

There's a knock at the door as I step from the shower. The two voices exchange words, but I can't make them out. Probably best. If I hear pain in her voice, I'm not sure I could go through with it. The door clanks shut and the apartment goes quiet again. I throw on sweats and a t-shirt and grab two Tylenol from the bathroom medicine cabinet. My head has the early throb of a soon to be awful hangover, only I haven't even slept yet.

"You had a visitor," Tatiana says, a question in her voice.

"Who was it?" As if I didn't know.

"The girl from the reality show. Kate."

"What did she say?"

"Nothing, really. She just sort of stared at me and then asked if you were home. I said you were in the shower. Then she asked what I was doing here." She walks to me and places her palms flat on my chest. "Nosey little thing, isn't she?"

"What did you tell her?"

"I said I was just about to strip and join you, then I asked her what she wanted." She tilts her head. "Such a prude. She took off after that."

Her hands lift to my neck and she clasps them behind it. Pouting, she whines, "You got done too fast. I didn't get a chance to suds you up."

I pry her fingers from around my neck. "Go home, Tatiana. I'm not in the mood."

Her eyes widen with shock at being turned down. I'd venture to guess it doesn't happen often—if ever.

"*You* invited *me* here."

"I told you. I needed you to sign the copyright release for the DVD rights sale."

"You could have messengered it over, instead of inviting me to your place at eleven at night."

I shrug. "Next time I'll do that. I drank a little too much and wasn't thinking clearly."

"And *now* you're thinking clearly?" she mocks me, annoyed and offended.

"Have a good night, Tatiana."

The slam of the door vibrates loudly a few seconds later.

My plan was effective, what I needed to get accomplished is now tied up in a neat bow. Yet in the end, I've effectively become unraveled myself.

chapter
thirty-four

Kate

The visual wasn't enough. I couldn't leave well enough alone. My heart was already bleeding, but it was the response to my three A.M. text that eviscerated any remnant of hope I'd clung to.

Why? was all I wrote.

His response came ten minutes later. *I thought I could do exclusive. I'm sorry.*

I dropped the phone, curled back into the fetal position and cried myself to sleep.

"You look ... like shit," Sadie says, sliding me a cup of coffee.

"Good morning to you too." I skipped the mirror after the shower. But I don't need my reflection to confirm what I look like ... I feel it *inside* of me.

"Sad because you're leaving one god behind to run off to a tropical island with another god?" She eyes me over her mug as she sips her coffee.

I stutter to say the words. "Cooper is sleeping with Tatiana Laroix."

"What are you talking about?"

"He wasn't answering my texts all day, so I went over there last night." I make a sound that's close to a laugh, even though it isn't funny. "I was worried something happened to him. Tatiana answered the door."

"Maybe she was there on business."

"She told me he was in the shower and she was about to join him."

Sadie's eyes bulge, then she does what I did half the night after I left … she grasps at straws. "Maybe she was lying. You told me yourself the woman was trying to dig her claws into him. I've seen the way he looks at you, he's got it bad."

"I texted him at three in the morning."

"And."

I slide my phone over to her. Her eyes go wide. "There has to be a mistake."

"What part of 'I'm sorry. I thought I could do exclusive' do you think I'm misinterpreting?"

Sadie sighs. Her shoulders slump, her posture looks every bit as dejected as I feel. "I'm sorry, Kate. I just … I thought he was different."

"So did I." A tear slips from the corner of my eye and streaks down my puffy face.

Seeing me cry, Sadie's face reflects the pain I feel inside. "I want to rip his balls off."

I swallow back sadness and allow anger to seep through in its place. "Could you bring them to me on a silver platter when you do that?"

"You got it. But you know what we need to do today, right?"

"Pack? My flight is tonight."

"Absolutely not. We need to go get makeovers."

"I'm not really in the mood." The mope in my voice depresses even me to hear.

"That's exactly why we need to do it."

"Don't you have to work?"

"Pffstt." She waves her hand. "I make the rules."

"Don't the partners whose names are on the letterhead make the rules?"

She winks. "I just let them think that."

We spend the next few hours at the salon. Sadie insisted I get the deluxe package, threatening the poor girl at the front desk if she didn't accept her credit card over mine. Everything I chose, Sadie overruled. I asked for a French manicure, Sadie made the girl paint them bright pink, saying it was more island appropriate. I told the hair stylist to give me a trim. I wound up with four inches cut and bold highlights, a heavy streak of blond brightly contrasting with my tanned skin.

I said regular bikini wax, Sadie demanded Brazilian ... we settled somewhere in the middle on French. Pretty much the only thing we didn't argue over was the shape of my eyebrows. In the end, I have to admit, Sadie was right. Although I still felt like shit, the primping and pampering made me look good on the outside, which raised my spirits somewhat.

It's nearly four o'clock when we finish. I study my reflection in the mirror as Sadie goes around and tips the dozen people who worked their magic on us. They really did do a remarkable job. The makeup artist even managed to bring the swelling down under my eyes and hide the dark circles.

"Looking good is the second best revenge after a breakup," Sadie says as she comes up behind me, admiring my new appearance.

"Should I bother asking?"

"Fucking a hot rockstar."

I smile and shake my head as we exit onto the street. "I'm not sleeping with Flynn."

"Why not? It might make you feel better. I know it would make *me* feel better to fuck him." She wiggles her eyebrows.

"I hate Cooper right now. But I'm also in love with him." I finally admit it out loud. Figures it takes me until after he breaks my heart to come clean with myself.

"I know." Putting her usual sarcasm aside, my best friend takes my hand in hers as we walk. "I'm sorry he hurt you."

"Thank you."

"But you know the old saying. When life hands you lemons, grab the salt and tequila."

"I'm pretty sure it's 'make lemonade.' But I get the idea." I bump shoulders with her.

"Seriously. Turn this into something positive. Remember the reason you agreed to do the show to begin with. I've been watching you walk around silently blaming yourself for something you had no control over for years, Kate. I can't even imagine what it will do to you if your mom loses the house and Kyle has to stop his therapy. The grand-prize money won't just help them. It will go a long way to make life easier for you to go back to living. Focus on winning. Don't let Cooper take that from you too."

The stretch limousine waits ten minutes while I finish packing. Between my jumbled mind and fragile emotional state, I'm not even sure what the heck is in the sixty-pound suitcase.

Sadie walks me to the car and peeks her head inside. "Wanna French kiss and totally blow their three empty minds?"

"Maybe another time." I hug her tight. "Thank you for today. For every day."

"Enjoy yourself," she whispers. "And focus. After everything you've been through, at least win the prize for your family."

chapter thirty-five

Cooper

The sweat drips from my brow as I turn the machine higher. It's been two days—two days of conjuring up ugly pictures in my head. Day one was thoughts of Kate being upset. Of her coming to the realization that I'm a total scumbag and crying over the loss of a man she thought she knew. It shredded me.

Then I started to dream up how she would get even. The visions of her in Dickhead's arms make me run faster. I press the button again and my run turns to a full-on sprint. I run faster and faster, chasing something I can never catch.

A knock at my door saves me from myself. It's Lou. I open it while I struggle to regain my breath.

"Working out hard, huh, Mr. M?"

"Just running. Helps me decompress." *Usually it does anyway.*

"Delivery guy dropped this off from Mile High. Figured it might be important." He hands me an unmarked small brown package.

"Thanks, Lou."

I consider tossing the thing in the garbage, actually getting as far as opening the drawer with the hidden trash can and *almost* dropping it in. Almost. But my curiosity wins out. What the hell could Miles send me after the shit he's pulled? Begrudgingly, I open the package. It's a clear jewel case with a DVD inside. I turn it over and find it marked. *Day 1 Barbados.* That sick, sadistic bastard. He's going to continue to send me the dailies.

I make it almost a full hour before I'm staring at the monitor. I mutter a dozen curses as I hit play. Five minutes in, the camera zooms in on her. She's sitting on the beach alone wearing a flowing cover up staring out to the ocean, her knees drawn to her chest. She looks sad. Lonely, even. I freeze the video and stare at the screen like a stalker.

I miss the feel of her skin and the sounds of her laugh. The way she comes back at me with a jab every time I challenge her. It pains me to see the feistiness gone from her eyes. Eventually, I muster the strength to hit play and, within minutes, I wish I could hit the rewind button and unsee what flashes on my screen.

Dickhead cozies up next to her. Wrapping his arm around her shoulder, he pulls her close to him, his hand rubbing her shoulder intimately.

"You feeling better today?" he asks.

"Yes. Sorry about not joining the welcome party last night. I really didn't feel well."

"You didn't miss much. Mercedes got drunk and Jessica decided to go skinny-dipping."

"Sounds like at least you had some fun."

He strokes her hair. "There isn't much fun when you're not around."

"Thanks. But I'm not very much fun these days."

"Well, I'll have to work on that." He grins at her and I get the urge to smack the con-artist dimples from his face. "My new sole mission in life is to see a smile on that beautiful face." *Yeah, and to fuck three other women. Dickhead.*

"Come on." He stands and offers her his hands.

"Where are we going?" She hesitates but puts her hands in his. He tugs her up and then, in one swooping motion, lifts her over his shoulder.

"Flynn!" she warns as he takes off running toward the water. She flails around and he splashes as he hits the water, but he doesn't stop until he's chest deep. He shifts, adjusting her from over his shoulder, and cradles her into his arms. Scowling, I clench the laptop in my hands so tight my knuckles go white.

I have to walk away to compose myself for a few minutes before coming back to shut the damn laptop off. I should have just let it play, because what I see hits me like a kick to the chest when I return. They're coming out of the water, holding hands, and she's *smiling*.

chapter

thirty-six

Kate

I t's day three post Cooper Montgomery and, while the world didn't end, there's a little piece of me missing. I've been doing better, smiling when it's appropriate, interacting with people—well, the staff and Flynn at least—and taking every available opportunity to leave the guest house.

We may have only been here for five days, but there's a memory at every turn. At night, after everyone goes to bed, I lay in the yellow room, replaying the last couple of months with Cooper over and over. Hindsight is supposed to be twenty-twenty. Yet I see nothing clearer as I look back than I did when it was happening in front of my eyes. Perhaps if I had seen it coming, it wouldn't cut this deep.

Yes, I was "dating" another man. The word hypocrite may even seem appropriate from the outside looking in. But we both knew what I was doing ... and *why* I was doing it. We'd even made promises to each other— rules we would follow until the show ended. No kissing on the mouth, no sex with anyone but each other ... he'd been the one to *make* the damn rules.

I believed him. I trusted him. Three days of looking for the clues I missed, has left me nothing but exhausted and clueless. Why now, when I look back, can't I see it coming? The only logical answer crushes me—I can't see the change because he never really felt what I thought he felt to begin with. I was seeing what I wanted to see all along.

I try the Sadie school of thought to get myself out of my state of perpetual melancholy. *If you don't feel good, at least look good.* Finally losing the ponytail I've worn since we arrived, I spend a full hour and half getting ready for our group date. I blow out my hair, do my makeup and put on a beautiful blue dress the show wardrobe designer swears was made with me in mind. Looking at my reflection boosts my spirits as much as it can.

When Flynn arrives, I hang back and watch from the hall doorway as the ladies greet him one at a time. Each fusses over him, making physical contact as they speak, flirting in that way that screams he wouldn't have to work very hard to be in their bed tonight. Flynn stands there, a sweet smile on his face, but the way he looks at them isn't a mirror of what they're feeling.

After getting a greeting from the third beautiful woman, I watch as he scans the room. His smile lights up when his eyes fall on me. He does that overt flirty sweep of me that he always does, and comes to me.

"You look gorgeous," he whispers in my ear after kissing my cheek. Unexpectedly, goose bumps break out on my arms.

"You don't look so bad yourself." He's wearing a linen dress shirt with an ocean blue knotted tie that brings out the azure in his eyes even more than usual. Perhaps it's the tattoos sticking out from the expensive shirt, but somehow he manages a look that screams casually elegant blended with rockstar. It works for him, and he wears it well.

We all pile into the SUV limo and head out for our first group date on the island. My heart lurches when we pull into a parking lot. Of all the places on this island, Miles had to pick the Saturday night beach fish fry. The same one Cooper and I went to the last night we were here.

"What can I get you to drink?" Flynn yells, his hand at the small of my back, leading me through the crowd to the bar. It's way more packed than the night I was here with Cooper.

"I'll have whatever you're having."

"You sure about that?" he questions. "I was about to order vodka tonic and I seem to remember you getting tipsy off a glass of wine."

I look around, the memory of Cooper and me slow dancing on the grass while everyone around us danced to a fast reggae beat causes a new wave of pain. Pain I need to dull, even if just for a little while.

"Vodka sounds good to me."

The effects are quick, my mind already numbed as I swallow the last bit of poison from the glass. "Let's dance." I grab Flynn's hand and lead him to the packed dance floor. Closing my eyes, I soak in the energy of the crowd and the heavy beat of the steel drum and begin to let my body sway to the music.

Bodies close in tightly around us—strangers reveling in the warm night air, moving with the sensual verve of the music.

"That's it." Flynn wraps his arm tightly around my waist and takes lead of my body. "Let the music take whatever burden you've been carrying for a while." In the moment, surprisingly, it's easy to do. The alcohol released some of the tension in my body, and the loud, hypnotizing beat of the drum, coupled with Flynn's hand leading my movement, allows me to forget everything else. By the end of the third song, I'm more relaxed than I've been in days. Even when Jessica cuts in, I'm still feeling no pain.

"Thank you. I needed that," I whisper and kiss him on the cheek as I leave him in Jessica's quite capable hands.

The problem with drinking alcohol when you're depressed is that you're always chasing that initial feel-good buzz. Sobriety starts to rear its solemn head, so you have another drink. But the second one doesn't affect you like the first, so you have yet another. And before you know it you're somewhere between feeling no pain and ostensibly obliviated.

I watch from a stool at the bar as Flynn dances with the three women surrounding him. He's having fun, but the more I get to know him, the more I realize he can pretty much turn anything into a good time. The antithesis of Cooper, Flynn is a free spirit—one who goes with the flow and emanates a casualness that sets the people around him at ease. Cooper, on the other hand, makes people sit taller when he walks into the room.

I order another drink to drown the thoughts in my head. A break in the music draws my focus to the stage. Flynn is peeling off his sweat-drenched shirt. The tattoos on his hard-ridged abs glisten, to the delight of the audience. The local women who had been dancing up a storm scream their praise in heavy island accents and catcall whistles. A dimple-baring crooked smile on his face, Flynn shakes his head, enjoying every minute of it, and takes the microphone from the bass player.

He doesn't bother with an introduction. Instead he begins to sing. Starkly different than the singer on stage just moments ago, his voice is incredibly soulful and seductive. A woman next to me comments to her friend how she'd like to trace his tattoos with her tongue. Staring at the stage, I can totally see the appeal. He's a ridiculously handsome man with an undeniable youthful charm. And that voice … it's throaty and sexy and travels straight through me.

I'm here, you're there.

Same time, same place,

Yet a million miles apart.

One last cry, let it go, release the pain of the past.

Feelings change, people change

I want your tomorrow, not your yesterday.

Feelings change, people change.

Take my hand, let me lead your way.

Standing beside you, lost in the forest.

Shadows of past bury you deep.

The sun glimmers in the distance

Mending broken dreams.

Feelings change, people change

I want your tomorrow, not your yesterday.

Feelings change, people change.

Take my hand, let me lead your way.

Sacrifice the past, give me today.

Walk to me, don't walk away

Hear the music, my words are a plea

Open your heart and let love sing.

Feelings change, people change

I want your tomorrow, not your yesterday.

Feelings change, people change.

Take my hand, let me lead your way.

The crowd goes crazy as the last note fades. Then the band picks back up with a song that has the mesmerized crowd grinding with heightened sexual appetites. I finish my drink and stand, but the sky begins to spin and my feet grow unsteady.

Flynn catches me as I wobble. "Woo … you okay?"

"I'm great." I fling my arms around his neck.

He smiles.

"I liked your song."

"I'm glad."

"It was sexy."

He chuckles, amused.

"Just like you." I push up on my tippy toes and lean into him, pressing my lips to his. He doesn't kiss me back.

"You're drunk," Flynn says when he pulls his head back.

"So? If Jessica tried to kiss you when she was drunk, I bet you wouldn't say no."

"That's because Jessica would kiss me when she's sober."

A little while later, I fall asleep in the SUV on the ride back to Sugar Rose, my head resting on Flynn's lap. He helps me out of the car and into my room.

The door closing behind us is the last thing I remember in the morning when I wake with a pounding in my head. I'm snuggled into Flynn, his arms tight around me.

"Morning," he says with a broad smile.

I'm quiet for a moment as I wrack my brain trying to remember what happened after we came into my bedroom. But my mind is completely blank. "Did we?" Too embarrassed to say the words, I motion between the two of us.

He responds with a devilish glint in his eye. "Did we what?"

"You know."

"Yes, but I want to hear you say it."

I roll my eyes. It's enough movement to cause my headache to worsen.

"Sweetheart, trust me, if we did, you'd remember it." He kisses my forehead and hops from the bed.

"Well, then, thank you. For … being a gentleman."

"Better look under the sheets before you call me a gentleman," he says sheepishly.

My eyes go wide and, hesitantly, I lift the sheet and look down. I'm wearing a t-shirt and underwear. I look up at Flynn and he shrugs and smiles.

"I might have helped you change." He winks and disappears.

chapter
thirty-seven

Kate

"How you feeling?" Flynn asks with a knowing smirk on his face after he returns from an hour-long beach run.

"Like death," I groan. I'm lying in a lounge chair near the water's edge, oversized sunglasses blocking the rays of light that cause the pain in my head to worsen. It's nearly five o'clock, yet I feel as queasy now as when I woke up this morning.

"How can you run after last night?"

He shrugs and takes off his shirt. "I'm better at partying than you."

"My idea of partying is drinking two glasses of wine in sweatpants after studying for four hours."

"Wild woman." He balls up his shirt and tosses it at me. "Come on. I need to walk to cool down." He extends both of his hands.

"The last time I took those hands, I wound up in the water against my will."

"You're safe with me today. I've had my share of hangovers. I feel your pain. I won't add to it. Just a walk."

He's sincere, so I take the hand he's offering. The first fifteen minutes we're both quiet, but I'm uneasy. "I'm sorry about last night."

"About what?"

"Kissing you."

"I'm not."

"But you didn't kiss me back."

"Only because you were too drunk." He halts. "You wanna try it again now, sober? See if I hold back?"

I smile and take his hand, tugging him forward. "Underneath that tattooed bad-boy exterior, you're really a good guy."

We walk some more in silence, hand in hand. Finally Flynn asks, "Can I ask you something?"

"Sure."

"Did I do something to turn you off?"

"What? No. What makes you say that?"

"When the show first started, I thought we had a connection. And then I kissed you and I felt it. I could swear you did too. But then things changed. We still had the connection, but you keep me in friend territory."

I sigh audibly. "I'm sorry."

"Don't be sorry. If it's not there, it's not there for you. I just wondered where we went wrong."

"*We* didn't."

"I don't understand."

"There was someone else in the room with us whenever we were together. Not physically. But I couldn't really be with you, when my heart was involved with someone else."

"*Was* involved. Not *is* involved?" He's astute.

"It's over now. I'm sorry. It should have never happened to begin with. What you felt when we first met ... when we first kissed ... you weren't alone. I felt it too. Then things got complicated and I could never move forward after that."

"And now? Are you available now?"

"Technically, yes. Honestly, you're a great guy. But my heart's broken. I wish we'd met under different circumstances at another time."

"Why don't we start over?" he says, taking my other hand and turning to walk backwards.

"How can we do that?"

He shrugs and smiles. "Easy." He lets go of my hands and extends a handshake to me. "Hi, I'm Flynn Beckham."

I shake my head, but play along. "Kate Monroe."

"Nice to meet you, Kate."

"Likewise."

"Listen. I hope this doesn't sound too stalkerish, but I've been stealing glances at you every chance I get. Would you go out with me the day after tomorrow?" We're already scheduled for our one-on-one date on Wednesday.

"I'd love to," I say and, for the first time since my eyes landed on Cooper Montgomery, I mean it.

The invitation that was delivered to my room this morning gave only a hint of the date that was to come this afternoon. The card read, *You make my heart soar,* although there was a bikini delivered with the gold-embossed invite.

I slip on the white bathing suit. It's simple, yet sexy—alluring long strings hang from the tie closures, almost a flirty invitation to anyone to tug and see what lies beneath. My skin is deeply tanned to a golden bronze after the last four days of lazily soaking up island sunshine. The image that bounces back at me in the mirror is pleasing—a flutter of hope that I won't be stuck in sadness forever finally starts to peek through.

Wardrobe outfits me with an almost see-through white cover-up dress and an incredible pair of high-heeled sandals. The only color in my ensemble is from the aqua bow on the brim of my straw sun hat. Mercedes and Jessica eye me angrily when I walk through the living room to answer the door for my date. It validates what I saw when I looked at my reflection.

"Wow. White's your color." Flynn's eyes pore over me and then he kisses my cheek.

"I don't think white is actually a color."

"Then what is it?"

"It's the absence of color."

"Well, then the absence of color looks hot on you, smarty pants." We both laugh.

"Likewise, your absence of color looks mighty handsome." Flynn's dressed in all white too. Well, except for the splash of color artistically running down his left forearm. All of his tattoos are black and grey except one. I'd never noticed it until now.

My handsome date leads me to the car and opens the door for me. "Is it a coincidence that we're both dressed in white?"

"Nope." He closes the door and jogs around to the driver's side. "It's symbolic. We're starting over. Remember? Today is our first date."

"Please tell me you don't expect me to go up in one of those?" We pull into a beach parking lot and a shack offering parasailing rides makes me suspicious. There are a few people floating around in the sky tethered to colorful parachutes above them.

"I do." He parks and smiles at me.

"I told you I was afraid of heights."

"We're starting fresh today. Remember? What better way to start off than to live a little."

"I'm all for living, it's the opposite of living that scares me and keeps my feet on the ground."

He opens my car door. "They set us up for a double harness. I'll hold you through the whole thing."

"Even when we splatter on the ground?"

He chuckles. "We won't splatter on the ground. Besides, there's water underneath us."

I look around and find the cameras already rolling. Taking a deep breath, I finally give him my hand. "What's your greatest fear?" I lean in and whisper to avoid my voice being picked up.

"Rejection." He kisses my cheek. "See, we're both conquering our fears today."

I'm still on an adrenaline high from our afternoon date as I get ready for dinner. Flynn was right, facing one of my biggest fears was somehow freeing. Leaving me to feel like today really was a fresh start.

As promised, Flynn held me the entire way. My body secured in a harness clipped to his, his muscular thighs straddled me, long legs wrapped tightly around my waist from behind the minute we lifted into the air. One strong arm fastened around my middle in a bear hug left me feeling secure as we soared high above the ocean. Even when I had finally relaxed enough to enjoy the breathtaking view of the crystal-clear aqua water below, his hold on me never loosened. Eventually, I found myself leaning into his embrace instead of clinging to it.

After parasailing, the boat took us to a sand bar in the middle of the ocean and we hand fed giant sea turtles and snorkeled amid schools of colorful fish. Today was a day made for reality television, yet I was so completely enraptured with everything we did, most of the time, I didn't notice the cameras.

The smile on Flynn's face when he arrives for dinner matches my own. His long hair is loose, framing an undeniably swoon-worthy face. But it's his smile that undoubtedly would have women throwing their panties at him on stage.

"What? I didn't even say anything yet and you're shaking that head at me like I'm up to no good." Flynn feigns innocence, although his eyes tell me his thoughts are anything but.

"That smile. I bet women drop their panties for those dimples."

He takes a step closer. The air between us shifts. "I hope so."

Unlike the playful carefree mood from this afternoon, tonight there's a tension that hangs thick between us. The challenge of navigating down the steep natural stairs of the dimly lit cliff to Bottom Bay is handsomely rewarded at the bottom. The serene beach, surrounded by tall privacy-ensuring cliffs is dark and empty. Until we walk a few hundred yards and pass a towering jut of a mountain to the other side. I actually gasp at the vision.

Leaning palm trees are bedecked with sporadically placed candles ensconced in hanging glass lanterns. A blanket is spread in the corner, an oversized picnic basket illuminated by a few candles surrounding it.

"Wow. It's beautiful."

Flynn looks at me pensively. "It is. Are you okay with this?"

The ice protecting my heart for the last week melts just a little. I look at him and smile. "I think I am."

We spend the next three hours eating, talking and laughing. With only the candlelight around us, it's easy to forget there are probably cameras set up all over. It's romantic and beautiful, and Flynn is a complete gentleman. I learn things about him I never would have guessed—things we have in common. We both were science majors in college, although his focus was astronomy and mine was biology. We both love Johnny Cash, but don't get the Beatles phenomenon. And our dads never met a casino they could walk past.

"What makes the stars twinkle, Copernicus?"

"Ahh. That is a common mistake of the layperson," Flynn says with some sort of accent. I assume it's an attempt at the dialect of the famous astronomer, but I know little about Copernicus other than he is the granddaddy of astronomy. "Stars actually don't twinkle."

"They don't? I'm not sure I want to hear this."

Flynn chuckles. We're both lying on our backs, gazing up at the sky filled with stars—some of them twinkling. He rolls from his back to his side and props up his head on his elbow with one hand. His other hand brushes a stray hair behind my ear. "It's just the angle we view them at. A ray of light bends slightly when it passes through the atmosphere, it deflects and we see it as a twinkle. If we were on the moon, we wouldn't see a twinkle at all."

I smile, captivated by the splendor of the twinkles above, even if they aren't really what they seem. "Well, then I'm glad we're here and not on the moon."

"Me too," he says quietly. My heart skips a beat meeting his direct gaze. We hold a long stare, his eyes filled with longing and intrigue, the candle illuminating the blue in his eyes. And his mouth … full and soft, perfectly kissable. He smiles staring down at me, revealing luscious dimples and a confidence that makes me think he absolutely knows what to do with a woman. His eyes drop to my lips and then return to mine with even more heat in his gaze.

The last thought I have as his lips meet mine is that this may be more than a game, and I'm either all in or all out.

chapter thirty-eight

Cooper—2 weeks later

Walking from the bathroom, a towel wrapped around my waist, I jerk to a halt when I hear the sound. My gaze is riveted to the TV I'd left playing, where her face knocks the air from my lungs. I stopped watching the DVDs after the day the camera zoomed in on them sleeping snuggled in a bed. In the yellow room, of all rooms.

I know I left her with no reason to think I was worthy of a second chance. But I guess I'd secretly hung on to hope that maybe, just maybe, we could be together after the show ended.

Dickhead comes on the screen. This must be the finale. My asshole brother must be in his glory. Ratings have been through the roof. I've caught glimpses of the advertisements in the moments before the remote could change the channel. He got what he wanted. America is dying to know if the longhaired, hippy-looking cocky bastard choses the temptress or his torch.

As much as I despise my brother, I have to hand it to him. He's turned the last week of the show into an advertising phenomenon. Women of all ages are on edge waiting to find out which of the two final contestants he picks. Jessica—the pinup girl who seduced him from the minute he met her—or Kate—the woman he set his sights on seducing from her first smile. I've even overheard Helen gossiping about who she thinks he'll pick.

Against my better judgment, I don't change the channel. Instead I stand and glare at the scene that plays out before my eyes. It's a recap of last week, Dickhead's in a tuxedo and Kate in a gown. She looks gorgeous, but nervous, as they enter an elevator. The doors slide closed and my heart aches as the camera pans to their hands. They're standing next to each other, but Dickhead's pinky reaches out and locks with hers and then they briefly turn and look at each other smiling.

The doors glide open again and the sign on the suite in front of them makes my blood boil. *Honeymoon Suite.* I can't bear to watch it, yet my eyes won't leave the screen.

He slips a keycard from his pocket and holds it up to her. Their gaze catches for a moment and she takes a deep breath.

Don't go in, Kate.

Slowly, she reaches down and takes the key out of his hand. The slow, wordlessness anticipation is killing me.

Shake your head no, Kate. Don't go in.

Key in hand, control of both of our destinies hanging in the wind, her eyes meet his once more. I hold my breath as she slips the key into the door. Dickhead hangs the *Do Not Disturb* sign and sound finally returns with the click of the door shutting behind them.

I feel hollow inside. Wounds that had only begun to heal are ripped open again. But seeing her move on, watching the door close behind them, is what I needed. It's symbolic of what I need to do. It's time. Forcing my balled fists open, one finger at a time, I stretch my palms wide. The door closing. Them walking inside. The end of the show. Finally, I let go. Closure.

chapter thirty-nine

Kate—1 month later

"No trucks outside today," Sadie says as she walks in, a shopping bag in each hand.

"I've bored them to death."

"You are kind of boring." She chides and unloads her bags. One bag from the liquor store, the other is lingerie.

"That's some combination you have there." My eyes point to her purchases.

"Isn't it? The funny thing is, too much of one leads to the removal of the other."

"I'm just glad you're wearing underwear again these days at least."

"Jared gives me a hard time if I don't."

"Which is pretty funny since that's how you met." Sadie's new boyfriend, Jared, is an entertainment correspondent who was filming out front of our apartment after the finale. The media went into a frenzy after I won *Throb*, setting up camp all over our building to try to catch a glimpse of me and Flynn. One afternoon it all got to be too much and Sadie was tired of people screaming questions at her as she navigated to our door. So she pulled up her skirt and mooned the cameraman—she wasn't wearing any underwear. That got the cameras off my back for a little while. But Jared, the reporter who'd caught the entire thing on the camera behind him, was hot on Sadie's trail instead.

It's been less than two weeks, but the two of them are already inseparable. Somehow he's even got her to do the unthinkable—wear underwear under her skirts.

There's a knock at the door. "That's Jared," she yells over her shoulder as she heads into her room. "Tell him I'll be ready in five minutes."

I open the door and find Jared. And Flynn. "Hey. What are you doing here?"

"Just met him in the parking lot." Jared smiles and I step aside for both men to enter. "Figures. I don't have a camera with me."

"No one is really interested in us anyway. We're just a boring old couple now, right, honey?" I say to Flynn.

"Yep." He slings his arm over my shoulder.

"Sadie will be out in a few minutes. You guys want a glass of wine?"

Flynn takes the bottle from my hand, grabs three glasses from the cabinet and takes over. Fifteen minutes later, Sadie emerges with a smile and an indulgent kiss for the new man in her life.

"We have to get going, we have reservations," Jared says.

"You two have fun." Sadie blows a kiss in our direction.

We hear their muted conversation as they reach the door. "You do have underwear on, right?"

"Sort of," Sadie elusively responds.

"Do I even want to know what that means?"

"You will later." The door closes behind them.

I tuck my feet under me on the couch and sip from my glass. "So, to what do I owe the pleasure of this surprise visit?"

Flynn gets up and tops off my wine glass, even though it's not even near empty. "Drink up."

"You came here to get me drunk?" I tease.

"No. But you're going to need that drink for what I came to tell you."

My head pounds, whirling with questions. I make Flynn repeat everything twice, even though I heard every word he said loud and clear the first time.

"Why would Miles tell you this now?" It doesn't make any sense.

"He had too much to drink. We were celebrating my signing on to do another show with Mile High."

"What show?"

"*Beat.* He's going to follow my band on our upcoming tour. Sort of a day-in-the-life with a rock band ... that lasts three months."

"He has to be lying."

"I don't think so. He was pretty proud of himself. Taking credit for breaking you two up so I could have you."

"But if it's true, why would he do it?"

"He said the finale needed to be between you and Jess. The audience loved the vixen-versus-virgin angle."

"I take it I'm the virgin."

"His words, not mine."

"And Cooper agreed to dump me, just like that?"

"Miles said he had leverage. He was pretty drunk, none of it really made sense ... but he babbled about a video of the two of you at a guest house in Barbados and your brother's trip to the emergency room."

"My brother? Kyle?"

"Yeah. Something about causing trouble with a clinical trial."

I barely make it to the bathroom when the two glasses of wine empty from my stomach. Flynn strokes my back gently. "You okay?"

"Not really."

He helps me to the couch and tucks me in, kissing my forehead sweetly. In the last month, I've grown to adore this man. "Maybe it's not too late for you two. I know you still have feelings for him."

"I'm sure he has feelings for me too. Some pretty powerful ones after watching that finale."

chapter forty

Cooper—1 week later

"There's a Mr. Beckham here to see you," Helen's voice announces over the intercom in my office.

"Who?" I had to have heard that wrong.

"Flynn Beckham. He was on your ..."

"I know who he is."

"Would you like me to tell him you're busy?"

I'd like you to tell him a fuck of a lot more than that. I hit the button to respond. "Tell him ..." I say angrily, but then think better of how I want my message delivered. I'll definitely take more joy in doing it myself. "Send him in."

Dickhead walks in and I have to fight the overwhelming urge to go straight to him and punch him in the face. I stay behind my desk; it's safer with a barrier between us. He walks to me and the idiot extends his hand for a shake. I look down at it and then back to him, my face clearly relaying my disdain as I fold my arms over my chest.

"What do you want?"

He lowers his hand. "I came to talk to you about Kate."

"I'm pretty sure you and I have nothing to discuss in regards to Kate."

"I just need two minutes of your time."

"The clock just started. Say what you came to say and get out."

Dickhead takes a deep breath. "I fell in love with her."

"That's what you came here for? You wasted your time, don't waste any more of mine. I really don't care to hear about your love life. I think you got the wrong brother." I pick up a stack of documents for my next meeting. But the moron doesn't take the hint. Instead, he sits.

"She doesn't love me."

I glare at him and say nothing.

"She loves you."

"Didn't look like it when she was leading you into that honeymoon suite." The words taste as bitter as they're spoken.

"It was an act." Dickhead rubs the back of his neck. "We cheated. She told me about her family and why she really did the show. We pretended to be together because that's what Miles wanted. I chose her so she could win the money."

"So you didn't spend the night together?" I have no idea why I ask, because anything but an unequivocal no is going to kill me.

"Dude, she made me sleep on the floor. Wouldn't even share the big bed with me."

"So the whole tension between you and Jessica and Kate was an act?"

"Well, not all of it."

I glare at him.

"Turns out Jessica was on your brother's payroll the whole time. He was paying her to stir the pot." He shrugs. "Plus, I ended up sleeping with Jessica after I figured out I had no chance with Kate. Probably wasn't the smartest move. I was wishing it was Kate the whole time."

"Quit while you're ahead," I warn.

Dickhead chuckles. "Anyway. She's a great girl. But I never had a shot. She's in love with you."

"A lot's changed."

"That hasn't."

Dickhead stands and extends his hand. This time I take it. He gets to the doorway before I call after him. "Hey."

He turns.

"Thanks."

He nods with a defeated smile.

"Maybe you're not such a dickhead after all."

chapter

forty-one

Kate—1 day later

Today I'm reminded why I did the right thing. The smile on Kyle's face when he returned home from spinal cord stimulation therapy is contagious. He's regained a small amount of voluntary control of his muscles, enough so that he could "flex" for me as I helped him back into bed. His hope shined so bright, a little even warmed me today.

Ever since Flynn came by to tell me about his conversation with Miles, I've regressed back to the depressing state I was in right after Cooper and I broke up. I feel like I'm missing a few pieces of the puzzle still. Even if it's true that Miles blackmailed Cooper into breaking things off, and he did it to save me from myself, how could he have turned to Tatiana so soon? Why wouldn't he have come to me? I spend hours trying to figure out why I feel like something's missing, but in the end the only thing I'm clear about is that I've lost a piece of my heart.

My phone buzzes and I smile seeing his name on the caller ID.

"What, you don't call, you don't write?" Frank's jovial voice booms loudly through the car speaker.

"You miss me, don't you?" I say.

"I do, kid. I do. Are you too big and famous to play cards with us anymore?"

"Is that an invitation or just a general question?"

"Can you come tonight? Eight o'clock." There's a smile in his voice. "Grip and Ben took all my money last time. I need you to teach the bums a lesson."

I laugh. "I'd love to come."

"All right, kid. I'll see you later."

I park and sit in the car for a few minutes outside the studio. The memory of the first night I played cards here months ago still affects me, even through my sadness. I had no idea who Cooper was, but the flex of his forearm almost had me losing hands a few times—my focus so thrown by the effect the man had on me from the moment I laid eyes on him.

Taking a deep cleansing breath, I push the memory to the back of my mind and lift the case of Stella out of the back of my Jeep and head into the studio.

"Frank?" My voice echoes in the cavernous empty hangar. The usual card table isn't set up yet. The large room is perfectly still, an invitation to my mind to run off and daydream.

The heavy steel door clanks open loudly, then slams shut.

"I was beginning to wonder if I had the wrong night." I turn, expecting to find Frank, and freeze—my gaze locking on brilliant green eyes. I ached to see him, dreamed of running to him, yet a tangled mesh of feelings stir inside me that keeps me rooted in place.

As he moves across the room with his usual confidence and grace, every emotion I forced down over the last month comes flooding to the surface all at once.

I missed him every second of every day, but seeing him before me makes me remember all the reasons why. The way he looks at me like he wants to devour me, his cocky confidence that borders on arrogance, his irresistible charm, the way he commands a room without having to say or do a thing.

My heart pounds in my chest.

My mind finally stops whirling with questions and goes blank.

Cooper stops as he reaches where I'm standing. I don't move an inch, my feet securely cemented to the earth.

I look at him. He stares at me.

His face is a mask. I can't tell if he's happy to see me or angry I'm here. While what's going on inside of him may be completely unreadable, there's a rash of emotions churning inside my own stomach that are impossible to ignore.

He folds his arms over his chest in a closed-off stance.

I don't know what to say or do. Maybe he's just as surprised to see me as I am to see him. His beautiful face is somber, and his green eyes are distant. It's physically painful to be this close, yet feel so far away.

The seconds tick by. I'm certain he must be able to hear the pounding of my heartbeat, it's so loud. Yet we just stare—neither of us saying a word. I long for him to open his folded arms and invite me in, but he doesn't.

Mimicking his stance, I wrap my shaky arms around my waist to occupy them. So badly they want to reach out and touch him—I'm afraid they might. My body has a mind of its own when it comes to this man.

"How are you?" Unable to take the deafening silence any longer, I finally speak. His green eyes darken with emotion. He's angry with me.

"How do you think I am?" The pain in his voice slices through me.

I close my eyes. Blinking back tears when I reopen them. "Do you want me to leave?" I ask softly.

"I wouldn't have arranged for you to be here if I wanted you to leave."

A spark of hope ignites in the darkness I've been shrouded in.

"I don't understand?"

Cooper blows out a rush of air. "Neither do I, Kate." He rakes his fingers through his hair, then regains his intimidating composure.

Our eyes lock in a challenging stare off, until I finally break. All the sadness I've been carrying, all the hurt and anger, bubbles to the top. My need to know the truth is greater than any silly race to win our stalemate. "Did Miles threaten you with things that could hurt me to make you break things off?"

He swallows. "Yes."

"Why didn't you tell me? We could have figured out a way."

"You said it yourself best. You couldn't give winning your all while we were together. If it were just me he'd ruin, I'd never have walked away. I'd have let him take everything I own to keep you." He pauses and his voice drops lower. "I know how much you love your brother. It was too much to risk."

He's right—I'd never have been able to connect with Flynn like I did if he didn't free me. Since Flynn came to see me, all I could focus on was how Cooper could tear us apart. I was upset he didn't trust me enough to figure it out together. But in this moment, I finally understand. My eyes well with tears. I've been so busy being mad at him for making the decision *without* me, I couldn't see what he really did. He made the decision *for* me.

"Tatiana," I whisper. "How could you have so soon?"

"I used Tatiana to chase you away. To set you free to do what you needed to do."

"So you slept with her for me?" There's a bitter edge to my voice.

"I didn't sleep with her." His jaw flexes and it looks like he's contemplating adding more.

"Truth," I remind him.

"I didn't lay a finger on her the night you came over and found her there. I went out with her once before we met. That's it." His eyes close and then come back to find mine. "I settled for less before you walked into my life."

"Then why didn't you come to me after the show was over?"

"I thought you were with him. You looked … happy."

The pain in his eyes when he utters his truth wraps around my heart and squeezes so tightly my hand reaches up to rub my chest. He acted so selflessly, without regard to his own happiness. It must have killed him to watch the show. The editors pieced together my small moments of joy to make them appear like I was blissfully in love.

Head bowed, he looks up through tortured eyes and asks, "Do you love him?"

"No."

He steps closer to me and I think I stop breathing for a second. "Remember when I asked you if you believed in loving something and setting it free to find out if it's meant to be?"

"You told me you were more of the school of if you want something you should pursue it aggressively."

"I finally understand the difference. If you *want* something, you pursue it aggressively and nothing gets in your way. If you *love* something, sometimes you have no choice but to set it free so it can find its way back to you forever. It killed me to let go, but I'd do it again if it meant your happiness in the end. That's how I know."

"Know what?" I whisper with apprehension, although my heart opens wide with hope.

One hand grasps my waist and his other rises to tuck a piece of hair behind my ear. "Know that I love you. In a way that is irrational and incomprehensible, but is the only thing that has ever made sense to me."

My eyes close, trying to quell the deluge of tears I'm no longer able to keep at bay. It doesn't work, the downpour comes. "I thought I'd lost you."

Cooper cups my cheeks, his thumbs catching the salty stream as he moves in closer. "Shhh … I know," he says. "I know. I'm sorry. But I knew you'd have given up anything for a chance for Kyle and I had to do it."

"I missed you every day." My soft cry intensifies. Weeks of pent-up emotions all break free at once. "When we went back to Barbados, I saw you everywhere I looked. Losing you felt like I lost a piece of myself." Crying turns to an ugly sob.

He lets me weep it all out, holding me tightly while it all washes away. Sadness, anger, regret, doubt, hurt. When I finally calm, he brings his hand to my face and wipes away every last tear. Silence falls between us as our eyes meet and I confess what I've known for months but never admitted out loud.

"I love you. So much."

His eyes close, relief softens his face as he draws me near. He kisses my forehead, then presses his to mine. We communicate with only our eyes for a long moment. I watch in utter amazement, completely captivated as a transformation in his gaze takes form. The golden sunflowers in the middle of his beautiful green sea blossom, coming alive again.

The allure of our attraction can't be denied and neither can the love. He cups the back of my neck with one hand, and the other strokes my cheek. Slowly, his mouth grazes over mine. It's a whisper-soft touch, but it's enough to awaken every nerve in my body. Lord, I want this man. Love this man with all of my heart.

"Remember the first night we met in this room? I had the little chip I always carry with me out for luck?" I push my lips against his again.

"Every time you swiped your little finger over it, you won."

I smile. "Winning wasn't luck. That was talent. I wished for you."

"You didn't have to wish," he breathes. "You had me from the moment my eyes landed on you."

epilogue

Kate—Six months later

"I'm calling last hand. I have an early meeting in the morning," Cooper says, leaning back in his chair with an easy smile. His stack of chips is nearly depleted—it usually is, but these nights once a month are some of the happiest and carefree times.

Last month, I decided to get a little daring with my bets. I'd come straight from school and didn't have anything of value to enter for the last hand. So, not unlike the first day I met Cooper, I tore a piece of paper from my purse, scribbled something and tossed the folded up paper into the pot.

I threw three kings face down to lose to Cooper's pair of fives. He mumbled something about what would have happened if Ben or Frank had won, as he guided my head down into his lap to collect his prize on the drive home.

But tonight I've come prepared. We'd spent the last two days arguing over the car he bought me. My Jeep broke down for the third time in as many weeks and he hates that I don't have what he calls reliable transportation. It's bad enough he won't let me pitch in toward any of the household expenses since I moved in a month ago. I certainly don't need him buying me a new car.

With a daring smile, I dangle the keys in the air for a second before dropping them into the center of the pile. Frank whistles, catching a glimpse of the Range Rover key fob, and tosses in a watch. Ben opens a bag on the floor and parks a tall awards statue in the middle of the table. Heads turn to see what Cooper will be anteing tonight.

Yielding a mix of anger and playfulness in his penetrating glare, Cooper takes a piece of paper from his pocket, scribbles something, and arches an eyebrow to me as he tosses it to the center of the table.

Frank and Ben drop out with a huff when I raise. I really want to win, although I'm not sure if the thought of Cooper having to keep the Ranger Rover or what's inside the folded-up note is a bigger incentive.

The luck I've had all evening runs dry as I peek at my crappiest hand of the night—not even a pair amongst the five cards I'm dealt. But I don't let that deter me at all. Keeping only the two red hearts and discarding everything else, I brush my finger over my old black lucky chip as I lift my three replacement cards.

Watching me intently, Cooper never says anything, but I know he doesn't believe in any of my lucky charms.

With a knowing grin, he turns over five different cards. A losing hand even if I hadn't been lucky in my draw and picked up the three tens that I did. I rake the pile in and ceremoniously drop it into my purse. Whatever prize is written on that paper is best read when we're alone.

"You know, you don't need to throw your game so I can collect the prize you're offering. I can beat you fair and square," I say, coming out of the bathroom after getting ready for bed. One of the things I love best about living here is the unfettered access to his dress shirts. It might be one of the things Cooper likes best too, seeing as I rarely button them.

"Who said I threw the game?"

I shake my head and walk to my purse to dig out what I've won. "Not even *you* play cards that bad. But it doesn't matter. I'm looking forward to collecting my prize anyway." It takes me a minute to dig the little folded-up square from my bag, my smile already in place anticipating what sort of perverted words I'll find.

Feeling Cooper's eyes burning into me, I unfold the note painstakingly slowly, a sort of mental foreplay. I wet my lips in anticipation, but they part finding what he's written: two words, and not the two that I expected. *Marry me.*

I stop breathing. Holding the paper to my lips, I turn and my already full eyes find Cooper. He's down on one knee, a black velvet box perched in the center of his hand.

I have no idea how my knees don't buckle when I take the two steps to walk to him. My beautiful, confident, loving man smiles up at me before he speaks, and in the moment, he shows me how vulnerable he is. A side I rarely see from a man who goes after everything in life like he's on a seek-and-destroy mission.

The hand not offering the ring box reaches out to me, and I place my trembling hand in his. "Kate Monroe. Even though I lose every hand to you, at the end of the day, I'm the big winner because you go home with me every night. I don't need a chip or a four-leaf clover for all my wishes to come true. I only need you. Marry me, beautiful."

Kate—Four months later—
on the eleventh day of the eleventh month

The big day has finally arrived. Parting the elegant drapery just enough to peer out at the crowd on the beach waiting below, I watch as the last empty seats fill with guests. It's certainly an eclectic enough looking crowd.

Cooper's side is filled with an interesting mix of Hollywood royalty—studio heads, directors, actors—sitting alongside lighting grips, secretaries, and security guards. Noticeably absent is one man I'd hoped to convince Cooper to invite, but he wouldn't budge in the least.

Miles isn't here. It saddens me the two couldn't reconcile. They're basically the only family left for each other. I know Miles is the one who did all the damage, but somehow I still feel guilty that it was my actions that gave him the ammunition for the gun he held to Cooper's head.

A few more people trickle in that I don't recognize, then a familiar face leisurely swaggers in. A few women do a double take, although he doesn't seem to even notice. He looks great, tanned and relaxed, with his trademark long hair pulled back into a ponytail. I smile, thinking how only a year ago seeing Flynn Beckham at my wedding was unthinkable.

But Cooper slowly warmed to him. Flynn definitely earned points by coming to see him, helping us reconcile after the show. But it was our staged public break-up that solidified that the bachelor wasn't such a Dickhead after all. As part of the deal we made so I could win the prize, Flynn and I had agreed we would say my returning to school and his leaving for tour was hard on our relationship and we were parting ways friends. But the media loved him and he knew they'd be horrible to me, blaming me for our demise with made-up stories. It also meant Cooper and I had to continue to keep our relationship quiet.

I called Flynn the day after Cooper and I reunited to thank him. The next day, Flynn took Jessica out to a very public lunch and then kissed her for a full five minutes while cameras snapped away in a frenzy. After that, I was free and Flynn was deemed a playboy who broke the girl-next-door's heart.

"Your brother was out there at seven this morning, practicing," Mom says, coming up behind me and looking out the window over my shoulder. Cooper had a wide wooden platform constructed that leads from the inside of the restaurant to the altar set up on the beach, so that Kyle would be able to walk me down the aisle in his wheelchair. All he needs to do is push a button to start and stop motion, but that's not always a feat he's capable of.

"He puts too much pressure on himself. I wish he would let someone wheel him down."

"He wants to escort you alone. He's stubborn. But he can do it."

Between the experimental drugs and promising therapy, my brother has made progress. But the progress isn't always consistent and he sometimes grows frustrated. Cooper and I had a custom wheelchair made for Kyle's birthday last month. I might not let my generous fiancé buy me cars, but chipping in for a ten-thousand-dollar wheelchair is more than okay.

The tick of the clock growing louder, Mom helps me attach my veil. There's a knock on the door as I take one last look in the mirror. "Who is it?" my mother asks, but the door creaks open before the response comes.

"I need a minute with Kate, Lena."

"No! Cooper. It's bad luck." She tries to shoo him out and shut the door, but she doesn't really have any idea who she's dealing with.

"It's okay, Mom. It's fine. He can come in."

Her eyes go wide as saucers. "Really? But it's bad luck." She can't believe what she's hearing. Oddly, me, the person who doesn't step on a crack for fear of breaking my mother's back, is actually okay with seeing the groom ten minutes before the wedding. It's kind of shocking even to me.

Cooper opens the door and my mother leaves the two of us alone. He eyes me in the mirror I'm still facing. "You look … gorgeous." I may not be the most beautiful woman in the world, but to him, I am at this very moment. He leaves no room for anyone else.

"Thank you. But you could have told me that in ten minutes." I turn, placing my palms on the lapels of his swoon-worthy tuxedo. "It must be important if you're willing to risk bad luck, knowing how I am."

"You know that none of that's true. You'd beat me at cards whether you had a lucky chip or not and we'll grow old together fifty years from now." He wraps his arm around my waist.

His nose nuzzles in my hair. "You smell good too."

"Cooper?"

"Hmmm."

"Did you come here for a reason? Because I am *not* having sex with you ten minutes before we are getting married."

"That sounds like a challenge," he says and I see that look growing in his eye. The one that both of us know I can't resist.

"Cooper …" I warn. "I'm kicking you out."

He takes a step back, his hands scrubbing the hormone-induced haze from his face. "No. I came to give you something."

"That's what I'm afraid of."

He grins. "Get your dirty mind out of the gutter, soon-to-be Mrs. Montgomery. I'll give you that after the ceremony. In the coat closet, on the way to the reception." He winks. I wouldn't put it past him for a second.

"Close your eyes."

"Seriously, Cooper, we …"

"Just trust me. Close your eyes."

I do as he asks. I feel him move around the room and then he's back in front of me. "Open your eyes."

He's kneeling down in front of me.

"Lift." One hand on my ankle, he guides me to lift my foot, then slips off my shoe. His finger goes to the toe and he removes the four-leaf clover I'd stashed there, but never told him about.

"But … I already tempted fate by letting you see me before the ceremony." Panic starts to rise.

Cooper lifts my bouquet placed at the floor next to him. I hadn't even noticed he put it there. He hands me the simple bundle of roses with a few silk ribbons cascading from the bottom. "Look underneath."

Confused, I turn the flowers upside down. Something sparkly affixed to the top of the ribbon captures my attention. It couldn't be. How could he ever find them?

"Are these ..."

He nods. "They're mine now. But I thought you might need something borrowed."

My eyes sting with tears I desperately try to hold back. "I can't believe you got these back for me." Securely fastened to the ribbon under my bridal bouquet are my father's lucky four-leaf clover cufflinks, the ones he had made when I was born. He wore them to all four World Poker championships—firmly believing they brought him luck each time he won. Sometime between his last win and next loss at the national championships, he lost them in a "sure thing" bet he made. A year later he died of a heart attack.

"I don't even know what to say. I love them. You found my father's lucky charm."

"I'm glad you love them. But you're wrong. I'm *marrying* his lucky charm in a few minutes." He kisses my lips softly.

"You're going to make me cry."

"No. I'm going to spend the rest of my life making you smile and giving you orgasms." He pulls me flush against his body. I have no doubt he'll do both. This man is a royal straight flush. A field of four leaf clovers. He's red skies at night. I need no other lucky charm, as long as I have him.

"Thank you, Cooper. I love them."

"And I love you."

Ten minutes later, at exactly eleven-eleven, on the eleventh day of November, I married the love of my life. As my husband said when he kissed me for the first time as his wife, "There's nobody luckier than me."

And just like that, the game was finally over.

Dear Readers,

f you liked Cooper and Kate's story, then please check out Flynn and Lucky's story! BEAT is coming summer 2015!

Dimpled smile of a boy

Hard body of a man

Sings like an angel

Fucks like the devil

I was stuck between a rock(star) and a hard place.

—*Lucky Valentino*

Sign up to receive a sneak peek at Beat!

http://eepurl.com/ba8vov

And please add Beat to your reading list!

http://bit.ly/1thI45l

acknowledgments

Thank you to the incredible community of bloggers that support Indie Authors! Without your help, my books would never have reached so many new readers.

A special thank you to some amazing ladies—

Penelope—for 6am chats almost every day.

Julie—for always keeping us snorting and never sleeping.

Dallison—for rocking it old school with a real dictionary!

Lisa—for putting up with my obsessiveness.

Sommer—for making the amazing cover that is Throb.

Carmen, Beth and the TF chicks—for friendship and support, always.

Finally, a huge thank you to all the readers. With so many incredible authors out there, I can't extend my gratitude enough for picking my story to read! I love your notes, emails and reviews, so please keep them coming!

Much love,

Vi

other books
by vi

Worth the Fight

http://www.vikeeland.com/mma.html

Worth the Chance

http://www.vikeeland.com/mma.html

Worth Forgiving

http://www.vikeeland.com/mma.html

Belong to You

http://www.vikeeland.com/cole.html

Made for You

http://www.vikeeland.com/cole.html

Left Behind

http://www.amazon.com/Left-Behind-Vi-Keeland-ebook/dp/B000JM92LI

First Thing I See

http://www.vikeeland.com/ftis.html

connect

with vi

https://www.facebook.com/vi.keeland

http://on.fb.me/1uxLPTH

Twitter—@vikeeland

Instagram—@vi_keeland

http://www.vikeeland.com

CPSIA information can be obtained
at www.ICGtesting.com
Printed in the USA
BVOW06s1313170517

484405BV00018B/327/P